GOING TO THE DOGS

Pierre Lemaitre

GOING TO THE DOGS

Translated from the French by
Frank Wynne

Headline's policy is to use papers that are natural, renewable and recyclable
products and made from wood grown in well-managed forests and other
controlled sources. The logging and manufacturing processes are expected
to conform to the environmental regulations of the country of origin.

HEADLINE PUBLISHING GROUP
An Hachette UK Company
Carmelite House
50 Victoria Embankment
London EC4Y 0DZ

www.headline.co.uk
www.hachette.co.uk

Neighbour
I'm sure she's an alcoholic
Have you seen the way she shakes?

Neighbour's husband
She's positively quaking. She must be in the grip of Evil
She must have serpents in her head

Gérald Aubert
A Difference of Opinion

1985

May 5

Mathilde drums a forefinger on the steering wheel.

The cars along the motorways have been engaged in a hesitation waltz for the past half-hour, and the Saint-Cloud tunnel is still at least ten kilometres away. The traffic remains at a complete standstill for minutes at a time, then, mysteriously, the horizon clears, and the Renault 25, almost grazing the crash barrier, moves off, 60, 70, 80 kph, only to come to another juddering halt. The accordion effect. Mathilde could kick herself. She wouldn't mind, but she took every precaution; she set off early, stuck to trunk roads for as long as possible, and joined the motorway only when the traffic reports assured her there were no tailbacks.

"All that to end up in this shitshow . . ."

Generally, Mathilde is polite and soft-spoken; not at all the kind of woman to be crude. She swears only when she is alone; it relieves the tension.

"Well, I would have had to go at some point or other . . ."

She is surprised by her own flippant tone. Never has she been so lackadaisical. To risk running late, today of all days. She thumps the dashboard, furious with herself.

Mathilde sits very close to the steering wheel because of her stubby arms. She is sixty-three years old, short, plump and heavy. A glance at her face is enough to know that once she was beautiful. Indeed, very beautiful. In some of the photographs from the war years, she is a young woman of surprising grace, with a sinuous figure and long blonde hair that frames a face that is smiling yet extremely sensual. Obviously, these days everything has doubled in size, her chin, her bust, her derrière, but she has retained the same blue eyes, the same thin lips, and there is a harmony to her features that evokes her former beauty. If, over the years, her body has begun to sag, Mathilde has been careful to preserve everything else, to focus on the details: clothes that are stylish and expensive (she can afford them), a trip to the salon every week, a professional makeup artist, and, most importantly, perfectly manicured hands. She can bear to see the advancing crow's feet and the accumulating kilos, but she could not abide her hands to be less than immaculately groomed.

Because of her weight (seventy-eight kilos on the bathroom scales this morning), she suffers in the heat. The motorway tailback is an ordeal, she can feel sweat trickling between her breasts, her buttocks feel damp, she is desperate for the traffic to move so that she can feel the faint breeze on her face. The return journey to Paris is almost as excruciating as the weekend she just spent with her daughter in Normandy, which was only just bearable. There were endless games of gin rummy. Her cretinous son-in-law insisted on watching the Formula 1 Grand Prix on television and, if that was not bad enough, on Saturday they served leek vinaigrette, which took Mathilde all night to digest.

"I should have headed back last night."

She looks at the watch and swears again.

In the back seat, Ludo lifts his head.

Ludo is a hulking, one-year-old Dalmatian with a gormless look but a gentle disposition. From time to time, he opens one eye, studies his mistress's thick neck and sighs. He never feels completely relaxed with her, she is prone to violent mood swings, especially lately. In their early days together, everything was fine, but now . . . it's not unusual for him to get a kick in the ribs for no reason he can comprehend. But Ludo is loyal to a fault, the kind of dog that stands by its owner even on their bad days. He has learned to be a little wary, though, especially when he can sense that she is on edge. As she is right now. Seeing her huff and pant behind the wheel, he prudently lies down and plays dead.

For the twentieth time since turning onto the motorway, Mathilde mentally traces a route to the avenue Foch. In a straight line, she would be there in less than fifteen minutes; but she still has to navigate the horrors of the tunnel at Saint-Cloud . . . This is why she is raging at the world at large, and especially at her daughter, though she is not to blame for this predicament. Not that Mathilde cares about such niceties. Every time she visits her daughter, she is shocked by the little country house that so reeks of narrow-minded bourgeois values it is almost a parody. Her son-in-law comes back from playing tennis sporting a broad smile and a towel draped casually around his neck, as though he were in a TV commercial. When her daughter tends the cottage garden, she looks like Marie-Antoinette playing the peasant at le Petit Trianon. It's a constant reminder to Mathilde that her daughter is no Gloria Steinem; if she were, she would never have married such a milksop . . . An American to boot. And dumb as a sack of hammers. But then again, he's American. It's a blessing they've never had children; Mathilde sincerely hopes her daughter is barren. Or her husband is firing blanks. Because she cannot bear to picture the children they would have . . . The sort of brats just begging to be smacked. Mathilde likes dogs, but she hates children. Especially girls.

Maybe I'm being unfair, she thinks, though she does not believe this for a minute.

It's because of the traffic jam. When she drives to work on weekdays, it's the same, she feels anxious and impatient; add to that the pusillanimous Sunday drivers and, well . . . Perhaps she could postpone until next Sunday . . . ? She considers the idea, but this particular task has to be done today. She has never been a week late . . .

Then, suddenly, for reasons no-one understands, the bottle-neck suddenly clears.

Unaccountably, the Renault hurtles through the Saint-Cloud tunnel and in a matter of seconds emerges onto the périphérique. Mathilde feels her limbs relax as she notices that, though the traffic is still heavy, it is flowing. In the back seat, Ludo breathes a long sigh of relief. Mathilde floors the accelerator, swerving to overtake a slowcoach, then just as quickly slows, remembering that the ring road is littered with speed cameras. Don't do any-thing foolish. She shrewdly pulls over into the middle lane, behind a Peugeot belching white smoke, and smiles as she passes the Porte Dauphine and sees the flash of the hidden speed camera in the left-hand lane.

Porte Maillot, the avenue de la Grande-Armée.

Mathilde wants to avoid the place de l'Étoile, so she turns right and heads along the avenue Foch. She feels calm now. It is half past eight. She is running a little early. Perfect. It was a close call; she can hardly believe her luck. Perhaps luck is part of the skill, who knows? She turns into the side street, pauses near a pedes-trian crossing, turns off the engine but leaves the headlights on.

Thinking they are home, Ludo stands up on the back seat and starts to whimper. Mathilde stares at him in the rear-view mirror.

"No!"

She does not raise her voice, but the curt, peremptory tone brooks no appeal. Instantly, the dog curls up, gives his mistress a repentant look, then closes his eyes, stifling a sigh.

Mathilde puts on the glasses that hang on a thin chain around her neck and rummages in the glove compartment. She takes out a piece of paper and is about to reread it when she sees a car up ahead drive off. Mathilde coolly pulls into the parking space, turns off the engine again, puts on her glasses, leans back against the headrest and shuts her eyes. It's a miracle that she made it here on time. She vows to be more assiduous in future.

The avenue Foch is quiet and peaceful; it must be nice to live here.

Mathilde rolls down the window. Now that the car is stationary, the air feels somewhat muggy, pervaded by the smells of Dalmatian and perspiration. She longs to take a shower. All in good time . . . In the wing mirror she sees a man in the distance walking his dog down the side street. Mathilde heaves a sigh. Out on the broad avenue, the cars flash past. There is not much traffic so late in the day. Especially on a Sunday. The soaring plane trees barely quiver. The night promises to be oppressive.

Although Ludo has not moved, Mathilde turns and jabs her finger at him. "Lie down! Stay! OK?" The dog complies.

She opens the car door and, gripping the frame with both hands, she levers herself out of the car. She needs to lose weight. Her skirt has rucked up over her considerable behind. She pulls it into place, a gesture that has become habit. She walks round the car, opens the passenger door, takes out a light raincoat and slips it on. Up above, a warm breeze gently stirs the tall trees. To her left, the man is drawing closer, while his dachshund sniffs the car tyres and tugs at his leash; Mathilde is fond of dachs-hunds, they have a placid temperament. The man flashes her a smile. This is how people sometimes meet each other, they have dogs, they talk about dogs, they strike up a friendship. Especially since the dog walker is a rather good-looking man in his fifties. As Mathilde returns the smile, she takes her right hand from her raincoat pocket. The man stops in his tracks as he sees the Desert Eagle pistol fitted with a long silencer. Mathilde's upper lip curls into an imperceptible sneer. For a split second she aims the barrel between the man's eyes, then allows it to dip and shoots him in the groin. The man stares in wide-eyed astonishment; the information has not yet reached his brain. He doubles over, spasms and soundlessly collapses. Mathilde trudges around the body. The brownish stain between the man's legs slowly spreads across the pavement. The man's eyes are wide open, his mouth agape, an expression of surprise and pain. Mathilde crouches down and stares at him. He is not dead. Mathilde's expression is a curious mixture of amazement and pleasure. Like that of a chubby little boy who has just discovered a rare insect. She stares at the man's lips as small waves of blood appear with a stomach-churning smell. Mathilde looks as though she is about to say something; her lips quiver with nervous agitation, her left eye twitches spasmodically. She places the barrel of the gun in the middle of the man's forehead and lets out a sort of wail. His eyes look as though they might pop out of their sockets. Unexpectedly, Mathilde changes her mind and shoots him in the throat. The impact of the blast seems to sever the head from the neck. Mathilde steps back in disgust. The whole scene has taken no more than thirty seconds. Mathilde sees the petrified dachshund frantically tugging at its leash. It stares at her dumbly and she shoots it in the head. Fully half of the dog is vaporised by the blast; what remains is a hunk of meat.

Mathilde turns and looks out at the avenue. It is as calm as ever. Cars impassively flash past. The pavement is deserted, as one would expect of a well-heeled neighbourhood at dusk. Mathilde climbs back into the car, puts the gun on the passenger seat, turns on the ignition and quietly drives away.

She pulls out of the side street and drives back down the avenue towards the ring road.

Ludo, roused by the sound of the ignition, stands up and lays his head on Mathilde's shoulder.

She takes one hand from the steering wheel, strokes the Dalmatian's muzzle, and coos:

"Good dog, good dog!"

It is 9.40 p.m.

It is 9.45 p.m. when Vasiliev finishes work. The office smells of sweat. The only advantage of working the late shift at the Police Judiciaire is that it gives him time to clear the huge backlog of reports demanded by Commissaire Occhipinti, who never actually reads them. "Just give me a summary, old man," he says, cramming handfuls of peanuts into his mouth. Just the thought of that face, that smell, makes Vasiliev want to retch . . .

He has barely eaten today, and now he is dreaming of opening a tin . . . A tin of what, he wonders. Mentally, he pictures his kitchen cupboards. Tins of peas, green beans, tuna, we'll see . . . Vasiliev is no gourmet, in fact he does not much care for food. It is something he readily admits: I don't enjoy eating. Whenever he says this, the people he is with turn and say, I don't believe it, how can you not like food? The French consider it an aberration, it is antisocial. It is unpatriotic. As for Vasiliev, he continues to feed on tinned beef, redcurrant jelly and sugary drinks all year round; he lets his stomach take the strain. Such a diet would make anyone else obese. Vasiliev has not put on a single gram in more than a decade. The real advantage is that there are no dishes to wash. There are no saucepans or utensils in his kitchen, only a dustbin and some stainless-steel cutlery.

But right now, he must put the tin and its contents to the back of his mind since he has to go to Neuilly to visit Monsieur de la Hosseray.

"He's been asking to see you for a while now," the nurse told him. "He'd be very disappointed if you didn't come."

The nurse, whose name is Tevy, has a strong Cambodian accent. She is a little woman in her early thirties. She is a full head shorter than him, but it does not seem to trouble her. She's been caring for Monsieur for a month now. Tevy is friendly and much more obliging than the previous nurse, a real termagant . . . A nice girl, Vasiliev thinks, though he has had no real opportunity to talk to her; he doesn't want to seem . . . well, you know . . .

"You have to understand," he said plaintively, "when you're working the late shift, you never know what time you'll get off."

"Of course," said Tevy, "it's the same for us nurses."

Her tone is not critical, but Vasiliev is quick to feel guilt. Tevy works with another nurse, but it is she who covers most of the shifts, and Vasiliev has never quite worked out her schedule.

"Call me when you're done," she says gently. "I'll let you know whether it's worth making the trip . . ."

Translation: whether Monsieur de la Hosseray is awake and

not too tired. He sleeps a lot, and his lucid moments are unpredictable.

When, at 9.55 p.m., his colleague Maillet comes to relieve him, Vasiliev has no choice but to head to Neuilly. He is craven enough to look for a pretext, but too honest to make up an excuse.

Grudgingly, he pulls on his jacket, turns off the light and trudges down the corridor, exhausted after a senseless day.

Vasiliev. René Vasiliev.

It sounds Russian because it *is* Russian. He takes his surname from his father, a tall, broad-shouldered man with a thick moustache, his likeness forever enshrined in an oval frame on the sideboard in the dining room. Papa's name was Igor. He seduced Maman on 8 November 1949 and died three years later to the day – thereby showing himself to be a fastidious, punctual man. During those three years, he drove his taxi through the streets of Paris, sired a little René for Maman, then fell into the Seine one night after a drunken binge with a few White Russian friends who had never learned to swim any more than he had. He was pulled from the river and died of severe pneumonia.

This is why René's surname is Vasiliev.

Vasiliev's first name is René because Maman wanted to honour her father. So it is that the police inspector bears the first and last names of two men he never knew.

From his papa, René Vasiliev inherited his height (one metre ninety-three); from his maman, his leanness (seventy-nine kilos). From his papa, he inherited a high forehead, a broad chest, a lumbering gait, a clear eye and a lantern jaw. From his maman, a certain tendency to indolence, boundless patience and an unfailing probity. It is curious that, although tall, lanky and somewhat gangling, he looks completely hollow – probably because he lacks muscle.

René's hair began to recede when he was twenty. Five years later, the perfidious retreat stopped as abruptly as it had begun, leaving a round, bald patch on the top of his head, the scars of the battle waged by his mother with unguents, potions, pickled eggs and miracle cures, a war of attrition Vasiliev placidly endured, one that Maman felt certain she would win. Today he is a silent, single-minded man of thirty-five. Since Maman died, he has lived alone in the apartment they once shared, which he has redecorated a little, but not too much. The best that can be said of what little family he has left is that their breath stinks. Aside from a navy jumper and a pewter hipflask he used to fill with vodka, Papa left him with nothing but the memory of Monsieur de la Hosseray, whom Igor had been driving around morning, noon and night – since long before he met Maman – acting almost as his personal chauffeur. When Papa died, Monsieur de la Hosseray felt so moved that he decided to give little René a bursary, since his mother was almost destitute. Thus, in memory of his favourite taxi driver, the beloved benefactor funded René's studies, including his law degree and his training at the National Police Academy. Monsieur de la Hosseray is reputedly childless (though this is debatable . . .) and has no family (or if he does, they are extremely inconspicuous, since Vasiliev has never known anyone to visit him). When he dies, all his goods and chattels will go to the government that he served conscientiously for forty-three years, most notably as a préfet in some département (Indre-et-Loire? Cher? Loiret? René can never remember), before taking a post as Minister of State, thereby elevating Igor Vasiliev to the status of VIP driver, i.e. a driver who transports a VIP.

Time was René wondered whether there had once been something between Maman and Monsieur de la Hosseray, because, let's face it, you don't give a bursary to a taxi driver's son! As a boy, he sometimes imagined that he was his benefactor's unacknowledged son. But he had only to think back to the shy, frightened, yet ostentatious primness of Maman's greeting when they visited to know there had never been anything between them; in a way, it is a pity, since it means that the debt owed – if any – lies with René, who cannot even share it with his mother.

Monsieur de la Hosseray may be very rich, perhaps even preposterously so, but he has appalling halitosis. René was forced to endure this fetid breath for two hours every month, on the days when Maman drove him to Neuilly to thank his beloved benefactor. Monsieur de la Hosseray is eighty-seven now. His bad breath hardly figures in René's weekly ordeal; what he finds overwhelming is seeing the man grow old and lose his taste for life.

Vasiliev walks past Maillet's desk. Nothing to report. He would happily hang around a little longer, but he has to go to Neuilly sooner or later, so he might as well get it over with.

What stops him is a phone call.

Maillet is all ears. They both stare at the clock on the wall, which reads 9.58 p.m. A murder on the avenue Foch. The colleague who calls it in is panting for breath, either because he had to run to find a phone, or because he's in shock.

"Maurice Quentin!" he shouts.

Maillet lets out a whoop of triumph and jabs a finger at the clock. 9.59 p.m. Vasiliev's shift doesn't end until ten o'clock – it's his case. René squeezes his eyes shut. Maurice Quentin. Even people with little or no interest in the stock market know the man. Public works, cement works, or maybe crude oil, Vasiliev is not exactly sure. He is a big-time French tycoon. The financial magazines call him 'President' Quentin. Vasiliev cannot picture his face. Maillet has already dialled the commissaire's number.

Even on the phone it sounds as though Occhipinti is masticating. And he probably is; the only time he is not stuffing his face is when he is asleep or talking to his superiors.

"Quentin! Jesus fucking Christ . . ."

Dealing with the commissaire is exhausting.

He shows up at the crime scene on the avenue Foch less than two minutes after his inspector, and within seconds he has everyone on edge with his panicked nervousness, his habit of flailing in all directions, and giving orders that Vasiliev quietly countermands behind his back.

Occhipinti is one metre sixty-three, and, convinced that this is not sufficient, he has shoe lifts. To Commissaire Occhipinti, humanity is divided into those people he admires and those he hates. He is obsessed with Talleyrand, whose aphorisms he attempts to quote from half-remembered books of quotations, novels by André Castelot and issues of *Reader's Digest*. He spends his day cramming peanuts, pistachios or cashews into his maw, which, in itself, is almost intolerable. But he is also a complete arsehole. He is one of those petty, two-faced public servants who owe everything to their stupidity and nothing to their talent.

He and Vasiliev are like oil and water.

Since they started working together, Occhipinti has been obsessed with the idea of taking Vasiliev down a peg or two because he considers the man too tall. The inspector is not temperamentally inclined to take against anyone, but his superior has curious fixations and, from the outset, has done his utmost to give him every rotten apple in the barrel. Like most people who have a chip on their shoulder, Occhipinti has a keen sense of other people's bêtes noires, and assigns Vasiliev the kind of cases he most loathes. This is how René came to be lumbered with countless cases of sexual assault followed by murder (or vice versa). He has become an expert in the field, which justifies the commissaire assigning all such cases to him on the pretext that he is the most competent officer. Vasiliev takes all this in his stride. He only looks as though he has the weight of the world on his shoulders. "That's why he's so stooped," Occhipinti says.

On the avenue Foch, the only moment of calm between the two men is as they study the body. Or what is left of it. They have seen it all before, but, even so, they are shocked.

"Pretty heavy artillery," says the commissaire.

"A .44 Magnum, would be my guess," Vasiliev says.

The sort of gun that could stop a stampeding elephant in its tracks. The extent of the damage to the pelvis and the throat make work difficult for the forensic officers who have just arrived.

Vasiliev is in two minds.

The MO suggests a crime of passion – you don't shoot someone in the balls without good reason. The bullet in the throat evokes something similar, it's not something you encounter every day. And then there's the dachshund, shot at point-blank range . . . On the other hand, the manifest cruelty, the desire to obliterate, suggests revenge, uncontrollable anger . . . But the choice of the time and the location, the use of a silencer (nobody heard a shot, a neighbour walking her dog happened on the body by chance), suggests a cold, calculated, premeditated, almost professional hit.

The forensic officers are taking pictures. Though no-one knows how they got wind of the incident, reporters have already started to show up with cameras and flash guns, a man appears with a mobile television camera and a determined-looking news reporter; the commissaire gobbles a fistful of pistachios – his nerves, probably.

"You can deal with the media," says Occhipinti, who only ever gets in front of the cameras if it is to his advantage. "But careful what you say, huh? No bullshit!"

Vasiliev dispatches officers to gather witness statements – if there are any, which seems unlikely.

The examining magistrate arrives. Vasiliev scuttles off. The judge calls him back and Vasiliev retraces his steps.

He is unfamiliar with the man barking orders. He seems young to be a magistrate, and is nervously surveying the rubberneckers and reporters behind the cordon manned by two uniformed officers.

"Give them as little information as possible!" he says to Vasiliev.

On that, everyone is agreed. Not that it will be difficult, since, aside from the identity of the deceased, there is no information he can give.

The magistrate and the commissaire will have to deal with the family. The area is milling with people now. Vasiliev will deal with the blood, the forensic team, the local officers, potential witness statements . . .

Stoically, he walks over to the news reporter who has been waving at him for some minutes.

All things, even the most unpleasant, have an end.

Eventually, the various officers come back more or less empty-handed; the forensic officers stow their equipment and have the body taken to the mortuary, the glaring spotlights are switched off and the avenue is once more plunged into darkness as the mild May night reasserts itself. It is 11.23 p.m. At least Vasiliev has managed to avoid a trip to Neuilly – always a bonus. A guilty conscience prompts him to call the nurse and promise to go tomorrow.

"You can come now," she says. "Monsieur is awake, and I'm sure he'd be happy to see you."

Some days there seems to be no end in sight.

Because he was once head of a Resistance group in south-west France, Henri Latournelle is still addressed as "Commandant" when he is present, and referred to as "the commandant" when he is not. At seventy years old, he has the dry, rather dispassionate manner that is common among egotists and obsessives, but also in people who endure great hardship and come through it stronger. He wears a silk cravat tucked into his open shirt. This, together with the shock of white hair, the chiselled looks of an Indian Army officer and the title "Commandant", gives him the rather louche air of the penniless aristocrats who hole up in luxury hotels and are referred to by hotel staff with a nudge and a wink as "Monsieur le Comte". But there is something about the angular features, the determined expression, that means no-one finds him ludicrous. The commandant lives alone in his family mansion near Toulouse and, contrary to popular stereotype, he does not ride horses or play golf, he never drinks and speaks little. Many men have a problem with ageing. They either refuse to accept it and seem pathetic, or they embrace old age and seem preposterous. Henri Latournelle falls into the latter category, but does so with a restraint that makes him less bumptious than others. Merely a little old-fashioned.

He is sitting in his armchair in the drawing room waiting to watch the midnight news. He is holding a large black-and-white photograph of a man in his fifties; exactly the same photo that appears on the television screen as the newscaster reads the late headlines. Blinding spotlights rip through the darkness and reveal a stretch of pavement on the avenue Foch. The TV crews arrived shortly after the police. The cameramen have had more than enough time to set up and film the forensic technicians, scuttling around like harried waiters, taking measurements and photographs of the victim. The night owls watching are treated to a few shocking images: the corpse, little more than a tangle of limbs in death, the plastic sheet pulled over the remains in a semblance of modesty before it is taken away, the stretcher being wheeled to the ambulance and the loud clank of the rear doors closing: end of scene, curtain. The cameras linger on the pool of blood trucking into the gutter with the delicate tact for which the media are famous.

The flashing police lights streak the facade of the building blue. The TV reporter at the scene has little information to give except this: Maurice Quentin, CEO of an international consortium and a man of considerable influence, has been murdered outside his Paris home. A senior officer, an inspector from the Police Judiciaire, mumbles something brief and incomprehensible. Henri bides his time; he is worried.

It is easy to speculate on the possible motives for such a crime, and to admit that, alas, there must be dozens of people who wanted the man dead, but right now, all that is known is that Maurice Quentin was walking his dog when he was gunned down. The manner in which the deed was done is almost as repulsive as the crime itself. There is no need to wait for the autopsy to know that Quentin died of multiple gunshots, including one to the groin and one to the throat, which, quite literally, made him lose his head. The fact that Quentin's dog also got a bullet in the head makes the crime seem personal. It feels less like a murder than a massacre. There is no such thing as an innocent crime, but some smack of hatred more than others.

The commandant sighs and closes his eyes and thinks: Fuck . . . A word that is not in his everyday vocabulary.

Mathilde has just eaten a tin of sardines. Needless to say, she is not allowed sardines, but this is the reward she allows herself after a successful mission. All of her missions have been successful. She sops up the oil as she watches television. The man looked better in real life than he does in the picture they show on the news, she thinks. Well, at least until he met her. She is sorry the newsreader has said almost nothing about the dachshund; viewers, it seems, are not interested in dogs . . .

She struggles to her feet and clears the table as the cameras zoom in on the blood trail on the pavement.

After driving away from the avenue Foch, she headed for the Pont Sully, her favourite bridge. She knows every bridge in Paris; there is not one from which she has not tossed a pistol or a revolver over the past three decades. Even when her mission was out in the provinces – though this is something she has never told Henri. It's like an obsession. She nods her head and smiles. She likes to dwell on her little idiosyncrasies; she almost seems to cultivate them. One such quirk is that whenever she has been sent on a mission to the provinces – in a flagrant breach of the rule that the weapon entrusted to her be discarded as soon as possible – she has always brought the gun back to Paris. To toss it into the Seine. It brings me good luck! I'll be damned if I'm going to give up my little ritual because of a stupid rule dreamt up by some clever dick! Another quirk relates to munitions. Mathilde refuses to work with small-calibre firearms, which, she firmly believes, are good only for bourgeois soap operas and adultery. Not that it was easy to procure big guns, she had to fight with the Supplies team, apparently the Personnel Director was reluctant. Take it or leave it, Mathilde said. And since she is an excellent worker, the Personnel Director capitulated. He is probably pleased with his decisions. With Mathilde, there is never a stray bullet, her work is clean and neat. Tonight was an exception. A little whim. Obviously, she could have taken the shot from a distance, done less damage; obviously she could have made the hit with a single bullet. What can I say? I don't know what came over me. This is what she will say if anyone asks. And anyway, who cares? All that matters is that the guy is dead, right? And when you think about it, it's probably a good thing. The cops will be chasing down false leads, they are less likely to be suspicious, meaning the client is protected. This is what she'll say! And what about the dog? Mathilde has a host of justifications: can you imagine the poor dachshund having to live on without his beloved master? If the dog could talk, I'm sure he'd have chosen to die rather than stay behind and pine. Especially since no-one else in the family cares about him, and they would be quick to drop him off at an animal shelter. That's it! That's what she'll say.

And so, tonight, she chose the Pont Sully.

She found a parking spot on the rue Poulletier and, as usual, she strolled across the bridge in her light raincoat, then leaned over the railings and tossed the Desert Eagle.

She is seized by a sudden doubt.

Did she actually throw the gun away or did she just imagine it?

Never mind; time for bed.

"Ludo!"

Reluctantly, the big dog gets up, stretches itself and pads towards the door she is holding open. He steps forward, sniffs the air.

It's so mild, thinks Mathilde, it's lovely. On the right, a cedar hedge separates her garden from Monsieur Lepoitevin's. An arsehole, in Mathilde's estimation. Neighbours often are. She has no idea why, but her neighbours have always been arseholes and this one is no exception. Lepoitevin . . . Even his name . . .

She finds herself toying with a piece of paper in her pocket and takes it out. Her own handwriting. The coordinates of the target on the avenue Foch. Normally, she never writes things down. When she's tailing a target to come up with a plan, she stores all the information in her head. The Personnel Director insists that nothing be written down. Well, I'm tweaking the rules, she thinks, but nothing too serious. No-one will be any the wiser. She crumples the piece of paper and glances round for somewhere to dispose of it. She'll do it later. The big garden is dozing. She loves this house; she loves this garden. She is only sorry that she has spent so long here living alone, but that's life. Such thoughts invariably bring her back to Henri. The commandant. Right, buck up, this is no time for self-pity.

"Ludo!"

The dog trots inside, Mathilde closes the door behind him, grabs the Desert Eagle fitted with the silencer that she put on the table when she got home. She opens a kitchen drawer only to find a Luger semi-automatic. I'll put it in a shoebox, she thinks. She switches off the lights, heads up to her bedroom and opens the wardrobe. My God, the mess! She used to be so tidy, but now . . . It's like the kitchen, everything used to be spick and span, never a blot or a mark. She knows that she's let herself go. She still does a little vacuuming, but she can't summon the energy for anything else. What she most hates are stains. Grease stains, coffee stains. Stains of any kind. It's the one thing she cannot abide. Cleaning the windows has become such an ordeal that she doesn't do it anymore. If she doesn't pull herself together, this place will become . . . She chases away the grisly image.

The first shoebox contains a .475 Wildey Magnum, the second a LAR Grizzly Win Mag, the third, a pair of beige shoes she will never wear again, her feet have swollen and shoes like these with little straps hurt like hell. She throws them in the wastepaper basket. To fit the Desert Eagle into the box, she has to remove the silencer. She probably has too many guns in this house; it's not as though she'll ever need them all. It's like the cash: she stuffed a lot of it into a bag in the wardrobe back when she thought she might need it, but she never has. She could get robbed; she really should put it in the bank.

As she brushes her teeth, she pictures herself on the Pont Sully.

But for the fact that she prefers the countryside, she would have loved to live on the île Saint Louis! She could easily afford to, with all the money she has tucked away in Lausanne. Or is it Geneva? She can never remember. Yes, Lausanne. Oh, never mind. She suddenly thinks back to the piece of paper in her pocket; she'll deal with it tomorrow. Oh, Mathilde might play fast and loose with the rules, but she's not one to take unnecessary risks. She forces herself to go back downstairs. Ludo is curled up in his basket. Now where did she leave that bloody piece of paper . . . ? She searches the pockets of her coat – nothing. Her dressing gown! It's up in her bedroom. With some effort she goes back upstairs. There it is. And the piece of paper. She goes downstairs, walks over to the fireplace, takes the box of matches and burns the note.

Everything is in order.

She goes up to her room and lies down.

At night, she reads three lines before falling asleep.

In theory, she likes reading; in practice . . .

Tevy opens the door before Vasiliev has time to ring the bell.

"He'll be so happy to see you."

She looks overjoyed, as though she is the one he has come to visit. Vasiliev apologises for showing up so late. Tevy just smiles again. Her smile is a language unto itself.

Usually, by this hour, the apartment is bathed in an oppressive gloom. All that is visible from the front door is a long, murky corridor and, at the far end, the faint glow emanating from Monsieur's bedroom. To Vasiliev it seems as though Monsieur's whole life is circumscribed by this room, where the lamp, which seems to flicker constantly, seems to long to be switched off. The long walk down the corridor is an ordeal.

But tonight is very different.

Tevy has turned on the lights in every room. It is not exactly cheerful, but it feels more habitable. René follows the nurse down the hallway; from Monsieur's bedroom comes the sound of voices . . .

Tevy stops and turns to René.

"I put the television in his room. Getting as far as the living room can be a real struggle for him . . ."

She says it in a whisper, as though it is a joke.

The room looks different. The television has been set at the end of the bed, there is a small bouquet of flowers on the night-stand, the various books and magazines have been arranged on the shelves, and the pile of newspapers neatly folded. The countless pills and potions (a real pharmacopoeia) are no longer strewn over the round table, but concealed behind the Japanese screen that Tevy has brought in from the living room . . . Even Monsieur looks different. First and foremost, he is wide awake, which is unusual at this hour. He is propped up on a mass of pillows, hands folded over the covers, and he smiles when he sees Vasiliev. His face is glowing, his hair is neatly combed.

"Ah, René, there you are at last . . ."

There is no reproach in his tone, merely relief.

As René goes over to kiss the old man's cheek he gets another surprise; the terrible halitosis is gone. His breath smells . . . of nothing. This is a vast improvement.

The television is on, Monsieur gestures to the chair next to him, Vasiliev sits down, but not before glancing around for some-where to leave his coat. Tevy takes it from him.

"I don't get to see you very often . . ."

Conversation with Monsieur quickly slips into a time-honoured ritual. The same phrases pepper all their conversations. Monsieur will start with "You're looking a little peaky", followed by "Oh, don't ask me about my health, we'd be here all day!", then "So, what's new in the forces of law and order?", and finally "Don't let me keep you, René, it's so kind of you to drop by, an old man's company is not exactly . . .", etc.

"You're looking rather peaky, my little René."

That's another thing: Monsieur has always addressed him as "my little René", though by the age of sixteen, his protégé had reached one metre eighty-two.

"How have you been?"

In recent months, Monsieur has taken to complaining less. Since Tevy's arrival, he seems to have more energy. He looks older, but less feeble.

Tevy has just reappeared carrying a tray with glasses and cups. She offers him chamomile tea, mineral water, "or something more . . . fortifying?" She is hesitant about certain words, and pronounces them with a trailing question mark. Vasiliev declines with a wave.

"It is the witching hour," says Monsieur. "Black stage for tragedies and murders fell!"

This is one of Monsieur's recurring jokes, though at least this time it feels appropriate, as the midnight news headlines scroll across the television.

Maurice Quentin is in the news.

René is sitting on a chair to Monsieur's right, Tevy to his left. Together they look like a tableau vivant.

Seeing him appear on the TV screen, Tevy glances at René, who is as shamefaced as when she ushers him into the apartment. She smiles. René turns to Monsieur. He has fallen asleep.

"I made noodles. Singapore noodles."

René was about to leave when the nurse offers to heat them up.

"I don't know if you like South-East Asian food . . ."

This is not a good time for René to explain his dietary regime.

"I wouldn't say no . . ."

They eat together at the huge round living room table; it feels almost like a picnic.

Tevy was surprised to see René on television, she acts as if she's flattered.

"So, you're in charge of a great investigation!"

Vasiliev smiles. The term reminds him of his mother, who firmly distinguished between music and *great music*, cooking and *great cooking*, writers and *great writers*. Now he has had greatness thrust upon him.

"Oh, you know . . ."

He tries to appear as modest as he feels, but cannot help but preen a little cheaply.

Tevy is much prettier than he remembered. Her laughing eyes accentuate her fleshy, sensual lips. Granted, she is a little plump, or rather . . . Vasiliev racks his brain . . . *cosy* is the word that comes to him.

She has a funny, sardonic way of telling the story of her journey from Cambodia, taking the boat with her family, the time spent in refugee camps, finding her nursing qualification was not recognised in France and having to repeat her studies. "And the French I learned in Cambodia was nothing like what you speak here."

Without knowing why, they are both speaking in hushed tones, as though they are in church, or trying not to wake Monsieur. René tries to eat neatly, something he does not always find easy.

"I have to say, I think Monsieur is in fine form," says René.

This is less a diagnosis than a compliment. Tevy either does not notice or turns a deaf ear.

"Yes, he's much better these days. He's the one who suggests that we go out. He's still steady on his feet. We go to the park, spend a couple of hours there, when the weather is fine. Oh yes, I forget to tell you: we went to the cinema!"

Vasiliev is flabbergasted.

"How did you get there . . . bus or métro?"

"Oh, that would have been too difficult for him, no, I drove us. My little Citroën Ami isn't much stronger than Monsieur, and it's about the same age, but the suspension is still good, and that's all that matters to him. We went to see . . . Oh, sorry."

She covers her mouth and giggles.

"Yes?"

"*Cop au vin* . . ."

They both laugh.

"He really enjoyed it. He said he hasn't been to the cinema in more than a decade, is that true?"

"I've no idea, but it's possible."

"So, anyway, he fell asleep before the end, but he had a nice day, I think. And then, the day before yesterday we went to . . ."

Tevy likes to talk.

As she walks him to the door, she says:

"My first name, Tevy, means 'she who listens', though I know it doesn't seem like that . . ."

May 6

On the telephone, the voice of Madame Quentin, the widow of the murdered man, is not particularly agreeable. The enunciation is pedantic, the tone condescending, the words painstakingly chosen: this is not a telephone conversation, it is an opportunity for madame to peacock.

The lobby of the apartment building is much like her voice: genteel and decidedly chilly. The carpet runs all the way to the heavy front door. The place is pristine, it does not smell of furniture polish like some bourgeois building. From outside the concierge's lodge, Vasiliev can see the sweeping staircase through the ornate copper banisters, and a carved wooden lift cage that is surely a listed monument. A man appears at the hatchway and stares mutely at the visitor. A hushed atmosphere reigns. Is this habitual, or because this is the house of a dead man? Inside the concierge's lodge, Vasiliev can glimpse a Henri II sideboard, a table draped with a lace cloth, a vase of flowers and, a few steps away, a little boy who stops playing with his cat whenever the door is opened. Vasiliev eschews the lift, preferring to take the stairs.

The parlourmaid, shaped by the unconscious imitation that causes domestic servants to resemble their masters, opens the door and holds it ajar for a long moment. She is a small woman in her fifties, with a wary look. Vasiliev introduces himself and stands, holding his warrant card, which the maid studies intently before reluctantly letting him inside and muttering, "Wait here."

An opulent apartment. The difference between opulence and mere wealth is evident. No interior designer has imposed her taste, because here the interior designers are time, the culture of the occupants, family heirlooms, princely gifts, exquisite mementos of foreign travels . . . No reproductions hang on these walls, only original artworks. Vasiliev steps closer to a watercolour of the port at Honfleur. The artist's signature means nothing to him. The subject is evocative, but Vasiliev finds something faintly unsettling about the painter's technique, how he contrasts the peaceful harbour with the looming threat posed by shadowy, flat-tiled houses. It is the widow's voice that wakes him from his reverie.

She is a striking woman in her forties, a woman who, since childhood, has wanted for nothing, especially not respect. Discreet makeup, a firm gait, the faintly harried air of the aristocrat who politely listens but has more important matters to attend to. Unconsciously, Vasiliev smooths the wrinkled lapel of his jacket, gives a little cough: the masculine equivalent of Maman's gestures whenever Monsieur de la Hosseray appeared.

The widow squints at the inspector, who is a head taller than she, though his shoulders are hunched and his suit has seen better days. She proffers her hand ("Good morning, Inspector" – she dispenses with "Monsieur") and leads him into a drawing room which, Vasiliev thinks, is about three times the size of his apartment. She settles herself on a sofa and gestures to an armchair, on which Vasiliev delicately perches one buttock.

The widow reaches out, opens a box, takes a cigarette, lights it with a table lighter, then, realising she has not offered her visitor one, wordlessly nods towards the box. Vasiliev makes a polite gesture of refusal. He feels like a stockbroker.

In grief, Madame Quentin looks more like a venerable madame than a woman who has been recently widowed.

"What can I do for you, Inspector . . . ?"

"Vasiliev."

"Indeed. My apologies, the name slipped my mind."

"Firstly, I would like to offer my sincere condol—"

"Please, don't trouble yourself. There's really no need."

Madame exhales a plume of smoke through her nostrils with a knowing smile that vanishes as quickly as it appeared.

"Your husband was . . ."

"My spouse."

Vasiliev does not quite see the distinction.

"The bonds between us were pragmatic, chiefly legal and financial, he was my partner, my spouse. A husband is a very different thing. Monsieur Quentin had a civil engineering company; my father had a number of cement works. And three daughters. Not that it mattered to my father. He married off the first daughter to a civil engineering firm, the second to Inland Water Transport and Management to ship and store his cement. The last he married off to the Crédit Immobilier in order to finance public works."

Although Vasiliev does not claim to know much about women, he has nonetheless encountered his fair share and, though he racks his brain, he can think of no-one who remotely resembles this woman who was widowed scarcely twelve hours ago.

"I imagine you would like to know more about my husband's life. And perhaps mine . . ."

"Well, the thing is . . ."

"Allow me to save you some time. You will soon discover that my spouse had a number of mistresses. As for my own lovers – of whom, to date, there have been three – I can furnish you with a list of names and thereby avoid wasting police time and resources at the expense of the taxpayer."

"You sound somewhat ... bitter about Monsieur Quentin. Would that be right?"

The Widow stubs out her cigarette and lights another. Vasiliev continues:

"Because the details of his murder suggest ... well, a crime of passion."

"Yes, I appreciate that. So, naturally, you will be speculating about possible conjugal motives and you will doubtless ask me for – what is the term? – ah yes, my alibi."

"As a rule, we simply talk about timelines."

"As you wish. Well, at the moment when my spouse was gunned down outside this building, I was at La Tour de Nesle, a private fetish club, with some friends. A most rewarding evening – I only wish there could be more like it. Many men and very few women. We carried on late into the night. Consequently, the details of my visit to the establishment can easily be traced; I am well known there, I would almost call it my 'second home'."

Unruffled by the Widow's attempts at provocation, Vasiliev takes out his notepad.

"Perhaps we might save the taxpayers a little more expense," he says. "If you could give me a list of these intimate friends before we visit the establishment, it would be very helpful."

The Widow merely gives a nod that is impossible to interpret.

"I know nothing about the practicalities of murdering people, Monsieur l'Inspecteur, still less what it is about my husband's murder that makes you think it was a crime of passion, but if I may just say ..."

She hesitates for a moment; or perhaps pauses for dramatic effect.

"Please go on," Vasiliev says encouragingly, "any useful information is welcome."

"Your investigation will quickly discover a tangled web of sordid relationships, fraudulent business dealings and highly suspect profits cunningly concealed by a veneer of perfect propriety. In a day or two, you'll be able to paper the walls of your office with the list of people who hated my husband enough to kill him. At which point, I am willing to wager that you'll see the manner of his death in a rather different light, one tinged more with rage than passion."

"I understand."

The Widow spreads her hands, are we done here?

Vasiliev purses his lips, I believe so . . .

The Widow makes it a point of honour to escort him down the long hall to the front door. A sudden and belated mark of respect intended to smooth out an encounter that she feels has not gone as well as it should.

"About your friends from La Tour de Nesle," says Vasiliev, "if you could send me the list sometime this evening?"

The commandant pulls on his coat, dons his checked cap and takes the car out of the garage. The skies are cloudless, but his mood is overcast. He has slept badly; that is to say, even less than usual. He drives some twenty kilometres to a village that glories in the mysterious name of Montastruc, pulls up next to a telephone booth a stone's throw from the main square, dials a number, allows it to ring twice, then hangs up and drives away.

The main road runs though the little valley of the Girou, a rivulet often referred to as a river on maps of the region. The wooded banks that line the road create patches of bright sunlight alternating with cool passages where the shade is almost crepuscular. The road is used only by a handful of regulars and is one of the commandant's favourites, so much so that, on the rare occasions he has the opportunity to take this route, he is sorry he does so only in exceptional circumstances. As is the case today . . .

He turns off towards Belcastel, stops at a phone box on the outskirts of the village, checks his watch, walks a few steps away. He is instantly recalled by the ringing of the telephone. With a touch of irritation, he notes that the prearranged schedule has not been followed. Three minutes early is *not* the appointed time. But he is in no position to point this out.

"Hello . . ."

"Monsieur Bourgeois?"

It was clearly not the commandant who chose this pseudonym.

"Yes."

"I was afraid I'd misdialled . . ."

"No, no, you've got the right number."

There. The ritual is complete. The first salvo does not linger.

"What the hell kind of shit was that?"

"Things don't always go exactly according to plan."

"I'd hardly call it a clean job. We need our operations to be immaculate. I don't want to have to keep pointing this out."

The commandant says nothing. From the far end of the village square, he hears a faint music, a tune that sounds vaguely familiar. He dispels the thought with a shake of his head.

"You are ultimately responsible for the missions assigned to you. But you know our terms and conditions," says the voice. "I decide whether the workmanship is up to standard and whether to sever ties with the operative."

In his life, the commandant has been faced with countless tricky situations and he has discovered that the more tense they are, the more detached he becomes. He mentally scrutinises every detail, noting any slight alteration that might change the context, and, regardless of the circumstances, he remains perfectly calm; Henri has a cool head on his shoulders.

"Should I make the call?"

"No, I'm prepared to vouch for the operative."

He had called Mathilde early that morning. Another breach of protocol – just now, the commandant's meticulously ordered life is beginning to spin out of control.

"No, don't worry, Henri, you didn't wake me!" She had sounded happy to hear his voice. Happy but surprised.

"Is there a problem?"

The question like a needle in Henri's ear.

"What do you think?"

His tone was curt, brittle.

Mathilde allowed a few seconds to pass.

"Oh, come on, you're not going to make a song and dance about minor details!"

She said this with a light-hearted chuckle, all the while thinking: Shit, I fucked something up – but what?

"It's not the end of the world, now is it, Henri?"

She racked her brain but could remember nothing. Best to let him make the running.

"I demand clean work!" said the commandant, realising that he was simply parroting the words of his superior.

What exactly did he mean by *clean*? For a brief moment, both seemed to be pondering the question.

Mathilde assumed that she had missed something.

"It's a little hiccup, Henri, nothing serious, it won't happen again . . ." she ventured.

The commandant listened intently, trying to capture every nuance. Mathilde sounded genuinely upset. Should he give her the benefit of the doubt?

"But *why* did you do it?" he said after a moment.

Mathilde smiled – from his weary tone, she could tell he was not going to read her the riot act. Phew.

"That's just the way it goes some days, Henri, it could happen to anyone."

She made the most of the brief silence to add:

"You never phone me – yes, yes, I know, it's protocol . . . But still, you hardly ever call me, and when you do it's always to find fault . . ."

What could he possibly say to that? He shouldn't have called her. Suddenly, it was his turn to feel tired. He had hung up without another word.

"Very well," says the voice on the other end of the line. "I don't want to have to raise this matter with you again."

"Understood," says the commandant.

Driving back, the road that winds along the banks of the Girou is much more tranquil than he is.

For her part, Mathilde goes downstairs, opens the door to let the dog out and makes herself coffee. She is upset by the phone call. Why would Henri call to criticise her work? Maybe this is about the Desert Eagle . . . Maybe he's wondering whether she got rid of it.

She smiles. You should know better, Henri – I always drive over one of the Seine bridges on the way back! Why ask me to start doing things differently?

The brutal murder makes the headlines of every newspaper. Since the only people to claim responsibility are a few insignificant groups unknown to the police, the investigation focuses on relatives of the victim. They rake over every detail of Maurice Quentin's life, and his widow's prediction proves correct. The tangled network of his contacts and relationships is dizzyingly complex, the number of businesses in which he had an interest or some role is almost incomprehensible.

Commissaire Occhipinti, initially convinced that he has landed a case that will launch him into the stratosphere of the ministry (a goal in keeping with his delusions of grandeur), quickly finds himself being sidelined for no apparent reason by all manner of experts who are working on investigations into fiscal and fiduciary offences, stock market trading and business malfeasance relating to senior politicians.

The murder took place in early May. Now, on the eve of his summer holiday, Inspector Occhipinti can't wait to be rid of this case, which stinks to high heaven.

As for Vasiliev, he was ousted by the end of the first week of gruelling and fruitless interviews of Maurice Quentin's various partners, secretaries, assistants, advisers and deputies. The civil servants who dismissed him did not mince their words: he was simply not up to the task. Vasiliev did not demur.

The most secret of the Republic's secret services shake down their network of informants only to come to the same conclusion as the police: this was a contract killing, and it is unlikely they will ever get to the bottom of it. Before long, it will have been filed away next to the dossier on ministers who committed suicide in highly suspicious circumstances, local préfets gunned down in the street in towns plagued by local mafiosi. In cases like this – which are more common than one might think – sometimes years pass before a clue accidentally comes to light that makes it possible to identify the hitman responsible, which in itself is not particularly useful, since more often than not the trail ends there, while those who contracted the killing can sleep soundly in their beds. Meanwhile, the general public, always happy to be flimflammed, is as happy to remain ignorant as to be bombarded with shock revelations. The common people have more pressing concerns. Will Platini be on the transfer list this season? Will Stéphanie finally marry her one true love?

But for the media, the case remains a thorny issue. On the one hand, they want to wallow in every sordid detail (the murder of a prominent businessman is akin to treason, they are reluctant to let the subject drop); on the other hand, they have nothing new to say. Not that such considerations have ever stopped a real journalist, but it becomes increasingly difficult to keep the fire burning. Several newspapers ran the headline "THE GRIM TRUTH ABOUT MAURICE QUENTIN'S MURDER", but with little conviction. Maurice Quentin, having been somewhat uncooperative in life, proved even less accommodating in death.

Vasiliev, who is glad to be out of the running, continues to read every article written about Maurice Quentin, because he saw the man's corpse and, despite his long years in the profession, he is still moved by such things: he is a sensitive soul.

He cannot know that, all too soon, the mystery of Maurice Quentin's death will come knocking at his door, trailing in its wake a string of tragic consequences.

September 5

The young woman is clearly very nervous. She is too quick to laugh and too loud. She is painfully thin. Constance is thirty years old. There is something curiously masculine about her manner, something not unusual in women who have spent time in prison. The woman from the orphanage watches as she struggles to close the bonnet of her car. As for Nathan, he watches the scene impassively, unmoved by Constance's laughter and her gesticulations. He is distant, almost cold; he has spent time in various children's homes, he is inured. Constance has just bought a child seat and has no idea how to install it.

"Let me help," the woman says.

"Don't worry, I can do it!"

Her tone is curt, almost offensive.

The woman shrugs; fine then, go ahead . . .

It is no easy task. Leaning over the back seat, Constance tugs on the plastic strap, trying to work out how it attaches, tries it first one way then the other; it's completely ridiculous, but if she can't do this, she will have failed as a mother. She already feels that she has failed at many things, almost everything, because she has not had time to learn. It's strange that she has been waiting almost five years for this moment, but she has not been able to prepare herself. Then again, a lot has happened in those five years. As she struggles to slot the child seat into the steel brackets, Nathan is only aware of the tightly clenched buttocks in her patterned trousers and her muttered invective. Constance suddenly turns, flashes the care worker an apologetic look, then smiles at the little boy standing behind her, arms by his side, a brand-new plastic figurine of Goldorak he does not know what to do with dangling from his right hand. The boy does not respond to her smile, he stares at her with a reticence that looks like indifference. Or resentment – Constance cannot tell, but it is certainly not friendly. She goes back to her task, shaken by the child's frostiness; it's only to be expected, they hardly know each other.

Nathan was taken from her when he was six months old; Constance punched the social worker who had come to check on their living conditions. Nine days off work. And since Nathan's father was listed as unknown, and Constance had spent time in prison, the authorities immediately took the child into care, she was not allowed to see him, she was sent before a magistrate, she begged and pleaded, but she had a long rap sheet, she wore a long-sleeved shirt to hide the track marks on her arms, but no-one was fooled. Nathan was placed in a care home and later with foster parents, Constance was not allowed to visit, she did not even know where he was. For more than six months, she hounded the authorities, trying to get custody of her son. She did everything they asked, filled in questionnaires, attended appointments, submitted to random blood and urine tests, which required constant juggling because she hadn't managed to detox. At the time she was living with a guy called Samos – she'd never known his real name. Then came the break-in at the rue Louvenne pharmacy and she was sent down for five years. Curiously, it was this which had given her strength to quit. Nathan's presence floated above her like a benevolent cloud. She found the strength to resist the brutal hard-sell of the inmates who dealt drugs inside. Although it really wasn't her thing, she slept with Mona, who was top dog on her wing, and Mona made sure Constance was left in peace. From time to time, she would get news of Nathan, sometimes a photograph, and every time she would cry. Fat Mona was moved by this, and although she pretended they were still together, she no longer asked anything of Constance, the two became close friends, or as close as people can be in jail. After three years, she was paroled with a six-month probationary period, with no chance of getting Nathan back. She returned to Seine-et-Marne where she had to move house twice, hooked up with a couple of dodgy guys, but, despite her troubles, she didn't relapse. She had only one goal in life: to prove that she deserved custody of her son. She finally found an apartment she could afford, with a bedroom for the boy. Constance had no qualifications, so she worked on the markets or as a cleaner, resolutely refused cash-in-hand jobs, she wanted pay slips, invoices, receipts, so that she could prove that she was legit, that she had done nothing illegal – a Herculean task when you're at rock bottom. Probation officers came to inspect the apartment, she showed them the child's room, freshly repainted, with a bed, a wardrobe, new clothes, a few toys, even. They subjected her to random blood and urine tests; she did everything they asked, she was a good little soldier.

What really helped was the Hatzer Agency, which provided temp work. Madame Philippon was moved by Constance's circumstances, inspired by her fierce determination. Constance's clients were delighted with her, perhaps because she channelled her rage and determination into her work with the sole aim of getting Nathan back.

And, in the end, it paid off.

The judge made his decision.

Constance can have custody of Nathan again.

She will be subject to supervision, she'll have to answer questions, fill in forms, put up with surprise visits, but she can go fetch her son. She can keep him with her.

She took a bunch of flowers to the agency, a cheap bouquet, but the gesture brought tears to the eyes of Madame Philippon, who had bought a toy for Nathan – she had a grandson about the same age . . .

Under the watchful eyes of the care worker and the boy, Constance continues to struggle with the car seat. She bought the things second-hand – child seats are pretty expensive. She wonders whether she's been conned, whether there's a piece missing, and at the thought that unless she can install this bloody seat she won't be allowed to take Nathan with her, she feels a wave of panic.

"Are you sure you don't want me to . . . ?" the care worker says.

On the verge of tears, Constance steps aside and the woman patiently explains how it works.

"Watch me, you slip the strap underneath here and . . . now slide your hand under here, no, a little bit further, you'll feel the little catch – can you feel it? Now, press the buckle in, and you'll hear a click. Go on, try it."

Constance tries it; it clicks into place – she is a good mother again.

She flashes Nathan a complicit smile but the child doesn't bat an eyelash. He doesn't know this woman, and he's had to deal with all sorts of people in his short life, he's not about to smile for nothing, he needs a reason.

In the boot of the car next to Constance's suitcase, he had seen a gift-wrapped package. Nathan is sure it's for him and wonders when she will give it to him. The minute she showed up she gave him the plastic robot from some TV series he's never watched; Nathan did not say anything, but he can't wait to be rid of it. If she put as much thought into the present in the boot of the car, it's not promising.

The child allows himself to be strapped into the child seat. Constance does not know what to say.

"Thanks ... thanks for ..."

The care worker smiles.

"Don't forget to buckle him in," she says.

Shit!

Constance leans into the car to grab the seatbelt, this is the first time she and Nathan have been physically close. Though it lasts only a split second, they both know this is a crucial moment, but do not know what to do. Constance sees Nathan's face in close-up, the grey-brown eyes, the little mouth, his chestnut fringe that falls over his forehead ... He is so beautiful that it terrifies her. Nathan can smell Constance's perfume, it's a smell he doesn't recognise, girly, a little sweet; he loves the smell, but is careful not to show it.

The drive does not go well. Almost three hundred kilometres to Melun.

"We could stop and get a pizza, what do you say?"

But Nathan would prefer a McDonald's Happy Meal. Constance talks endlessly about their life together, all the things they can do now that they are together again, for ever. But the boy speaks only to find fault with the sweets she bought him, the comics she picked out ... By the time Constance finally gets to Paris around midnight, her nerves are shot. Only then does she realise she forgot to give him the present; she left it in the boot of the car.

Nathan has spent the long car journey thinking of little else. By the time they arrive, he is fast asleep.

Constance had been looking forward to this homecoming, had imagined Nathan discovering his bedroom, the furniture, the toys, but here he is, sound asleep in her arms. He really needs to go to the bathroom, brush his teeth. If he doesn't, then I'm a bad mother. But she simply undresses the boy and slips him into bed without waking him. It was a gruelling drive! She wouldn't have put up with such behaviour from anyone else. There had been stressful moments, the whole pizza-versus-burger showdown – Constance could kick herself. A child's trust is something you have to earn . . . This was what the judge said to her when she applied for custody.

It's late now. Tomorrow, they will have the whole day together, she has everything planned, the movie, the picnic, but just now, she worries about everything.

She uncorks a bottle of Bordeaux. She is shattered.

Vasiliev now visits twice a week. Still, Monsieur de la Hosseray grumbles: "You don't come and see me very often . . ." Tevy stifles a snigger. René offers an embarrassed apology. Temperatures have been soaring all summer, and Tevy has had to draw on her considerable ingenuity to keep the house aired and Monsieur cool, though he never complains about anything. "We go to the park a lot," says Tevy. "Monsieur likes to read the newspaper." Vasiliev hasn't seen so many newspapers in the house for years. Time was, Monsieur's desk groaned under the weight of them, then he tired of reading them, now it seems his enthusiasm has returned.

Thinking about it, Vasiliev is amazed by the extent of the young nurse's influence. Everything in the apartment has been marked by her presence: the new cushions, the reorganisation of Monsieur's bedroom, but also the new lamps ("I mean, you could hardly see your hand in front of your face, could you?"). And all the amulets and gris-gris. Tasteful and discreet, but, as Tevy confesses with a laugh, she is very superstitious. She surrounds herself with all manner of good-luck charms, she can't help it. And so, betel-nut boxes shaped like birds, gilded offering bowls, figures of apsara dancers, a terracotta copy of the bas relief of Avalokiteshvara from the Plaosan temple have laid siege to Monsieur's collection of nineteenth-century bronzes, alabaster ashtrays and delicate engravings. Her superstitions amuse René and provide a distraction to Monsieur. For example, she has never really liked the apartment. Not that it is uncomfortable, but the staircase has an odd number of steps: "It allows ghosts to enter the house." She laughs at herself, but she believes it nonetheless. A few nights ago – René does not remember how they got onto the subject; he certainly didn't bring it up – Tevy informed him that a man should never sleep with a woman who shaved her pubic hair: "It will lead to terrible trouble for the man, oh yes." René had blushed, not Tevy.

On the subject of Maurice Quentin's murder, Tevy is adamant that he would not have died if his body had been armoured by sacred tattoos.

"I'm not sure a tattoo is a particularly effective talisman against a .44 Magnum," said Vasiliev.

"You can't know that, René!"

He asked if she had considered a sacred tattoo for her own protection. Tevy blushed; René did not know where to put himself . . . Since then, he has been troubled by the idea that, somewhere on Tevy's body, there is a sacred tattoo. He cannot help but think that it is in a secret place, and the thought is profoundly unsettling.

Although they are on first-name terms, they are very formal.

They had ended up talking about Maurice Quentin not because there are any new developments in the case, but because Monsieur de la Hosseray met him once.

"It was at the Jockey Club, at a gala dinner, I don't remember the occasion . . . A curious cove. He spent positively ages telling us some story about a safari he hadn't even been on . . ."

Vasiliev's visits play out according to a pattern that owes much to Monsieur, but also to Tevy. Both are very attentive to routine, convention, ritual. They make small talk over drinks, dine on noodles or on vegetable soup, and afterwards they sit at the big living room table and play Nain Jaune. Tevy usually wins. René suspects that she cheats, he never tries to catch her out, but he would like to think she cheats. When he can, he lets her win; Tevy is happy, her victory confirms all her beliefs and superstitions.

Tonight, Monsieur once again brought up the subject of the Maurice Quentin case.

"I haven't paid much attention for a while now," René said.

"Another scandal hushed up," said Monsieur.

"Hushed up," Tevy said. She makes a mental note of unfamiliar expressions, and repetition helps her memorise them. Later she tries to use them, with varying success; René corrects her with an apologetic gesture, Tevy is never offended.

After their game of Nain Jaune, when Monsieur has dozed off, René and Tevy sit chatting in the living room; sometimes René stays late into the night.

"Having met Monsieur, you know my whole family," Vasiliev says, "but you've never told me anything about your family . . ."

"They're not very interesting."

Seeing that René is waiting for her to say more, she adds:

"I mean, they're nothing special, families are all the same, aren't they, whether they're in Cambodia or in France?"

It is a subject that she clearly does not want to talk about, and in fact she changes the subject, talks about Monsieur, goes over the game of Nain Jaune they have just played, which reminds Vasiliev that he intended to make a suggestion.

"I thought . . ." he says, "I thought maybe some night we could take a photo, what do you say?"

"A photo?"

"Yes, a memento of the evenings we've spent with Monsieur. For when the time comes that . . . Well, you know what I mean . . ."

"Oh no!" says Tevy.

She seems so outraged that Vasiliev cannot help but wonder how he has offended her.

"You should never take a picture of three people; it brings bad luck. One of the three would surely die!"

They are both thinking about the same thing – Monsieur's advancing age – and suddenly they burst out laughing. It is an enjoyable evening. His evenings here are always pleasant, not to mention that twice a week René gets to eat food that has not been tinned or frozen.

As Tevy is showing him out, Vasiliev says: "Tell me something, Tevy . . . Has Monsieur . . . has he got a screw loose?"

Tevy frowns at this unfamiliar expression and René taps his temple with his finger.

Twice this evening, when talking about Maurice Quentin,

Monsieur had suddenly said, as though he had only just remembered:

"I met him once. It was at the Jockey Club, at a gala dinner, I don't remember the occasion . . . A curious cove. He spent positively ages telling us some story about a safari he hadn't even been on . . ."

Tevy remembers. She does not tell René that she has noticed various other signs of Monsieur's decline. She simply laughs, her hand over her mouth.

"Yes, sometimes his screw is a bit loose . . ."

As he takes his leave, Vasiliev bends down and they kiss each other on the cheek.

Ever since last May and the disastrous Quentin affair, Henri Latournelle has been preoccupied by Mathilde. Needless to say, he has not phoned her again, in fact, as is often the case, he has had no news of her, but this time, for reasons he cannot understand, he is worried. It is perfectly normal for them not to be in touch; protocol stipulates that any contact be the exception rather than the rule. It is the uncertainty that worries him. Is something wrong? Something that might cause problems in future operations? But this is not his only worry, his chief concern is Mathilde.

Though he dare not admit it even to himself, it troubles him deeply. How much does he love her? The question merely adds to his misery. He has loved her passionately. But always from afar.

1941. Mathilde is barely nineteen and utterly ravishing. Nothing like the fat frump with the wizened face she has become.

She was brought into the Resistance movement by Coudray, a comrade who was killed shortly afterwards. Henri, who has just set up the Imogène network, gives her minor missions, suitcases to carry, addresses to investigate, messages to deliver, and she proves her worth.

In 1941, in the guise of a nurse, Mathilde plays a key role in the successful escape of three comrades from the Gestapo in Toulouse. It was her coolness that impressed him; she was fearless.

Then comes the day in 1942 when the network is broken up due to an unfortunate coincidence which is no-one's fault, but which decimates the workforce. Henri still remembers that frantic day when the surviving members mobilised to prevent a brutal breakthrough by German intelligence. They have to move fast, very fast, to recover documents, warn other comrades, manage escape routes, organise arms shipments, notify other networks, ensure there are no leaks . . . That day, Mathilde performs miracles. Being totally overwhelmed with other tasks, Henri asks her to check whether a cache of weapons is under Gestapo surveillance. Only much later, when the storm has passed, is he able to reconstruct the sequence of events. At the depot, Mathilde spots the discreet Gestapo surveillance unit. She is running a twofold risk: the entire cache may be seized, but, if she tries to save it, she could be arrested. There is only one Nazi vehicle. The German intelligence service may be quick, but the reinforcements they need to secure the trap are not yet in place. Mathilde calls Roger, a strong man always ready to be of service, he shows up with his empty fruit and vegetable van, and together he and Mathilde load up the cache in less than twenty minutes. "She didn't say a word, the lass, not a word," says Roger, appreciatively. They set off. Roger is reluctant to take the main street since there is always a Nazi unit there. "She seemed completely confident."

In the end, nothing happens. "I was scared to death . . ." The surveillance car does not move. Half an hour later, when Nazi reinforcements arrive, they find the two guards in the front of the car with their throats cut.

Henri does not approve of this piece of initiative. And reprisals are swift. But he has to acknowledge that the arms cache has been saved. The balance sheet of war is something he has always struggled to resolve. But after this incident, he looks at Mathilde very differently. She is still the same: quiet, pretty, not particularly talkative. It's insane how much Henri yearns for her. They flirt constantly, their fingers brush against each other, but nothing happens. Henri wants to know everything there is to know about her life, but she tells him very little. He cannot reconcile the image of this girl as lissom as a wildflower with the slaughter of two men. It is something that haunts him, but he does not pose the question because he is afraid of the answer. She would have to have climbed into the back seat, slit the first officer's throat and instantly killed the other . . . Or perhaps she used two knives, one in each hand . . . ? Did she use her feminine wiles to get close to them?

Afterwards, it was too late, other matters took precedence, the episode with Gerhardt . . . A handsome man, pure Aryan, self-confident, a fanatical Nazi. "Let me do it." Gerhardt was already in a bad way and the comrades dealing with him had given up. They were in a remote barn, everyone had to get back home, the plan was to dispose of the German before nightfall. "Let me do it," Mathilde said decisively, without a flicker of hesitation. Henri had been weak, he had agreed, though he had insisted on one condition: that an armed Resistance fighter stay behind with her. It was Gilles who stayed behind, the name came back to him suddenly. Everyone else headed off, leaving Gerhardt and Mathilde alone while Gilles stood guard. "Can you drop by my parents' place? I don't want them to worry unnecessarily."

Henri had gone to see Dr Gachet, though it was the doctor's wife he saw. He reassured them; they trusted him.

He barely slept that night. The following morning, he had been the first to arrive, shortly after daybreak. Gilles was dozing in a hayrick at the entrance to the path. The roar of the car woke him.

"He's dead," the sentry said.

He looked dazed, probably from exhaustion.

"Where's Mathilde?"

He nodded to the barn without a word.

Henri ran over and ripped open the door, waking Mathilde.

"You startled me," she said, getting to her feet.

She smoothed her skirt as though she had just finished dinner. She handed him a piece of paper, he recognised her handwriting, saw the dark marks beneath her fingernails – there was no water on the farm, the well had long since run dry. "It's all there," she said. Two names, a date, a location, a dozen words. Henri goes to the far end of the barn, which is lit only by a bare bulb that dangles from the beam. The floor around the table is squishy, the hay has soaked up a lot of blood. The German soldier lying on the ground is pale and bloodless as a fish. Henri throws up. The man's fingers and toes have been tossed into the bucket used to milk cows back when there was a farm. Together with the eyes, the ears, the testicles and various things he cannot identify.

"I'm tired, can you ask Gilles to drive me home?"

Mathilde is there, smiling – is she expecting a compliment? No, that is not what she wants. She gathers up her things, then turns and stares at Henri. And it is her expression in that moment that will forever linger in his mind, that rises up every time it seems likely that something might happen between them. It's not the face of a woman in pain, it is an expression of sheer . . . satisfaction.

Henri goes outside to join Gilles.

"I had to get away . . ." Gilles says by way of apology. "I couldn't stand there listening to that . . . you understand?"

"Shall we go?" says Mathilde.

Gilles bows his head and walks around the barn to where his car is parked. Mathilde plants a kiss on Henri's cheek and walks away. She has a figure that would tempt a saint.

After that, nothing in the group was ever the same.

Mathilde was . . . Henri gropes for a word. But several words are needed to talk about Mathilde, the woman of the war years. The members of the unit had been shocked by the incident of the slaughtered Nazis, but Mathilde's night in the company of this German NCO left them completely dumbfounded. From that moment, the unit divided into those who avoided working with her and those who would not work with anyone else. She was at once ghost and muse, saint and succubus, goddess and demon. What surprised Henri was how many men were attracted to her. Did she succumb to their advances? If so, no man ever bragged about it.

None truly knew Mathilde. There was never another Gerhardt, but when it came to killing Nazis or collaborators, she was always there. As if it were her right. And she had a penchant for knives. "Quieter, more discreet," she would say. Whenever there was blood, Mathilde was sure to be found.

And later . . .

1947, Mathilde marries Dr Perrin. A beautiful ceremony. After that, she and Henri lose touch. In 1951, he receives a card announcing the birth of Françoise. They arrange to meet in Limoges, where Mathilde is teaching French, but the meeting never happens. Such is life. They are brought together in 1955 when they are presented with medals by the minister.

Five years later, they meet again when Dr Perrin dies. There is a huge throng of mourners. Henri is lost in the crowd, but Mathilde sees him from afar and comes to him, shakes his hand as though he were an old comrade. As the dignified widow, Mathilde is irresistible. Henri does some mental calculations: she is thirty-eight. She has never seemed so beautiful, so alluring; black becomes her. For several weeks, Henri wonders whether to declare himself. Is there someone else in her life? A dozen times he picks up the phone to call, takes a pen to write, but every time he gives up. Deep down, Mathilde terrifies him.

At the time, Henri is spending much of his time travelling. He is seeking out and hiring specialists he refers to as "the scum", former Resistance fighters, men who have been drummed out of the Foreign Legion and have turned to crime; he finds it difficult because a true professional is almost impossible to find, there is always some flaw, and there are few competent people you can truly trust.

In 1961, the idea comes to him. He doesn't know how, but it seems obvious. A stroke of genius. What more perfect collaborator could he have than a well-heeled widow with an impeccable past as a Resistance fighter? He gets in touch with her; her eyes well with tears at the prospect. She executes her first mission. The Personnel Director is very happy with her work. As a result, they barely see each other – a necessary precaution, they cannot be seen to associate; Mathilde understands.

From time to time, they call each other from telephone booths. One mission follows another, three or four a year. Some of them outside France.

Mathilde sometimes takes her daughter, Françoise, with her, leaves her by the hotel swimming pool, goes and shoots a woman in the head as she is rummaging for her car keys, then reappears, dressed to the nines, with bags of groceries and presents to take back to Paris.

In the course of twenty years, they meet three times. Henri always credits these encounters to luck, as though luck plays any role in his life. They meet in Paris in 1962 and again in 1963 – a tricky period when new protocols had to be put in place. "We're taking a cold hard look at everything," is the message from Personnel. All operatives must be re-interviewed, every dossier carefully re-examined; some operatives Henri will never see again, Mathilde passes with flying colours ... They meet again in 1970. Mathilde, in her fifties, is exultant, she still has the same lithe figure, the same unmistakeable gait, waist thrust slightly forward on the side of the extended leg, there is something liquid about the way she moves. They have dinner at the Bristol. Mathilde is radiant. To Henri, she is an unfathomable mystery. A day earlier, she was in Frankfurt – an urgent mission, not a second to lose, triple the usual rate, the client was desperate, fine, someone will deal with it – and Mathilde was selected for the operation. She walked into a hotel room, there were three people present, one man, two women, three bullets in three seconds; within four minutes, she is out on the street while the gun and the glove that held it are in a bin in the hotel lobby.

"Well, I just took the lift!" she says to Henri when he asks how she managed to leave without a hitch. "You hardly thought I was going to walk down the four flights of stairs in heels, did you?"

She laughs heartily; she is irresistible. This is Henri's big day. Never before has he been so convinced that something will finally happen between them, that they will tell each other . . . But, nothing . . . As she gets into the taxi, Henri feels himself dissolve. That was fifteen years ago.

And the older Mathilde gets, the more perfect her cover becomes.

She has become slow and sturdy, her eyesight is poor, she perspires at the slightest heat, drives with her face almost pressed against the windscreen; she looks like anything but what she really is.

Beyond suspicion.

Until recently.

Then the thought comes back to Henri like a boomerang: the Quentin operation – was it just a hiccup? That's what Mathilde said, though she sounded rather vague. Or was it more of an organisational problem? This nagging worry makes it difficult to decide. There's another contract in Paris in a few days. He's a little hesitant to give it to Mathilde. This is the first time he has ever hesitated.

Mathilde is daydreaming. Sometimes, when the weather is fine, she takes a garden chair and sits on the covered terrace outside her house. Like an old biddy, she thinks. She gazes at the trees in the garden, the straight path that leads to the front gate. She can sit here for hours, lost in thought, waiting for night to draw in. *I'm bored stiff* . . . But she has another reason to sit out here, doing nothing: the funny turn she had this afternoon. All the way back from Paris, her heavy features were animated by a series of tics as her expression shifted from irritation to sadness, and – with no transition – from abject misery to a crafty smile, depending on whether she was thinking about Henri – dear Henri! – and the contract he will soon give her (it's tedious, waiting around, doing nothing) or about the state she left the house in, it is getting to look like a pigsty – I really should do something about it, but, well . . . She had popped into a home help agency in Melun to hire a cleaner. The idiot woman across the desk asked for a detailed description of the work.

"It's cleaning, cleaning a house, I assume you know what that involves?"

This, apparently, was not enough; further details were required.

"Have you ever cleaned your house?" said Mathilde. "Well, it's like that, except it's my house . . ."

Perhaps it was this conversation that had unsettled her. When she left the agency, she was jittery.

The woman from the agency had jotted down the address of a girl who lived nearby and was looking for work.

"Does she know how to clean?"

"Everyone knows how to clean."

"True, true," said Mathilde, "but there's many as know but don't want to do the work. Like me, for instance. And I don't want to be hiring someone like me."

The woman sighed.

"She's a young, single woman who needs work, she's dedicated, very conscientious . . ."

Her name was Constance something – Mathilde can't remember now whether they agreed that she would phone, or the girl would call her . . .

She was still frazzled when she pulled into the supermarket car park and it was then that she felt a sudden wave of exhaustion. Her legs felt like jelly, she felt a twinge in her chest.

The seizure hit her as she was getting out of her car. She was looking at the people, at the overflowing trolleys weaving up and down the aisles, but the images all seemed distorted. She had to hang onto the car door for several seconds and wait for the dizziness to pass. Sadness replaced the pain in her chest; she decided she'd do the shopping some other time, that she'd be better off going home. Being back in the car was reassuring, it felt almost like home. She set off back to La Coustelle. This was the name her husband had given their house, a name he borrowed from another house where he had spent part of his childhood. At the time, Mathilde had not much liked the name, and she found his tendency to cling to his past annoying. She had agreed because, deep down, it didn't really matter. Except that now, she is the only one to use this name that she has never liked. It is Dr Perrin's legacy. Even her daughter doesn't use it much, she doesn't really like the house, she doesn't like anything – and her husband is worse, he hates anything that's not American . . .

Now, the day is drawing to a close, Mathilde is sitting on the terrace in her rocking chair. Ludo, lying at her feet, is snoring like a pile driver.

She counts off on her fingers. Four months with no news from Henri, four months since he assigned her a contract. Then again, June, July and August are always quiet – the business tends to be seasonal . . . No, that's not right. Mathilde shakes her head, no, the contracts come in clusters. There will be nothing for three months, and then she'll have two in quick succession. So, something should come about now, or maybe in September . . . The real question is whether Henri is angry. Was he just pretending not to be annoyed? She can't really remember what it was that irked him, it's already so long ago, she only remembers that he sounded a little curt on the phone. And, why didn't he come to visit her? She would love to see dear Henri again. They have made such wonderful memories together . . . Henri is the polar opposite of her husband. She never truly felt any desire for her husband, they did the deed because it had to be done, but aside from the fact that he was a hopeless lover, it was a question of skin, they just didn't fit. They had got on well, and she had mourned his death as she would that of a childhood friend. But she burned with passion for Henri. The first time he shook her hand, she had felt the thrill ripple though her whole body. She had never said anything. She was a doctor's daughter, a good middle-class girl, there are some things you simply don't say to a man. And, given his position, he could hardly . . . He was the boss, he was in charge, the commandant! He could hardly start screwing his female comrades between bombings . . .

And then, after the war, life went back to what it was before.

But the least he could do is realise she's been fretting and give her a job!

An ungrateful bastard, that's what you are, Henri!

"Madame Perrin?"

It's not like I'm asking for the moon – just something to do! To make myself useful! Oh, you get to travel, you give the orders, you have lots to do, why should you give a thought to anyone else, especially your dear old Mathilde! I'm not as rusty as you think! I might just surprise you!

"Madame Perrin!"

Mathilde looks up.

Monsieur Lepoitevin, her cretinous neighbour. His house is only about fifty metres away. They can't see each other because of the boundary hedges, so from time to time he pops round on the pretext of bringing vegetables from his garden for which Mathilde has no use – she politely accepts them and throws them in the bin at the first opportunity. What does he expect me to do with two kilos of courgettes, the fool . . .

She recognises the figure at the gate: a short, thickset man, the kind that sweats, even his hand is clammy, Mathilde finds it faintly disgusting. She waves him in. He pushes open the gate – the latch hasn't worked for ages, it needs to be fixed, but she has so many things to think about. Ludo stirs, senses a presence and gets up, already wagging his tail at the prospect of greeting the newcomer, he's a gentle dog, he would never do as a watchdog.

"Ludo!" Mathilde says brusquely.

If she lets him, he'll launch himself at Monsieur Lepoitevin and lick his hands – that's all she needs. Ludo meekly lies down again.

Mathilde sees her neighbour is carrying his wicker basket. What a pest.

"Not disturbing you, am I?"

"I was just relaxing. Lovely evening, isn't it?"

"Indeed. Not a breath of wind. Some lettuces," he says, setting the basket on the terrace.

Well, obviously, I can see they're not beetroots, you moron . . .

"That's very sweet," she says with a smile.

In his fifties, brown moustache, as staid as a pensioner before his time. She knows very little about him, and cares less.

They chat a little about the forecast.

Mathilde wants to talk, but not with Lepoitevin, it's so

unrewarding. The weather, the joys of the countryside, the pleasures of having a dog . . . A couple of nights ago, he was gushing about a German shepherd he had for thirteen years. He gave details of the paralysis, the incontinence. When he came to the part where he had to take it to the vet to have it put down, there were tears in his eyes. If that's the kind of conversation he wants, he should stay at home.

Mathilde endures this nonsense for an interminable fifteen minutes, then it becomes a little chilly and Monsieur Lepoitevin decides it's time to go home.

"You won't mind if I don't walk you to the gate," says Mathilde.

He loves this sort of situation, which allows him to smile and seem like a gallant man who understands such things.

"Not at all, Madame Perrin, not at all!"

He gives a loud laugh.

"It's not as if I don't know the way!"

As he walks past the railings, he gives a last little wave; Mathilde does not respond.

I cannot abide that man . . . Not that she has anything against him, but that sort of obsequiousness often hides something depraved . . . I'm going to watch out for him, she thinks.

"Come on, inside."

The dog doesn't need to be told twice. Mathilde shivers, she has been outside a little too long, and all because of that idiot Lepoitevin, he must want her dead – there's no other explanation.

Before she heads upstairs, she hunts around for her glasses. She may not be a bookworm, but if she doesn't read a little at night, she can't get to sleep. She finds them in one of the dresser drawers. Next to them is a folded sheet of paper. As she opens it, she feels a surge of joy that makes her heart beat faster.

"Oh, thank you, Henri! You're such a sweetheart! You see – you remember old Mathilde, don't you?"

She reads. It's written in her handwriting, though she cannot remember writing it, and since, according to protocol, she is not supposed to make notes, she dismisses the idea. She feels so overcome that she goes over and sits in the armchair. She turns on the little table lamp and reads the note again: "Constance Manier, 12, boulevard Garibaldi." That's in Messin, a small town very near Melun – almost a suburb. So that is why Henri has assigned her the job, it's close to home, he probably doesn't want to bring someone in from elsewhere to save on costs . . .

She is delighted.

"Come, Ludo, come here."

The dog warily approaches, she strokes his muzzle and, feeling more confident, he lays his head on her lap.

"Good boy, good boy . . . We've got a job. Henri has assigned us a contract. After all this time."

Relieved. This time, she wants Henri to be happy, not to phone her afterwards making cryptic remarks she doesn't understand.

"What do you say, Ludo? We'll make a good job of this one."

September 6

She is woken by the sound of fighting. Shots. Guns. She jumps
out of bed, her heart pounding, and rips open the door. Nathan
is sitting in front of the TV. Onscreen, the characters are riddling
each other with machine guns. She cannot stop herself.

"What the hell is this . . . ?"

It is the word she remembers, not the gesture. She grabs the
remote control; instantly, silence is restored. Nathan is staring
at her. She sleeps in her knickers and a short T-shirt. Indecent.
She goes to her room and pulls on a baggy jumper. This makes it
worse, it's too sexy, but she can't bring herself to go back again
so she stands there, staring at him.

"You need to ask before you turn on the TV."

"Ask who?"

"Me."

"I was bored . . ."

"Well . . . Surely you can wait until I get up, can't you?"

"What time do you get up?"

Constance has a sudden doubt. A glance at the clock. Christ,
it's half past ten! Did she sleep through her alarm or what? There
is a reproachful silence in the room.

"I bought some stuff for breakfast . . ."

She goes to the kitchen: the cereal box is still on the table.
Nathan has already had breakfast, washed and dried the dishes

and put them away; Constance doesn't know what to say. He is staring at her legs. She needs to do something.

"Have you had a shower? Come on, I'll show you."

She takes him to the bathroom, shows him where to find the soap and the towels, she is beaming now, her enthusiasm has flooded back, but she feels intimidated by this child.

"It's fine," he says to reassure her.

She closes the door, takes a deep breath, sees the rain lashing the windows. She'd been planning on the zoo, then a picnic – what an idiot.

The suburb is like a wasteland sprouting hulking tower blocks. The patches of grass look like slashed tyres. During the day, there are a lot of cars outside – the people here have cars, but no jobs. So, they tinker with their cars; this is how they spend their time. Factor in the drug dealers, and there are always people with nothing better to do than watch who's coming, who's going, who's parking. For Mathilde, this makes her stakeout more complicated. Especially since her brand-new Renault 25 will attract attention. Initially, she drove past as though she had lost her way. She checked out the surroundings. The only discreet observation post was a street on the corner of the boulevard Garibaldi where the target lives.

It's been raining since early this morning, there are not many people out in the streets, it's quiet, she has to turn on the air conditioning from time to time because of the condensation.

There is something troubling Mathilde. This is far from her first mission, but she's never had a target like this. This Constance woman is in her thirties, thin as a rake, and looks a bit like a lesbian – but she's got a little brat in tow, so it can't be that.

She lives on a council estate blighted by unemployment, where the only shops not boarded up and covered with graffiti are a scattering of pound shops . . . It is a far cry from her usual target. Then again, she thinks, everyone's got the right to die, why not her? But when Mathilde is stalking a victim, deciding on the perfect time, the perfect angle, the perfect location, she's never able to stop herself wondering why someone has taken out a contract on this target. With this Constance, it must be something to do with drugs and dealers, or maybe it's a sex thing.

Whatever the reason, it must be a good one since the cash spent on bumping her off is probably more than she gets to live on in six months.

The rain puts paid to everything. She has no plan B.

Out of weakness (she knows it is a bad start . . .), she allows the boy to watch television while she showers and dresses; the morning slips past, there is no sign of the rain stopping.

Then, suddenly, she gives up. The pressure is too much.

Around noon, she says:

"I was planning for us to have a picnic after we'd been to the zoo. But . . ."

They both look at the windows.

"We'll just have to eat it here."

She sets the paper bags down on the table, and purposefully takes out the fruit, the foil-wrapped sandwiches, the crisps, the family-size bottle of Coke. Now that she has stopped trying to pander to Nathan, he seems more relaxed.

"I don't mind," he said. "And anyway, me and zoos . . ."

"Really, you too?"

The tin foil was a bad idea, the bread is soggy and unpleasant – it's a disaster . . .

They eat sitting face to face, making small talk. Despite the soggy sandwiches, everything turns out better this way. Nathan devours the crisps. She thinks he looks adorable and she smiles.

"Why are you smiling?"

"I was just wondering if you're planning to leave me any crisps . . ."

"Oh . . ."

He hurriedly hands her the remains of the pack, he is clearly upset, he apologises. There remains the problem of what to do with the day.

"How about a movie?" Constance says.

Nathan simply nods – OK. In the weekend paper, she finds a listing for the local cinemas.

"*The Never-Ending Story?*"

"Is *Gremlins* on anywhere?" Nathan says.

Constance scans the list, no, not right now . . . So they agree on *The Never-Ending Story* – it'll be fine.

"Right, then," says Constance, "if we're going to the movies this afternoon, I'd probably better go buy something for tonight's dinner . . ."

She is talking to herself, going round in circles.

"I can't really drag you out shopping in this rain."

She is visibly hesitating. Nathan looks at her quizzically.

"It's just that leaving you here on your own, well . . . It's not . . ."

She means "not appropriate". Can you leave children his age home alone? The rain is still lashing the windows. Do you drag them to the supermarket during a downpour?

"Oh, I don't mind staying," Nathan reassures her. "Unless it means I can't watch TV . . ."

It makes them both laugh.

As she is leaving, Nathan says:

"The picnic was really amazing."

He sounds sincere. He seems about to say something else. Constance feels as though she might faint. She longs to hug him, but she stops herself. It's not the right time, not yet . . . Nathan needs to adjust, and it has to come from him . . . There are so many reasons not to hug him – but she aches to pull him to her, she's been waiting for that moment for weeks, for months, for years. And still it hasn't come. It's choking her. But she's afraid she'll ruin everything.

She pulls herself together and acts as though he said something pleasant but trite.

"Yes, it was nice."

"Especially the crisps . . ."

They smile at each other.

Constance heads towards the stairs filled with a joy she hasn't felt since . . . A joy she's never felt.

Under normal circumstance, Mathilde should have called Supplies. She decided not to do so. She has a lot of ironmongery to get rid of. The whole house is littered with guns that for some reason she can't remember didn't end up at the bottom of the Seine. They're everywhere: in boxes, in drawers, hardly a day goes by without her stumbling on another one. She settles on a Wildey Magnum she last used two or three years ago. She likes this pistol, it's perfectly balanced with a lovely wooden fore stock. The barrel is long, making it a bit unwieldy, but it's a lovely pistol, which is probably why she kept it. And it has the large calibre she prefers.

She is still wondering if this Constance Manier can really be the right target.

Should she call Henri to check?

There is something not right about the whole thing . . .

In cases of emergency, there's a number where she can leave a message, Mathilde knows it by heart, Henri always calls back promptly.

She turns on the windscreen wipers, rummages in her pockets for the crumpled piece of paper, smooths it out and reads it. No, everything seems in order.

Mathilde is in a quandary. She cannot bring herself to believe something she knows is correct. Indisputable. Her target has been clearly identified, but still she has a nagging doubt.

In that same moment, Constance appears at the end of the street.

She's wearing a nylon raincoat, something light that she pulls tighter against the rain and the wind.

Mathilde doesn't hesitate.

She climbs out of the car, dashes to the other side, already soaked to the skin. She opens the passenger door, leans in and rummages in the glove compartment. By the time she stands up again, the young woman is approaching, head bowed. She dodges to avoid the open car door, then suddenly looks up at this plump, elderly woman wearing nothing to protect herself from the rain, and stops dead when she sees the pistol with its impossibly long barrel. She has no time to wonder.

Mathilde puts a bullet in the heart at point-blank range.

Her hair plastered to her face, her clothes clinging to her skin, Mathilde climbs back into the car.

Less than thirty seconds later, she pulls away.

A figure comes running down from the end of the street, head covered by a newspaper, and screams at the sight of the body sprawled on the pavement and the blood streaming into the gutter . . .

Mathilde turns onto the main road and heads back to La Coustelle. With the back of her hand, she wipes the condensation from the windscreen.

"Pain in the arse, this rain . . ."

September 8

Before leaving the office, Vasiliev opens the slim file on the Tan family. Tan is Tevy's surname. In her reluctance to talk about her family, he sensed not simply modesty, but embarrassment. How much does he actually know about her, beyond the fact that she is a nurse, a qualified carer, who lives near the Porte de la Chapelle and owns an antediluvian Ami 6?

So, he had a file sent up from the immigration department.

If Tevy's name appears only on standard bureaucratic documents (visa on arrival in France, application for the recognition of overseas qualifications, enrolment in university, etc.), her brothers are well known to the police. The twins, born in 1958, have been arrested on numerous occasions. They formerly ran a fairly small network of drug dealers, but in the past two years they have become involved in prostitution. A pair of brutal thugs, inured by their status as immigrants, desperate for their place in the sun.

Vasiliev realises why Tevy was unwilling to talk about them to a cop like him . . .

Whenever he goes to Neuilly, Vasiliev always glances at Tevy's Ami 6 parked outside the building. The bodywork is battered and dented; everything about it looks antique. A fluorescent Buddha dangles from the rear-view mirror and the front and rear seats have been covered with Khmer fabrics. The car looks like a Buddhist shrine.

"I see your Ami 6 had an altercation with a bus . . ." he says as Tevy lets him in.

"Ah, yes . . ."

She puts up a hand to stop him for a moment.

"I don't want you quarrelling with Monsieur, promise me . . ."

René is a little confused.

"Wait there a minute!"

Tevy has already disappeared into the living room, René hurries after her.

"What has he got to do with anything?"

Tevy nervously shifts her weight from one foot to the other.

"I didn't tell you about it because, well . . . He just wanted to give it a try."

"Try what? Driving your car?"

"He showed me his driver's licence!"

"Which was issued when, exactly?"

"In 1931. Alright, it's a little old, it's true, but it's valid!"

"And where did he drive it . . . ? On the street?"

"Well, at first, just on the paths through the park."

"Where the children play?"

He is panicked.

"Yes, but only ever when they were in class! And I always kept hold of the handbrake. Any sign he was swerving, I'd pull on the brake!"

She drops her voice to a whisper and leans towards him.

"Seeing as it's you, I can say that, at first it was a disaster . . ."

"At first . . . Wait a minute . . . He's still driving?"

"He's made wonderful progress. I wanted it to be a surprise when he drove us somewhere one day, but . . ."

Vasiliev is waiting for the other shoe to drop.

"He's really not up to it, I can't see him driving through the city, it would be a bit . . . well, reckless."

Vasiliev is speechless.

"And he crashed the car?"

"No, no! He just pranged a concrete bollard on the corner, no big deal, I don't want you quarrelling with him about it. He's paid for the repairs, I just need to find a time to take the car to the garage . . ."

Vasiliev feels he needs to have a serious talk with Tevy, but she has already disappeared.

Even Monsieur has noticed that René is coming more regularly, and no longer makes snide remarks about his infrequent visits, contenting himself with "Ah, it's you, my little René, it's nice to see you . . ."

René is all the more worried about Tevy and Monsieur's activities because he feels that things are deteriorating. Over dinner (South-East Asian food – that's all they ever eat here), the subject of Maurice Quentin crops up when he's mentioned on the evening news.

"A queer sort of customer, I always thought . . ."

The meeting at the Jockey Club episode seems to have completely slipped his mind, as has the name Maurice Quentin . . .

Later, while they are playing Nain Jaune, Monsieur can go two turns without discarding any cards, or does so twice during a single turn. It's nothing serious, but his forgetfulness seems to be worsening. At first, René flashes a smile at Tevy, who has also noticed. Later, he doesn't smile, he tries to cheerfully carry on, but he's worried and it shows. They watch the late-evening news and when Monsieur falls asleep, it is Tevy who broaches the subject.

"Yes, he is a little worse than he has been. That's why I let him drive the car. Very soon, it won't be possible . . ."

Vasiliev understands.

"There have been other incidents, haven't there?"

Tevy nods, but she feels bound by professional confidentiality. René doesn't really want to know too much. Moreover, he is haunted by a nagging thought he doesn't know what to do with.

Would he and Tevy still see each other if Monsieur passed away?

A glorious surprise: Henri has been in touch!

Though, actually, it was hardly a surprise! The contract on Constance was flawlessly executed, and in record time, and Henri is clearly satisfied. So, he has assigned her another job!

It comes in the form of a Paris postcard, sent from Paris. A picture of the Eiffel Tower. No message, no signature, just a postmark from the day before.

Mathilde heads back down the long driveway from the mailbox by the gate towards her terrace. She is overjoyed! At having work, of course – everyone likes to feel useful – but mostly because she now knows Henri isn't angry with her.

Monsieur Lepoitevin spends his days in his vegetable patch by the hedge, and she hears him shout, "Good morning, Madame Perrin!" Ordinarily, she avoids this guy like the plague, but today she's feeling perky, so calls, "Hello, Monsieur Lepoitevin!" in a bright, cheery voice.

Ludo pads alongside her, he's gambolling near the hedge. Attracted by the presence of Monsieur Lepoitevin. Does he feed my dog things when I'm not there, she wonders. What kind of things? She pauses, stares at the hedge. There's something amiss about her neighbour. Something not quite above board – she's known this from the start.

"Here, Ludo, come!"

She walks on towards the terrace.

A postcard means that at noon tomorrow she needs to be in a public phone box. There are five postcards: a monument, a group of people, a street or avenue, a sepia-tinted image or a collage of different locations. Each postcard designates a different phone box near Mathilde's house.

Suddenly, she stops. A monument – which one does that indicate?

Which phone box did she go to for the guy on the avenue Foch? And for Constance? It seems to have slipped her mind, it will come back to her.

But it doesn't come back. She spends the day fretting, makes a list of the five nearest phone boxes but cannot match them with the postcards, it doesn't come up. At first, she worries she is losing her memory. But no, that's ridiculous, it's simply that after a long period with no work, she had to fulfil a difficult contract (the race to get to the avenue Foch, the stress . . .); in her shoes, anyone would be a little frazzled, so it's not that. Evening comes, and then the night. She falls asleep, wakes up panicking about the monuments of Paris, picks up the list she left nearby, but everything is confused, she turns off the light only to turn it on again after an hour spent tossing and turning.

In the morning, she is exhausted as she drinks her coffee in the kitchen.

"Oh, just leave me alone!"

Ludo goes and lies down in his basket, it doesn't occur to

her to open the door for him to go out and do his business, he whimpers desperately.

"Shut up!"

Mathilde tries to concentrate.

It's completely useless, after the sleepless night she's had, she can barely string two thoughts together.

Ludo whines.

"I said shut up!"

Normally, she should get to the phone box by noon, find a slip of paper with the details of her new target behind the receiver, memorise them, then tear up the paper. If she cannot get there by noon, there is a second chance at the same phone box at six o'clock. Should she not make it, and the paper is still there, the contract is cancelled – i.e. it is passed on to someone else.

Ludo gets up, pads over to the door and whines. Mathilde is exasperated with the dog.

"You can be a real pain, you know that?"

She goes over to him, the dog retreats, his head bowed.

"Well, go on, then. Leave me in peace!"

She opens the door, the dog slinks out and runs to pee on the grass. Mathilde is struggling to think. The phone boxes are some distance apart. She checks the map. They form a large square of several kilometres with her house at the centre. She formulates a plan: she will get to the box at about ten minutes to midday. She never knows what time "the postman" drops off the instructions, but probably shortly before noon. Ten minutes before seems reasonable. She has worked out that, driving at top speed, she can make it to the second box in twenty minutes. Ten minutes to for the first, ten minutes past for the second – it's doable. If it doesn't work out, too bad. She'll just have to try the same ruse at the six o'clock pickup, but she'll have to floor the accelerator and risk causing an accident . . .

Where to start? She has to pick two phone boxes, but which? As she climbs into the car, she still hasn't made up her mind. Let's go with Bastidière. Twenty kilometres away.

She gets there at 11.40 a.m. – too early. If the "postman" should see her pick up the paper and read it, it would cause complications. She drives around the village, then back to the phone booth for ten to twelve. Her heart in her mouth, she gets out of the car, steeling herself to jump back in the car and take off at top speed towards . . . She picks up the receiver, slides a hand down behind and finds the folded slip of paper. Right first time! It's a sign! Thank you, Henri, she could kiss him. She stuffs the paper into her pocket, goes back to her car, discreetly unfolds it and pretends to memorise the details, though in fact she is blindly scribbling them in her notebook in letters big enough that she will be able to read them later. Then she folds the piece of paper, adopts an expression intended to signal that she has memorised the contents, gets out of the car, she is cheery, almost grinning. She steps into the phone box, picks up the receiver, pretends to dial a number and waits as she slips the torn scrap of paper behind the phone, then goes back to the car.

Under normal circumstances, she should put a call in to Supplies tonight, but she's decided to use the weapons she has to hand rather than running around – they always leave the hardware in preposterous far-flung places.

When she gets home, she looks for something that will fit the bill. Ah – there's the Desert Eagle semi-automatic, she hasn't used it in a long time and it's a lovely pistol, does a neat job.

On the kitchen table is the notebook where, in a large trembling hand, she wrote: "Béatrice Lavergne, 18, rue de la Croix, Paris 75015."

It's not every day that the Melun police have a murder like this on their hands. Not that people around here don't stab and punch each other as much as they do anywhere, but such crimes are largely confined to the tower block estates blighted by high unemployment where a disproportionate percentage of immigrants are settled so that other neighbourhoods don't feel overrun – all in all, an ordinary microcosm of France. Rival gangs settle scores, drug dealers engage in turf wars, but a thirty-year-old woman being gunned down with a .44 Magnum in the middle of the street is uncommon.

All available evidence has been laid out on a desk.

The commissaire, a tall man not far off retirement, is studying photographs of the victim. Next to them are mugshots taken before her first spell in prison. Pretty, slim, obviously high-spirited. In the mugshots taken later, drugs have clearly taken their toll. The photos of her body sprawled on the pavement are particularly poor. Attempts were made to shelter the scene with tarpaulins, but it was raining so hard that by the time officers arrived and got themselves organised . . . The wind made things difficult, the tarps were blown away, the forensic unit had to cobble things together and if the case goes to trial, this may well complicate matters – but we are a long way from that yet.

Right now, the veteran commissaire is puzzled by the weapon. A magnum is big, cumbersome, and very rare. And the single shot went right through the heart.

The woman had her ID card in her handbag, and when officers

visited her apartment, they found a startled little boy in front of the television. A young female officer took him aside and explained what had happened; the kid started to cry, so social services were contacted and the boy will be sent back to the children's home he recently left . . . What can this Constance woman possibly have done that someone would have her mown down in the street? Could it be a message – but to whom? From whom? She had been working for a domestic cleaning agency run by a Madame Philippon, who burst into tears at the news. She insisted that Constance had turned her life around, that she had quit drugs, turned her back on her seedy friends: all she wanted was her kid back. What a story . . .

There is something very strange about this case.

The commissaire files away the evidence and tells his team to carry on digging, to put in a call to other local forces to check whether they have anything featuring a similar MO and weapon: a large-calibre semi-automatic, a single bullet to the heart. Maybe it will ring a bell with someone, you never know . . .

September 11

Mathilde always takes her tools with her, even when she's casing a location. With the hit on Constance, this had proved useful: she scoped out the area and did the job in a single visit. It's not always that simple. Sometimes you have to shadow the target for days, something Mathilde doesn't like very much. She's become impatient with age, she wants things done quickly. If scouting the location and tracking the target take more than ten days, there's a protocol for informing the Personnel Director; it's a little complicated and Mathilde isn't sure she remembers how it works. Not because her memory is faulty, but because the situation hasn't arisen in a very long time. The avenue Foch contract took exactly a week, Sunday to Sunday. Constance whatshername was done and dusted so quickly that it's hardly surprising Henri is over the moon. She has no intention of hanging around with Lavergne either.

The target is a beautiful woman in her mid-twenties. Papa is clearly minted. That much is clear from the way she walks, and the way she shops. Her handbag is stuffed with cash and she has a gold card that she flashes at every opportunity. She lives in a genteel neighbourhood.

Mathilde spends three whole days shadowing her, watching and waiting. The university term has not yet started, so the girl is making the most of it: swimming, jogging, retail therapy . . . She's certainly not preparing her doctoral thesis.

Mathilde finds tracking a target exhausting: the hours spent waiting around, the need to make a note of everything, analyse everything, double-check everything. Every day, the girl goes jogging in the Bois de Boulogne. She leaves her Austin Cooper in a car park, does a little warm-up, making sure everyone can see she has a nice arse, then she goes for a run, which usually lasts a good two hours. There is no way that Mathilde can check out her route in search of the perfect location; she'll have to do it differently.

Mathilde thinks the girl's life is dull and meaningless. Although she doesn't know who hates her so much that they've ordered the hit, she can sympathise: the woman is insufferable, she's vermin. Mathilde will wipe the smile off her face.

Except that, at the end of day two, Mathilde still hasn't come up with a plan: there's no useful routine, no obvious place where she can lie in wait. It's all very ordinary, which is why Personnel allocated a ten-day window for the hit ... By the morning of day three, Mathilde is frustrated. She's eager to be done so she can move onto a more interesting job. As she tails the girl's car through the leafy streets of the fifteenth arrondissement, thinking about this notion of an "interesting job", the little Austin Cooper suddenly turns into the car park of a shopping centre. Her every sense on high alert, Mathilde follows the Austin down to the second level, braking sharply when she sees Lavergne stop about ten metres from the pedestrian stairwell and the lifts. This, she instantly realises, is the perfect opportunity. It's not yet 10 a.m., the car park is almost deserted. In a few minutes, when she has parked the car, the girl will get out and walk past the line of cars towards the stairwell. At that point, Mathilde can pick her off. She stops her own car diagonally opposite, and no car comes and beeps for her to keep moving. The moment she sees the girl, she will start her engine, drive towards her, draw alongside just as she reaches the exit. She grabs the Desert Eagle, shoves it between her thighs, lowers the passenger window through which she plans to fire, then bends down to rummage for the silencer in the glove compartment.

From this point, things will go very quickly and very badly for Mathilde. Because she failed to accurately gauge the time the Lavergne girl would need to get out of the car and reach the exit. Mathilde always needs to take off her glasses, gather up her things and put them in the boot where they won't be noticed. But the Lavergne girl simply picks up her handbag, slams the car door and, before Mathilde has time to grab the silencer, she's walking down the central alley.

Mathilde starts the car in first gear and drives at top speed, the engine roars, the Lavergne girl turns to look at the fast-moving car, she ducks aside and presses herself against the wall, still staring at the car.

When she draws alongside, Mathilde slams on the brakes – she's given up on the silencer.

The Lavergne girl is stunned at the sight of this woman stretching her arm through the passenger window, pointing an impressive pistol whose barrel looks like a rolling pin, but she does not have time to wonder; a shot to the pelvis slams her back against the concrete wall between two cars. The thunderous blast echoes around the columns and is amplified by the low ceiling – it sounds as though the car park has been hit by an earthquake.

This kind of impact to the groin is agonising, guts spill out, there is no prospect of survival, but it is not over yet. Mathilde opens her door, bounds out of her seat and, gun in hand, walks around the car and finishes the job with a bullet to the throat, whose blast joins the echoes from the first.

And, in that instant, there is a scream.

A shriek so shrill, so piercing, that even Mathilde is shaken. It is coming from somewhere to her right. Mathilde wheels around: in the next bay, a woman of about fifty is getting out of her car. She witnessed the scene and only now realises what has happened.

She stares, dumbfounded – but not for long, because Mathilde instantly shoots her though the heart.

Panting for breath, Mathilde gets back into her car, tosses the gun under her seat, revs the engine that she never switched off, drives off in a squeal of tyres, taking a sharp right onto the exit ramp. Having reached level one without encountering any other cars, Mathilde slows the car and rolls up the windows. She is now Madame Perrin, sixty-three-year-old widow of this parish, heading home.

The devil, they say, is in the details, if you believe such things. So is luck. And luck is on the side of the police because the attendant at this car park is calm and methodical. He hears a blast, then a second and a third. There is no doubt that it's gunfire. As he is about to close the gates to check out what is happening, a younger colleague radios in and breathlessly tells him a woman has been murdered on level two. The guard presses the panic button; the siren wails. He grabs the phone, calls the police, then lowers the exit barriers in front of the departing cars, whose drivers have no time to react before he seizes a large bunch of keys and runs off.

Mathilde's car is in this queue. The two drivers in front of her have opened their doors – anyone know what's going on? No-one knows. Now Mathilde opens her car door. She thinks she heard a blast . . . It sounded like a gas explosion. That's not very likely, says someone else, it sounded like gunshots . . . Guns, Mathilde shrieks, her eyes wide.

Meanwhile, the security guard is racing down the concrete ramp. On level two, he finds the body of a woman in a pool of blood. Already a small crowd has gathered.

"There's another one over here!"

The security guard pushes forward, suppresses the urge to retch when he sees a second woman with a gaping wound slumped between two cars.

He runs to a metal cabinet marked "Service".

"Give me a hand here," he shouts to his younger colleague.

It takes less than two minutes to roll out the red and white barriers they usually use to mark out work areas. The older man tells his colleague to guard the scene and let no-one through. Under any circumstances. This man knows what he is doing. He heads back up the ramp. From around the car park comes a deafening roar of horns as drivers on every level fume that they cannot move or leave. As he reaches the exit barrier, he calculates there are about twenty vehicles in the queue. The police will be here soon. He goes back into the security hut and picks up where he left off. Drivers are quizzing him, what's going on? Were those gunshots we heard? The security guard is evasive, the ramp needs to be cleared as quickly as possible, that's the most important thing . . .

It takes the emergency services a little time to get to the car park, and the police car and ambulance have difficulty reaching the crime scene through the bottleneck of cars and the blast of horns. On the scene, the forensic officers are taking photographs, witnesses are being questioned . . .

The ambulance will not be here long, this is not a job for para-medics: the coroner's office will remove the bodies once the crime scene investigation is complete.

Just as she reaches the guard to pay for her parking, Mathilde asks:

"What's going on?"

"There's been a murder down on level two!"

"Oh my God! That's appalling!"

"Absolutely appalling . . . That will be four euros fifty, madame . . ."

As he strides into Vasiliev's office, bellowing: "Gather round, there will be blood!", Occhipinti is in a state of excitement close to frenzy. In his manic state, he stuffs two handfuls of pecans into his mouth. In the four months that he has been officially responsible for the Maurice Quentin case, everyone has gone before him, or gone over his head: the secret services, the chan-cellery, the Ministry of the Interior, the judiciary, the politicians, the spooks – they have all meddled in the case, and blamed him for the lack of results. Now, finally, he has another lead: a double murder in a car park in the fifteenth arrondissement. The same kind of high-calibre pistol used in the Quentin murder, the same modus operandi (a bullet to the groin and a second to the throat); the investigating magistrate believed these similarities warranted dispatching Occhipinti's men.

Within twenty minutes they are at the crime scene where forensics are hard at work. The crime was committed an hour and a half earlier, the two bodies have just been removed to the morgue, but as he stands next to the pool of blood seeping into the concrete, Occhipinti is given Polaroids of the two victims. He gobbles a handful of peanuts.

"Right," he sighs.

Impossible to say whether he is referring to the photos or to the peanuts.

The investigating magistrate takes his elbow and leads him a few steps from the crowd.

Vasiliev hears the words "highly sensitive", "I could be wrong", "move quickly". The usual clichés. Meanwhile, he tries to assess the situation. He begins with the young woman gunned down next to the stairwell. Judging from the photograph, the gun was a high-calibre pistol fired at point-blank range. He turns around. By his reckoning, the shooter would have been standing just the other side of the aisle.

A few steps away, there is a second brutal scene. Were the two women together? No, it seems unlikely.

Vasiliev surveys the perimeters where uniformed officers are trying to clear the crowd of rubberneckers. The most likely scenario is that the shooter (or shooters) came and went on foot. Probably using the emergency exit that can be opened from the inside. Anyone coming by car could not be sure of making a clean getaway, they could wind up being trapped and the murder weapons being discovered during a search of the vehicles.

So, he concludes, the shooter or shooters came and left on foot.

From the women's handbags, they can identify the victims as Béatrice Lavergne, twenty-three, law student, and Raymonde

Orseca, forty-four, a sales assistant working in a nearby shoe shop. All available evidence indicates that the Orseca woman was here purely by chance. Vasiliev ponders the possible motives for murdering a law student in a shopping centre car park.

The first officers on the scene conducted routine interviews, but the very nature of the place is that people are constantly coming and going, so evidence is hard to come by.

Vasiliev leaves the commissaire and investigating magistrate to go about their business and walks back to the pay booth. Here, uniformed officers are still noting the drivers' details and number plates of exiting cars.

It's probably pointless, there are more useful things they could be doing, but he does not have the authority to say so.

He steps into the booth where the car park attendant is still hard at work. He is a man in his fifties, square-jawed, square-shouldered, square hands.

"No-one to take over your shift?" says Vasiliev.

"No, not at this time of day. But carry on, I'm listening."

The inspector sits on the only available chair. The attendant continues to take tickets and give change.

"Where were you when the shots were fired?"

"Right here."

"What time was it?"

"Two minutes past ten. (You don't have anything smaller than a ten-euro note?) Every ticket is time-stamped, so obviously . . ."

"When you went down to level two, did you notice anything unusual?"

"Cars, what do you expect? That's what you usually see in a car park . . . (Six euros fifty, madame, thank you.)"

Vasiliev doesn't know if it's humour.

"Did you lower the barriers?"

"Of course I did!"

If there was only one shooter, it's possible he came by car, even if it meant running the risk of being locked in . . . and he would be among the first to leave. If he managed to drive off before the police arrived – which is more than likely – then we've lost him.

"Are there no CCTV cameras?"

"Too expensive, they tell me. Everything is too expensive to listen to management, even the pittance they pay us. (Eight euros sixty, thank you.)"

"Why did you reopen the barriers? Couldn't you have waited until the police arrived?"

This time the attendant pauses and turns to the inspector.

"If I hadn't reopened the barriers, the line of cars would stretch through every bay on every floor, all the exit ramps would be blocked and some people would try to drive out via the entry ramps and block them too. By the time the police arrived, the whole car park would be in gridlock, it would have taken two hours to clear it, and in the meantime, the drivers would likely get out of their cars to go have a nose around. And you'd wind up with—"

"Alright, alright!"

The attendant raises a hand, have it your way, and goes back to his job. "And nine euros fifty makes ten, thank you, madame."

"And that means . . ." says Vasiliev, "that the killer might have made the most of it to get clear before the police arrived."

"If he did – Nine and ten, have a nice day, monsieur– he'll be on here."

Without pausing, he passes Vasiliev a list of vehicles: make, model, colour, number plate and, in the last column, "nose", "tortoise", "fringe".

Vasiliev is dumbfounded.

"What's this last column?"

"Distinguishing feature, if I spotted one – That's ten euros exactly, thank you, madame – big nose, tortoiseshell glasses, stupid floppy hair, that sort of thing. To help me remember when you interviewed me. (Eight, nine and ten, have a nice day, monsieur.)"

Vasiliev runs a finger down the list. "Fat old biddy." Not particularly polite. But effective.

"Thank you," he says as he leaves the booth.

"Happy to oblige . . ." says the attendant. "Nine euros eighty, thank you, madame."

Number 18, rue de la Croix is a pot-bellied building constructed in the late nineteenth century. On the facade, a line of caryatids in soot-blackened loincloths prop up balconies teeming with pigeons. The lobby is impeccably polished. On the right, the concierge's lodge smells of butter sauce.

Vasiliev flashes his warrant card to a neat, plump woman in her fifties who is clearly thrilled at the prospect of being questioned. It's amazing how they love to gossip, he thinks as he trudges after the concierge.

"When I heard it on the radio, I was dreadfully upset! Such a tragedy . . . a beautiful young girl like that. And so quiet, let me tell you! Never any trouble with her! I used to see her in the morning, not so often in the evenings, I tend to go to bed early, you wouldn't believe the amount of work we have to do. She always said hello."

When Vasiliev doesn't answer, she wonders whether this doltish policeman has ever arrested anyone. She unlocks the door to the girl's apartment, and, in the wheedling tones of an estate agent, announces:

"Here you have the living room, on your right is the bedroom. Very bright and . . ."

"That's fine, thank you."

The concierge shifts her weight from one foot to the other, hesitating over which mien to adopt, finally opting for a tight-lipped pout. She walks to the door and says:

"Well, I wouldn't want to take up any more of your time and—"

"Thank you," Vasiliev cuts her short. "Madame . . . ?"

"Trousseau. Madeleine Trousseau," she says with a laugh. "For a concierge, you have to admit it's—"

"Hilarious," says Vasiliev.

Then he closes the door as gently as possible and takes a long, deep breath. The homes of the recently deceased have a characteristic silence, an intense, unsettling stillness found nowhere else, and perhaps brought there by the interloper. To Vasiliev it feels creepy, almost obscene, that he can walk into the home of a woman whose remains now lie in a refrigerator at the city morgue.

The apartment is indeed bright and spacious. A rare thing in such an old building, he thinks, including his own. There are three windows in the living room, a fact that tells Vasiliev that two apartments have been knocked into one. The furniture is contemporary, which is to say the antithesis of modern. The living room, with its simple green wallpaper, is gracefully but discreetly complemented by white furniture and a pale-grey carpet. The few curios and trinkets have been chosen with taste. Expensive taste.

Vasiliev opens a cupboard next to the front door and discovers an impressive array of sportswear: shorts, tracksuits, trainers, headbands and tennis rackets. But, down in the car park, she couldn't run fast enough . . .

He walks over to the wall lined with bookshelves and considers Mademoiselle Lavergne's reading material. Troyat, Desforges, Cauvin, the memoirs of Jean Piat, a collection from the book club France Loisirs. He quickly leafs through her record collection: Alain Souchon, film soundtracks. Hidden behind a sliding door, he finds a colour television and the latest TV guide. Apart from that, the surfaces are covered with unused ashtrays, glossy magazines and an impressive collection of alcohols to suit all tastes.

The bedroom. Very feminine, and heavily perfumed, drawers full of underwear and framed posters by David Hamilton. Vasiliev sits on the bed and takes a moment to study the stylish, silken decor, then gets up and goes into the bathroom. No surprises here. Potions, fragrances, beauty creams, hair products. There is something not quite right. Back in the living room, he stands, shoulders hunched, turning this way and that, letting his eyes wander over the walls, the collection of porcelain figurines on the glass shelf. The place is curiously stark and impersonal. It is impeccably clean, nothing is missing. In the little kitchen equipped with the latest gadgets, he finds crockery, basic foodstuffs, a collection of coffee cups with various patterns. This is how he pictures the luxury hotel suites he has never stayed in. Soothing to everyone but designed to please no-one.

There are photos of the girl, in which she is more attractive than in the car park Polaroids. A pretty face, delicate features, full lips, a set of dazzling, perfectly aligned teeth. Not his idea of a law student. And besides, where are the course books, the

Dalloz legal manuals, the desk, the notebooks? So, Vasiliev takes half an hour and turns the whole apartment upside down. Finally, he happens on some pictures that could not be used to illustrate a postgraduate thesis, photographs of a naked Mademoiselle Lavergne in a series of languid poses, lips parted, legs slightly splayed, nipples erect, and printed in the lower left corner, white on black, her name and a telephone number.

Vasiliev sets down the photographs. He is one of those people to whom deep thought seems an unnatural process, one that requires energy and produces wrinkles. He visualises this girl's life, the appointments, the precautions she has to take, the money changing hands, the clients ... The apartment would indicate that Mademoiselle Lavergne was a freelance escort. And, to judge by the opulence of the surroundings, she found her clientele from the most exclusive milieu and priced her services accordingly.

Hearing the inspector's footsteps, Madame Trousseau turns. He looks like a complete lummox.

"Can I lock up again?"

"You can."

Then, without asking permission, he settles himself in an armchair and studies the concierge. What a nerve, she thinks, and it shows. She thinks of him as a mangy old dog. Probably because he is bald.

"Madame," he begins in a deliberate, measured tone, "you knew Mademoiselle Lavergne well ..."

"Oh, well enough, I suppose, as I told you, I don't deal with ..."

But, seeing the inspector rise to his full height, she pauses. The old mutt suddenly looks imposingly tall. And not at all friendly.

"Madame Trousseau, I know I look like a fool – no, no, don't protest, I know that I look like a fool – but even I can tell the difference between a whore and a law student."

The concierge's lips form a perfect O as she flushes to the roots of her hair.

"And I cannot believe that the procession of gentlemen, however selective, that such a woman inevitably attracts when working from home could go completely unnoticed. My guess is that you got your Christmas bonus every Saturday. I could be mistaken, and, if so, I apologise for offending you . . ."

The concierge's face goes from powder pink to deep crimson. Vasiliev is already at the door.

"And if I am not mistaken, I'm sure that you will come to the police station to give us a detailed statement, am I right?"

A gruelling day. God, the chaos in that car park . . .

I should have gone about things differently . . . I'm too impatient, too impulsive, that's my problem. Well, maybe I do get carried away sometimes, Henri, but I get the job done, you can't deny that! The Lavergne girl is dead as a doornail! No two ways about it. And let me tell you, it's no loss, because she was a little whore. Oh shit – the bridge! Should have tossed the Desert Eagle off the Pont Sully! Never mind, I'll do it tomorrow. Cross my heart, Henri, I'm just too tired to do it right now . . . And did you see me at the car park exit? I sailed through, huh! That was your idea: no-one would ever suspect old Mathilde! Yes, yes, I know, the other woman, alright, I admit, she took me by surprise, she wasn't part of the contract, but did you hear her screaming! Did you hear her, Henri? I had to shut her up, didn't I? I mean if you heard her screaming like that you'd feel like giving her a slap in the face, wouldn't you? Of course you would. It's a natural instinct, so don't go making a song and dance about it!

Although Mathilde has cranked up the heating in the car, she can't seem to get warm. Perhaps she's caught a chill. She can't wait to get home and take a bath.

But that won't be for a little while. The dog is bored. For the past three days, she has had to leave him out in the garden (I have a job to do, I'm not a retired civil servant on a fat pension like that idiot Lepoitevin – well, yes, in a way I suppose I am . . . oh stop it, Henri, you're confusing me) and from the garden gate she can see the holes the Dalmatian has been digging in the lawn.

It's not that she particularly cares about the garden, but if she lets him, Ludo will turn the place into an obstacle course within six months. Mathilde is a little irritated. Especially since all she wants is to soak in the bath.

With all the rain there's been these past few days, Ludo is as filthy as a pig in shit . . . And he knows he's been naughty – dogs are funny like that, they tuck their tails between their legs, they flatten their back and their ears . . . Ludo was cowering next to the door. Mathilde flew off the handle, she screamed. Sometimes that's the only thing they understand, there's no point trying to reason with them. The positive effect of rage is that it takes you out of the daily gloom, it's like an oasis of life in a desert of aggravations. Now it's all over, Ludo is lying under the hedge. He's buried his head between his paws; he's not so cocky now.

She rocks in her chair as night draws in, still blaming herself. I'm such a hothead . . . The rain has washed the sky clear, there's a little warmth in the air again – but it's September, the weather can only get worse, it is September.

I must remember to go to the Pont Sully. Or another bridge. The Pont-Neuf? The Pont Alexandre-III? It doesn't matter as long as it's done properly.

I'll have to get a gardener to fill in all these holes. If it's not too cold, the grass should grow back before winter, so it's no big deal.

"Madame Perrin!"

Oh God, not him!

"Yes!"

She sees him striding down the path in his rubber boots, he's going to start blathering about the weather again, how rain is good for the garden, him and his vegetable garden . . .

"You never pop round to visit, Madame Perrin!"

"I know," says Mathilde, "I always intend to, but you know what it's like . . ."

He raises a hand; he knows what it's like.

"Just a few potatoes."

To Mathilde, the potato is Monsieur Lepoitevin personified.

"Potatoes, really?" she says in astonishment.

There is a full basket, every one mottled with black spots; she picks one up and feels it – hard as a rock. So, vegetables, fruit, the weather, the garden. Their topics for conversation have been exhausted.

"Did you hear about the tragedy in Messin last week?"

"No, what happened? You know me, I'm the last person to know! What tragedy?"

"A young woman brutally murdered in the street. No-one saw a thing. Terrible, they say."

"Who murdered her?"

"No-one knows, Madame Perrin! She was found lying on the pavement near the boulevard Garibaldi, do you know where that is?"

"Vaguely . . ."

"It doesn't matter. Apparently, she was shot several times!"

"Dear God!"

"If you ask me, it will turn out to have something to do with drugs, or prostitution, or gangs, or something, it's everywhere these days. But honestly, Madame Perrin, women being murdered right on our doorstep – people don't do such things."

"I'm afraid it appears they do, Monsieur Lepoitevin."

He is delighted that she's referred to him by name. Invigorated, the neighbour.

"And that's not the whole story . . ."

He turns and sees Ludo still lying by the hedge.

"At least he doesn't have to worry about these things."

"He is being punished. Just look at that . . ."

She nods towards the lawn. Lepoitevin, who had not noticed, surveys the carnage.

"My God!"

Gardens are sacred to Monsieur Lepoitevin, so it is hardly surprising that he is shocked to see all the holes.

"Did Ludo do this?" he says.

"If it wasn't him, it could only have been you . . ."

"Me? Haha! You're pulling my leg!"

He is unsettled by Mathilde's answer. He could not say why, but the joke makes him uncomfortable. Especially as she continues to stare at him silently. He glances back at Ludo.

"If we left dogs to their own devices . . ."

He can think of no way to end this sentence, so gives a little wave and heads back towards the gate. From his heavy, shuffling tread it is obvious that he is suddenly finding the garden path very long. He feels as though he is being watched. He is discomfited by Mathilde's eyes boring into his back.

After the gate has closed and Lepoitevin has gone home, Mathilde finally sits up and steadies herself on the arms of the rocking chair.

"Come on, Ludo, let's go inside!"

In the half-light, she thinks she can see him flinch under the hedge, but he doesn't get up. He's sulking. It is hardly the first time: it's in his nature. Well, if you think I'm going to beg, Mathilde thinks. Will he dig more holes in the garden if she doesn't let him in? No, he falls asleep as soon as it's dark and doesn't wake before dawn.

She looks at him through the glass door. From here she can only see his hindquarters. Deep down, she is not really surprised that he doesn't want to come inside. He's stubborn, that's the thing about Dalmatians . . .

In fact, the reason that the dog doesn't trot inside is because he no longer has his head. It is under the hedge, several centimetres away, held on only by a bloody length of spine that did not break when the kitchen knife sliced through his throat as through a farmhouse loaf.

September 12

Things are going from bad to worse, and he has no-one to blame but himself. Why did he cave in and assign a new contract to Mathilde? What on earth possessed him? This would be a worthy subject for contemplation, but he does not have the time. He listens intently to the radio news bulletin.

A bloodbath in the fifteenth arrondissement.

A shoot-out in the car park of a shopping centre.

Two women murdered. One of the victims was a shoe-shop assistant, the other has been named as Béatrice Lavergne, a twenty-three-year-old law student.

But that's not the most shocking part. Henri listens, every sentence like a stab wound to the heart.

"The two women were shot at point-blank range by a large-calibre weapon, a .44 Magnum. According to ballistics experts, the Desert Eagle used in the attack was the same weapon used to shoot Maurice Quentin. What possible connection can there be between the two cases? What could link this young law student and one of France's most important CEOs? Were they having an affair? Even this hypothesis does little to answer the crucial question: who benefits from the murders of Maurice Quentin and Béatrice Lavergne five months apart?"

News travels faster than he does.

Henri could ask Supplies what weapons Mathilde requested, but that would be tantamount to admitting his ignorance to

Personnel, which would not look good, especially as the information is already out of date ... Too late.

Mathilde must surely have her reasons. Her last mission was a bit messy, but she's carried out so many others successfully ...

She has to explain herself, otherwise his hands will be tied. Personnel will quickly demand that Mathilde be stood down.

He has to go and talk to her.

As he is about to leave, he goes to his cache to get his pistol, a 7.65 mm Mauser HSc.

Henri is a traditionalist.

Vasiliev has just finished reading the article linking the murders of Maurice Quentin and Béatrice Lavergne. He doesn't wonder how the information was leaked – he had only to take one look at Occhipinti strutting around, guzzling pistachios, clearly spoiling for a fight. It's evident that he's taken his revenge. Which, with him, invariably entails pissing off everyone else.

The front page features a photograph of Béatrice Lavergne. One of the snapshots Vasiliev found in her apartment. The kind of girl who appeals to readers when they've just died.

It is raining in Paris, something he doesn't realise until he leaves the station. He glances up at the lowering sky. He uses the newspaper he's still holding to shelter himself as he heads towards the métro. There is a certain poetry to the rain falling on the Seine. For some unknown reason, perhaps because it is still mild, he walks past the métro station and carries on along the riverbank. His brain is teeming with conflicting ideas. I've got serpents in my head, he thinks. He thinks of them in the plural because there are several.

The first is a fat, lazy python called Occhipinti. The kind that lurks in corners, and feeds on all manner of disgusting things. Slithering around, trying to find a patch of sunlight in which to bask. A loathsome beast who will squeeze him to death as soon as he is no longer needed.

Shaking his head beneath the sodden newspaper, Vasiliev thinks of the other serpent, the one flaunting herself on the front page of the newspaper, the pretty little viper from the rue de la Croix who's dead now, but used to slink up the stairs, undulating provocatively, as she led wealthy industrialists and property magnates up to her minimalist bordello under the maternal eye of the concierge Madame Trousseau. What a mess . . .

The little viper who once showed off her assets now lies in a refrigerated drawer in the morgue, her body filled with holes the size of footballs, while her picture, endlessly reproduced, is being offered up to the jaded readers of the evening papers, a sopping copy of which covers the head of that great wet dog Vasiliev, who, undecided about taking the métro, carries on walking.

As though he is going to face down another serpent, one that is lurking in its lair, in some hotel room perhaps, readying its arsenal, its venom.

Vasiliev has little faith in Commissaire Occhipinti's strategy of splashing the case all over the media in the hope of flushing out the snake. He leaked information to the press not to facilitate the investigation, but out of a quixotic desire to take control in a case where he feels he has been treated like a doormat. But Occhipinti still does not understand anything. This great serpent will move only when it feels the need. It is cunning and powerful. The driving rain and the soggy photo of Béatrice Lavergne will not force it into the open, flickering its forked tongue.

It is curled up somewhere, quietly digesting its prey, waiting for the hour when it will appear again, waiting for the storm to pass.

And when it re-emerges, there will be more newspaper headlines in the paper, another victim with a gaping wound in their stomach. Because it has a curious way of doing things, this great serpent, it has a particular aversion to little snakes, this is why it targets its venom at their crotches, this is a big snake that despises anything smaller. It is not the kind to plug a single bullet between the eyes, oh no, this serpent aims two bullets at the twin centres of gravity, whether the victim is a man or a woman makes no difference. It needs a shrink.

Under the damp newspaper, Vasiliev nods uncertainly. He can imagine psychiatrists falling over each other to diagnose the snake as a high-calibre killer, attributing his predilection for blowing people in half to serious sexual issues, a difficult childhood, a troubled relationship with gender, a killer who destroys himself by proxy. All of which might well be true, but does not help Vasiliev much. He tosses the wet newspaper into the bin, surprised to discover he has finally decided to take the métro. Serpents in his head, so many messengers from the other side.

In that very moment, Vasiliev feels a cold sliver in his heart, a sliver of the terrifying silence of Monsieur de la Hosseray between games of Nain Jaune, when, at the end of the evening, he heads to his room, to his bed. And he sees himself bowing his head to receive a kiss on his forehead from those cold lips, sees the pallid old man who is patiently waiting for another great serpent to wind its cold, death-dealing body around his throat.

Vasiliev is not in the best of spirits. He is brimming with sadness and a terrible sense of waste. He is watching helplessly, mournfully, as around him things furtively slither and creep, and he does not know where it is coming from, this sense that things are ending that he did not see begin.

Next to him, he sees Béatrice Lavergne's breasts, folded over, on the newspaper of someone engrossed in a crossword. Meanwhile, from the adverts plastered on the sides of the carriage, a bevy of Béatrices delight in their roll-on deodorant, their women's magazines, their lingerie and the summer sales at BHV.

The Widow lights a cigarette.

She is already familiar with the photograph of the dead woman, it has been on every front page, but this is the procedure, he has to show her again.

Then he takes another photo from his inside pocket. Béatrice Lavergne, with her legs spread, hands cupping her breasts. He could have been more delicate, could have hidden the bottom of the photograph and shown only the face, but he feels this is an appropriate response to her needling at their last meeting. She is keenly aware of this and feigns composure.

"I am obliged to ask whether you know this person . . ."

The Widow sets the photo down on the coffee table.

"No. The woman's picture has been in all the newspapers – had I recognised her, I would have been in touch . . ."

"We do not know whether this young woman knew your husband – I mean your spouse. But the similarities between . . . They were shot with the same gun, so you see . . ."

"Inspector, I think I can save both of us some time. I was not acquainted with all of my husband's mistresses – I say 'not all', I shall leave aside the more blatant. Although this young woman's face does not ring a bell, she would have been very much to his taste. She looks strikingly similar to all the others that your fellow officers – with varying degrees of delicacy – have brought to my attention over the past months. My husband had many . . . liaisons."

"Yes, we discovered as much in the course of our investigation, but there is one small detail that troubles us. Among his liaisons, there were no other, shall we say, professionals."

The Widow stubs out the cigarette she has only just lit.

"Monsieur Quentin was a deeply conventional man, Inspector. Preoccupied by decency and propriety, aware of his responsibilities, but unaccustomed to resisting temptation. He died at fifty-four – the age when men cease to be attractive to the women they desire. And he was a singularly pragmatic man. Had he died ten years later, doubtless the ratio of professionals to amateurs among his mistresses would have been reversed."

"I see . . ."

The photo of Béatrice Lavergne is still on the coffee table. Vasiliev stares at this face as though it were one of those pictures in a children's book where the big bad wolf is hidden amid the tangle of branches. His thought process involves allowing ideas to take shape and unfold. But nothing comes. A good minute passes in the comfortable silence of the flat, where servants probably glide like Japanese dancers behind closed doors. This haughty woman, this indeterminate space . . . Suddenly, he longs to be somewhere else, to breathe air, real air. Is her amorality a reaction to her husband's life? Or does she see love as an individual pastime and sex as a collective sport?

"I don't wish to press you, Inspector, but do you have any other questions?"

He hesitates, then gets to his feet. He apologises for bothering her, he is terribly sorry, no matter, she completely understands, she is also sorry she cannot be of more help, but she expresses the hope that "the investigation will one day reach a conclusion", a last kick in the teeth as she extends her hand to let the visitor know he is dismissed.

And then, who knows why, just as he is leaving the drawing room, Vasiliev feels the urge to say more.

"Your husband and Mademoiselle Lavergne were not merely shot by the same weapon, they were killed in the same manner. The first bullet was aimed at the young woman's genitals. As a rule, killers take precautions to shoot their victims quickly and discreetly, using a weapon of reasonable calibre; it is extremely rare to shoot the victim in the genitals with a bullet that could stop a rhinoceros."

Vasiliev glances at a watercolour in the hallway and carries on as though thinking aloud:

"Because when you shoot someone in the crotch, the damage is spectacular, but death is not instantaneous. Which is probably why the killer delivered a second bullet to the throat. In both cases, part of the skull was blown away, and what remained was attached to the torso by a few shreds of muscle. High-calibre bullets cause tremendous damage. Especially, as you can imagine, at point-blank range. In the case of Mademoiselle Lavergne, it almost looked as though the body had been cut into three sections: bottom, middle and top. It was quite *savage*, if you'll pardon the expression."

He looks at the widow.

"But I'm boring you with trivial details, I wouldn't wish to disturb you any further."

"You have not disturbed me, Inspector."

Her voice is choked.

As he goes downstairs, Vasiliev is aware that his revenge was petty and despicable – and what was the purpose of it? When he does these things, he could kick himself.

Tonight is not one of the nights when Vasiliev is supposed to be visiting Monsieur – well, actually, Tevy. He is keenly aware he no longer goes just to see his former protector, he goes there to see his protector's carer, and he's ashamed. It feels like a betrayal. Vasiliev has never had much luck with women; they have come along when he has least expected. So, the happiness he feels in the presence of this young woman feels sinful.

Usually, when he leaves, he says, "See you Thursday?" or "See you Tuesday?"

The same question, invariably addressed to Tevy, though she always answers, "Of course, of course . . ." It's as if it were now her home rather than Monsieur's, and he needs her permission to visit.

Last Sunday when he left Neuilly, he simply said, "See you soon." There is something going on in his head that he doesn't understand. Can it really be so difficult to tell a young woman that . . .

After visiting the Widow Quentin, he decided to go to Neuilly.

But first he went home to Aubervilliers.

To smarten himself up.

In fact, he looked no smarter than he did an hour earlier, but he felt cleaner. While at home, he rang to ask for news of Monsieur. Would Tevy invite him round? He had put on the nice blue suit he saves for special occasions – the last time was for the funeral of an officer gunned down by a drug dealer under the ring road.

Then it came out of the blue:

"Would you have time to come over tonight, René?"

It was not the calm, cheerful response he was expecting.

"Is there something wrong?"

"Let's just say that things are not getting any better and there have been . . ."

"Yes?"

"There have been a few difficult moments . . ."

In an instant, he was in the taxi. He should have changed; he looks ridiculous in this suit.

When he gets to Neuilly, he automatically looks for the Ami 6 with the dented wing.

He rings the doorbell, this is their usual ritual, except for the fact that Tevy sees that he is wearing a suit and says nothing, she simply steps aside to let him in. He turns to her.

"He has absences . . . it's been very sudden. There are times he doesn't know who he is. He doesn't recognise me, he pretends to, but I can see he's trying to remember and he can't. I told him you were coming, but I don't know if he understood."

When he goes in, Monsieur nods, as though he were a doctor he doesn't recognise. When René bends down to kiss his forehead, Monsieur doesn't know how to react. He smiles beatifically, he is clearly ill at ease. So, René stays with him and they watch television. It's excruciating. René struggles under the weight of the suit . . . If he'd turned up holding an anvil, he couldn't have felt more awkward.

Tevy says she could heat up some soup and there is some prawn salad, and René says, why not – he's not hungry, but what else is there to do? Monsieur doesn't say a word, he doesn't seem to have heard Tevy's offer of supper. He is not himself all evening.

At around eleven o'clock he decides to go to bed, but doesn't know where to find his bedroom. Tevy shows him the way. Monsieur is disoriented, quiet, worried, it is as though he's walking on eggshells.

Then, suddenly, he turns to Vasiliev and says, "Good night, my little René . . ." It's very perplexing.

The end of the evening is quieter than usual.

"He's not always like that . . . This morning, for example, he was chatting away quite normally."

This is intended to reassure Vasiliev, but it doesn't.

"After these episodes, does he remember what's happened?"

"When he comes to, I can tell he's embarrassed. He knows something has happened, but he doesn't know what exactly."

They sit in silence for a long moment.

"If he gets worse," Tevy says, "we'll probably have to . . . Well, you know what I mean . . ."

Vasiliev knows only too well, so he takes the plunge. "But I'll still get to see you?"

And Tevy instantly responds.

"Oh yes, René, yes, I think so . . ."

September 13

There is a comment next to each vehicle, usually a single word, but always well observed. Rarely polite, but well observed. Vasiliev hopes that if there is an arrest, the car park attendant will be as efficient at the line-up as he was at making his list.

Thirty-three vehicles, it's amazing the throughput of a car park in Paris.

Vasiliev has shared out the names with his colleagues, and they plan to question every one. If the drivers can't come to the police station, they will visit their homes or their places of work. Only three officers are assigned, so it will take several days, which is a complete waste of time since it will be utterly pointless.

The first thirteen witnesses all said the same thing. They heard bangs, explosions, gunshots – the words varied a little, but their statements were identical: they saw nothing, realised nothing, and only found out what had happened from the newspapers.

Vasiliev is particularly intrigued by two of the vehicles.

The first is a foreign car. Dutch. The driver headed straight back to Utrecht. Vasiliev has been in contact with his Dutch colleagues. It's difficult, since no-one in his station speaks Dutch or English, and nobody there speaks French: so much for an international investigation! He doesn't yet know what the driver was doing in Paris, or why he was in this particular car park at 10 a.m. He will find out in a few days . . . maybe.

The second entry is a woman. "Fat old bitch – makeup",

according to the attendant's notes. What intrigues Vasiliev is not so much the comment as the call that went out from the Melun police department, five days earlier, on 8 September regarding the murder of one Constance Manier, who was gunned down in the middle of the street. The use of a large-calibre weapon has unsettled his colleagues in Seine-et-Marne, and he can understand why: if guns of this size start circulating in the département, policing is going to become an extreme sport.

The weapon used in the car park shooting was also a high-calibre, Vasiliev suggests. Not particularly probative, according to Commissaire Occhipinti (the foul mood was tangible; having run out of peanuts, he wasn't really himself).

What Vasiliev does not mention is that on this list there is a female driver who lives three kilometres from where Constance Manier was shot. The commissaire would doubtless point out that thousands of people live within three kilometres of any given crime.

The inspector is simply puzzled by the fact that the driver who lives near the first murder scene was in the car park a week later when two other women are shot.

The police don't share life's cordial relationship with chance. And it is in the nature of an investigator to be suspicious.

Vasiliev does not tell anyone about his misgivings, because the driver's record does not exactly lend itself to his suspicions: a sixty-three-year-old widow, awarded both a Chevalièr des Arts et des Lettres, and a medal for fighting with the Resistance . . .

Which is why he tells his fellow officers that he will deal with it, purely as a formality – he doesn't want to look like a fool.

*   *   *

Henri caught the first plane, hired a rental car at the airport. By 11 a.m. he is driving through Melun, and twenty minutes later he arrives outside La Coustelle, where he parks up and turns off the engine. He sits for a long time. Then he gets out of his car and walks towards the gate, where there is a little bell on a small chain. He pauses one last time. He has spent the whole journey considering what he knows, what he doesn't know, what he dreads finding out, then, as he is about to ring the bell, he pictures Mathilde and is overwhelmed by the fear of the irrevocable. After a long, deep breath, he pulls the chain.

He is just about to ring again when, finally, Mathilde appears in the doorway at the far end of the garden path. She tilts her head to one side, unsure of what she is seeing, then a beaming smile lights up her face. He hears her say:

"Oh my word, it's Henri!"

She sounds as though she is talking to someone else. I hope she's alone, thinks Henri. He sees her shiver, then take a shawl and drape it over her shoulders.

"Come in, Henri, it's open!"

She stands on the terrace watching this dapper man approach, his gait calm and resolute. It's Henri to the life: he is wearing a blazer of midnight blue with a matching pocket square and a club tie, such a handsome, elegant man ... But in Mathilde's mind, lights begin to flash and, as she draws the shawl around her tightly with both hands, she wonders what he's doing here, it is a clear breach of protocol. He must have a very serious reason to show up, unannounced, with no official pretext. As he approaches, Henri sees each of these thoughts, these worries, these questions flicker across Mathilde's face and, just as he reaches the terrace, she remembers a 9 mm Luger semi-automatic in the drawer of the kitchen dresser.

"Oh, Henri, what an unexpected pleasure . . ."

He stops at the foot of the terrace and smiles.

"I'm afraid I've come empty-handed."

I very much doubt that . . .

"Well, come give me a little kiss."

Henri steps up and, taking her in his arms, gives her a long embrace. As she buries her face in the crook of his neck, she is thinking, if he were carrying a gun, she would surely feel it, but Henri is a smart guy, he always has more than one trick up his sleeve.

"How did you get here?"

"Plane, then rental car. I parked it a little way away, I wouldn't want to compromise you."

She laughs, compromise me . . .

With his arms around her shoulders, he peers through the glass door: kitchen, hallway to the right, window to the left, dog basket – always be wary of dogs.

"Have you got a dog, Mathilde?"

"He died yesterday, poor thing . . ."

Her voice is suddenly hoarse, Henri could swear she is about to sob.

"The neighbour," she says. "He poisoned him."

Henri frowns, why would he do such a thing?

"He never barked," Mathilde says, "good as gold he was, so well behaved . . ."

He turns towards the garden and looks at the lawn pock-marked with holes.

"Well behaved . . ."

"Oh, that – that's nothing! It's just something puppies do! I mean, you don't kill a dog because it dug a hole!"

Henri is baffled. Why would the neighbour poison a dog because it dug holes in someone else's lawn? He feels a little lost, but Mathilde shakes him.

"Come on, don't just stand there, come inside!"

She turns and goes into the kitchen.

"Can I make you some coffee?"

"I wouldn't say no . . ."

As she takes out the cups, Mathilde babbles quickly, there is an almost childlike excitement in her voice.

"You can't imagine what a pleasure it is to see you, Henri! All these years and never a thought for Mathilde. Tut-tut-tut, I know what I'm talking about, you tossed me aside like an old sock!"

She is right to talk about "all these years".

Their last meeting was fifteen years ago, dinner at a restaurant in Paris. Since that time, Mathilde has put on weight, she walks more heavily. She looks ten centimetres shorter and ten centimetres wider. Her face has started to sag, her chin droops a little. But her eyes are as amazing as ever, with their extraordinary clarity and lucidity.

Even sitting, Henri looks elegant, thinks Mathilde. These are strange circumstances for a reunion; Henri is smiling, friendly, relaxed, but with him you can never tell what that means.

She pours the coffee and they sit in the kitchen. She had considered suggesting the living room, but the kitchen is better, the dresser drawer is just on her right, and Mathilde is right-handed.

"Well, Henri, you didn't just emerge from your lair to sample my coffee . . ."

"Indeed, Mathilde. As you know, coming here is against all the rules. But, well, you and me, it's not the same . . ."

"Not the same as what?"

"Not the same as the others, we're old friends."

"And?"

Henri blows on his coffee, turns away, then looks back at her.

"The avenue Foch . . ."

"What about the avenue Foch?"

"I'm still puzzled by what happened . . ."

"We've already talked about that. Why do you have to rake over old contracts?"

Her spoon rattles nervously in her cup making a tinkling sound.

"Because you tried to set my mind at rest, but you never really explained why you went about it the way you did."

Mathilde bends over her cup. Suddenly it all comes flooding back, she can see the man, she knows his face, she's seen it a thousand times in newspapers, on television. She remembers the avenue, remembers him walking slowly towards her, he has—

"It was the dog."

"What about the dog?"

"Yes. The dog wanted to stop and the man was tugging on his lead, viciously dragging him along, that sweet little cocker spaniel, and—"

"I thought it was a dachshund?"

"Yes, sorry, a dachshund."

Mathilde tries to picture the dog, but the memory does not come. No matter.

"Well, that got me angry – I couldn't help it, you know how much I love animals."

"In that case, why kill the dog?"

Mathilde has tears in her eyes.

"Oh, Henri, I saw clear as day! With her master dead, the poor dog would have been miserable."

Henri is studying her, yes, yes, I understand. Reassuring her. He turns his head towards the terrace and the garden.

"You have a lovely place here, so quiet!"

Ouch. When Henri does small talk, it is rarely a good sign.

"Do you look after the garden yourself, or do you have someone come in?"

"Cut the crap, Henri, what else is there?"

"That car park . . . Personnel is furious, as I'm sure you can understand . . ."

Mathilde bows her head, her face flushed with remorse.

"You've come to kick me out, haven't you, Henri?"

"I would never do that, Mathilde! But I need an explanation for Personnel, and I couldn't see myself talking about it on the phone, so I decided to come in person so we could talk about it calmly. But first and foremost, how are you, Mathilde?"

She stands up and leans against the counter.

"I'm not going to pretend, Henri, old age is starting to wear me down."

"It's the same for all of us."

"I'm not sure, when I look at you, it seems it's not as hard on men as it is on women . . ."

They smile.

"May I?" says Henri, nodding towards the coffee pot. Without waiting for her answer, he pours himself a second cup.

"I don't want to rake over old history, Mathilde, but that contract was for one target, not two . . ."

"Look, I was interrupted!"

She shouts – not so much to lend credence to her story, but out of relief because she remembers the scene. She recounts the incident in detail. Only with specific points of fact can she hope to reassure Henri.

He listens attentively. Her account is convincing.

". . . a woman started screaming, she came out of nowhere, I couldn't believe it! And so, I wheeled round and . . ."

He can never give Mathilde another mission, she doesn't have the cold-blooded calm it requires, she will put everyone in danger. She is not up to it anymore; she needs to stop. But no-one retires in this job. Personnel will insist that he deal with Mathilde.

It could happen within hours.

If they are to avoid this, thinks Henri, she has to disappear.

He doesn't know whether this is good news, he wonders how she'll take it.

Because he will have to disappear too.

In the decades he has been doing this job, he has had more than enough time to put a plan together: false passports, money in an offshore tax haven. He has to be honest with Mathilde and to prepare himself for the worst. Explain: "I have my escape planned, Mathilde, and not just mine, yours too. We need to run away together."

". . . I decide that going in and wandering around the shopping centre would be pointless, so I play my trump card: being Mathilde Perrin. So, I start the car and . . ."

He made his plans fifteen years ago and renewed the passports whenever they expired. "We're going to leave together," he will say, "but don't worry, we don't have to stay together!" And it's true. Once they are out of this mess, they can do as they please. Who knows? Mathilde might want to start a new life . . .

When she has finished, Henri nods, he completely understands, a clusterfuck of unfortunate circumstances.

Mathilde knows she's on a tightrope. If she has persuaded Henri, he will leave her alone, if not, Personnel will be furious, which means . . . She shakes her head; she refuses to think about such things.

She notices that Henri has said nothing.

"Just one thing, Mathilde . . . Do you remember the weapons protocol?"

"Don't take me for a fool, Henri. Of course I remember!"

Mathilde's head is spinning again, she no longer understands anything about these stories of guns in drawers and boxes, in the Seine, the Pont Sully, the Pont-Neuf. If Henri keeps on grilling her, she'll open the drawer of the dresser she's leaning against and put a couple of bullets in his head, that'll teach him.

"Well then, tell me," he says, "why did you use the same gun in two different contracts?"

Mathilde sighs, she comes back to the table, sits down and takes Henri's hands in hers, how warm they are, it is one of the things she's always loved about him, these large veiny hands – where was I? Oh, yes . . .

"I have to tell you something, Henri."

"I'm listening."

"I know it will come as a surprise, but it's Murphy's Law."

Henri nods. Let her talk, wait and see what she comes up with.

"It might sound strange from where you're sitting, but it's true: I simply forgot! I was so upset after the contract on the avenue Foch, having to kill the cute little dog, that I left the gun in the car, I didn't notice it until the next day, there you go, a simple oversight."

"Murphy's Law?"

"Exactly! First, I forget to dump the weapon, then there's this woman screaming in the car park – it's always the way, things go smoothly for years on end, then suddenly everything goes pear-shaped, but that's all over now, Murphy's Law, I mean. And you know why?"

Henri shakes his head.

"Because you came, Henri."

She smiles.

"You wouldn't believe how happy I am to see you again! Thanks to you, I know I can start again. Oh, Henri . . ."

Her voice breaks, she grips his hands across the table. He is lost in her eyes.

"I never did tell you how much I cared, did I? I can tell you now because we're old and . . ."

She hesitates, her lips trembling. Henri feels deeply uncomfortable. She is clasping his hands so tightly, and there is something heart-breaking about this moment.

"I don't know if I can bring myself to say it, Henri . . ."

"Say what, Mathilde?"

Her voice is different, Henri scarcely recognises it.

Come come now, he thinks, this is getting ridiculous.

"I can't do it," she says, "making silly declarations at our age . . ."

No sooner has the magic moment come than it is gone.

Their relationship has always been based on a tried and tested formula woven from intimations and missed appointments.

As a result, everything is back on the table. Mathilde's decision not to make her declaration opens up the possibility of them disappearing together.

"And anyway," she says, "you've come here to find fault, to haul me over the coals, but—"

"Not at all, Mathilde."

". . . but you never bother to tell me when you're happy with my work! The contract on the Messin girl, you never said a word, you haven't even mentioned it! But you have to admit that you've never seen a mission so quickly and cleanly executed! And it wasn't easy, let me tell you! The rainstorm that day . . ."

She feels his hands stiffen. Henri is leaning towards her, hanging on her every word – at last, he can see how talented I am!

"Oh, yes, the young woman who . . ."

Henri is not sure he understands. Is Messin a surname, a town, a place? He treads warily.

"Tell me all about it."

"I got into such a panic, Henri, you wouldn't believe it!"

"Really . . . ?"

He gives her a broad smile.

"I very nearly went through the verification protocol! You'll laugh . . . At the last minute, I had doubts. No, honestly. A run-down neighbourhood full of small-time drug dealers, that girl, thin as a rake . . . I thought, wait a minute, Mathilde, you could be making a mistake, she may not be the target. But I had the details on paper, I checked them, and phew . . . I was in a terrible state, you know?"

"I can imagine!"

He smiles easily, reaches into his pocket for a pack of cigarettes – he smokes two packs a day. Silently he asks Mathilde, may I?

"But you had the details on paper, so you felt reassured . . ."

"Yes, luckily I'd brought it with me, I found it in my pocket. It's strange, there are certain signs you can't ignore: just as I found the piece of paper, the woman appeared at the other end of the street. Well, you know the rest. I hope you were satisfied."

"Impeccable work, as always, Mathilde."

He gives a little laugh.

"Well, *almost* always!"

He stresses the word to show that he's joking, to make it quite clear that he's joking.

Mathilde shot a young woman in some suburb whose name he can't remember, she takes notes, she keeps details of her contracts. Just as she keeps guns and then uses them for imaginary contracts on genuine victims. Exactly how many have there been? Henri's plans for them to leave, to disappear, have exploded in mid-air. He is dumbfounded. The killing machine created by the system is out of control.

Mathilde watches him smoke, approvingly. In him, even this simple gesture is extraordinarily elegant. She forgot to put out an ashtray. Hardly has he lit it than he crushes the cigarette out in his saucer. If I didn't know him, I'd think he was nervous, but I know Henri like the back of my hand, besides he's beaming.

"I'm glad we've had a chance to clear things up, Mathilde."

"You were worried about nothing, Henri!"

"Yes, I can see that . . ."

"But you're happy now?"

"Absolutely."

"Then again, getting you a little worried is what brought you here to see me . . ."

She looks coy. Henri pretends to scold her:

"Don't let it happen again . . ."

Beetling brows, like a schoolmaster. He gets to his feet.

"Well, well, I'd better go. It's bad enough I broke protocol to come here, I really shouldn't hang around, I'm sure you understand."

"Really?"

There is panic in Mathilde's voice. Henri makes a helpless gesture – what else can he do?

She takes the plunge.

"Can I ask you a favour?"

He spreads his hands carefully.

"Could you hold me, Henri, the way you did earlier?"

Without waiting, she goes over and hugs him. He is almost a head taller than she. He holds her tightly, feeling like a coward because he is about to leave. Under normal circumstances he would come back tonight and surprise her. Deal with the problem straight away. Mathilde has descended into a madness that can only get worse, best to cauterise the wound. But he knows that he will never be able to do it. Mathilde isn't really herself; she's gone off the rails. She's a danger to everyone and it can't carry on. But the idea of doing it himself – it's impossible, he couldn't point a gun at her and fire, it's beyond him.

He will find some other way to solve the problem.

And when it is done, he will urgently need to disappear.

"Time to go, Mathilde . . ."

But she doesn't move. He could swear that she is crying. He doesn't ask her, but when, finally, she pulls away, she quickly turns around so that he can't see her face. She snuffles, blows her nose.

"Go on," she says in a whisper, "get lost . . ."

Henri makes to say goodbye, she shrugs him off, don't bother. Eventually, she turns around.

They look at each other, her eyes are filled with tears.

Henri turns on his heel, steps out onto the terrace and, without looking back, walks to the gate, then to his car, and drives away; he is shattered.

My God . . . How wonderful it would be . . . If only it were possible! (Mathilde washes up the cups, the spoons, the coffee pot.)

Henri coming here like that, without so much as a by-your-leave.

He would come on the pretext of telling me off, there's always something to criticise, no contract ever goes exactly to plan, that's just how it is. He would show up and give me the stink eye, but actually he'd be coming so we could talk, so we could be together. Wouldn't that be lovely . . .

She finished doing the dishes, she should probably eat, what time is it? One o'clock! Here I am sitting daydreaming that Henri is coming to court me and I have nothing ready . . .

She sits down heavily. She doesn't have the strength.

She has left Ludo's basket in the corner of the kitchen. Poor bastard, dying like that.

The early afternoon passes very slowly, her waking dream of Henri has left her exhausted. She feels terribly alone.

At around three o'clock, she decides to go and buy a new dog.

The traffic doesn't help matters: suburban commuters are heading home after the daily grind, so everything is bumper to bumper. The drive is interminable. It is half past six by the time he arrives.

La Coustelle is not easy to find.

Vasiliev parks the patrol car a few hundred metres away. He walks back to the house, looks into the letterbox, then, glancing around to check he's not being watched, he takes a pen and fishes out the letters. Among them is a summons from Melun police station. This he stuffs into his pocket, then puts the others back in the letterbox and decides to do a tour.

At the corner of the street, he is passed by the cream-coloured Renault 25, registration HH 77, driven by a middle-aged woman wearing large glasses. Casually he walks on, only to quickly retrace his steps and look up the driveway of the single-storey house where he sees the driver, a short, stout woman, get out of the car and stretch her limbs before opening the boot. As Vasiliev continues his tour of the property he hears the sound of shears from the garden next door. Seeing a man, he stops.

"Would those be pear trees . . . ?" Vasiliev ventures, spotting a couple of fruit trees in a corner of the garden.

A garrulous gardener, this is the message sent by the beaming smile addressed to Vasiliev.

Inevitably, there is a lecture on the comparative advantages of different varieties of pear.

"Would you like a taste?" asks Monsieur Lepoitevin.

"I wouldn't say no," says Vasiliev, thereby rising twenty places on Monsieur Lepoitevin's dance card.

Passing quickly over the compliments exchanged about the pear, the praise lavished by the taster, the self-effacing smile of the grower.

"Next door – would that be Madame Perrin's house?" says the inspector.

"Ah, you've come to see the lunatic?"

Vasiliev frowns as Monsieur Lepoitevin steps back to study him with a new and sustained attention.

"You're police, aren't you?"

Before the inspector can reply, he adds: "I can always tell a police officer. I used to be an auctioneer."

Vasiliev doesn't see the connection, but his real interest is in the "lunatic".

"Why do you say she's mad?"

"On account of her dog. Buried him without his head, she did."

Vasiliev does not quite understand.

"So," Monsieur Lepoitevin patiently explains, "her dog died, don't ask me how, but you'd think even a dead dog still has a head on its shoulders. Well, not hers. I saw her bury it – I was looking through the hedge – the head was three metres away. It's probably still there. It's not what I'd call rational – would you? The dog was a Dalmatian, and they're about as dumb as you get, but even so, how did it come to be beheaded?"

"You didn't ask her?"

"Oh, you know how it is with neighbours, you just say hello, you can't be dealing with what goes on in other people's lives."

"You were looking through the hedge ..."

"I looked because I could hear her panting. I wondered whether maybe she needed a hand. Digging a hole the size of a dog, even a headless one, that takes serious effort. When I saw what she was doing, I thought, oh, no! I'm not getting mixed up in this."

"I completely understand. And you're sure the dog was decapitated?"

"Is that why you're here, because of the dog?"

"No, I came to drop off a summons, nothing very serious."

"A summons . . . about the dog?"

The man clearly has a bee in his bonnet.

"No, it's not about that, but now that I know, I'll be sure to ask about it. Thank you for the pear."

Lepoitevin watches the inspector walk away: he doesn't have much faith in this cop.

Madame Perrin is sitting on the terrace, she is bending down, seemingly talking to herself, but Vasiliev is too far away to hear what she is saying.

"You'll be happy here, darling."

Puppies are adorable at that age. True, they piss on the cushions, they whine in the car, but they're warm, they're fragile, they're loveable. A cocker spaniel. Mathilde went to the pet shop. The owner was a canny saleswoman, she thrust the little bundle of fur into Mathilde's hands and managed to sell her the puppy, a dog basket, a collar, a leash, enough kibble for a month, a nine-page pamphlet summarising European regulations – in short, just about everything Mathilde had bought a year earlier when she left the kennels on the avenue Malesherbes with Ludo. The cocker spaniel is called Cookie. She'll live with it. Right now, he's curled up in a ball in the basket.

She runs a finger through the puppy's fur. For a lonely woman like her, at least it's company. She'd shed all the tears she had for poor Ludo – who was as dumb as a bag of spanners – so it was time to get another and hope it's not as stupid.

Sensing someone's presence, Mathilde looks up and sees a tall man standing behind the gate. A sales rep? He pulls the chain, the bell tinkles . . .

By rights, she should march down there and send him packing, she has no intention of being bothered by some huckster, but something tells her he's not selling anything. For a start, he has no bag, no case, nothing, he's just standing there helplessly – even at this distance, he looks like a clumsy oaf.

At her feet, the puppy is trying to crawl out.

"You stay right there . . ."

She puts him back in the basket and he curls into a ball. She strokes his silken fur.

She turns back to the gate and gives a vague wave. Vasiliev pushes open the gate, comes in. As he gets closer, he seems much taller than she thought. He's hunched over, she can't abide men who stoop, just look at Henri, ramrod straight, though he hasn't got the height, whereas this man has the height, but he's dressed any old how.

Here he is at the bottom of the terrace. He introduces himself and shows his warrant card. Mathilde's eyes widen, she is awestruck.

"Police Judiciaire, oh my Lord!"

"Oh, it's not important, madame . . ."

"What do you mean, nothing! The Police Judiciaire is very important!"

"That's not what I meant."

"Then what did you mean?"

Vasiliev has come to ask questions and here he is being interrogated by this old biddy. He studies her. She was clearly beautiful once – although he is not one with an eye for the ladies, even he can see that.

"Well, come up all the same . . ."

Vasiliev doesn't know what she means by "all the same".

Mathilde is wearing a long-sleeved print dress and, over it, some sort of pinafore with a large front pocket, like a gardener's apron. Vasiliev thinks back to the neighbour. He turns around. Instinctively, he darts a glance towards the hedge the man mentioned. His macabre story . . .

"I've come about . . ."

"Please, take a seat."

She settles back in her rocking chair.

Vasiliev takes the folding metal chair.

"So, what brings you here?"

Vasiliev is determined to overcome his first poor impression. This woman is self-assured, which makes him uncomfortable. He sees the basket and the puppy's head sticking out.

"You've got a new dog."

He goes over, kneels down and runs a cautious finger through the fur of the cocker spaniel, whose head is nestled between its paws.

"What makes you say that?"

"It's a cocker," says Vasiliev, getting up.

"Yes, I know that, thank you!"

She is annoyed, he can hear it. Vasiliev has an advantage, his height. Mathilde has another one, she thinks very quickly.

"How do you know I've got a 'new' dog? Because he's a puppy?"

"No, because your neighbour mentioned it. You used to have a Dalmatian, apparently."

"This time I got a cocker spaniel. I can't be without a dog, I'm sure you understand, a single woman like me . . ."

"Mind you, a cocker spaniel isn't much of a guard dog . . ."

"I got him for the company. So, what brings you here, Commissaire?"

"Inspector."

"I'm assuming your rank doesn't change the reason for your visit."

"Very true."

He gropes for words. Mathilde stares at him, waiting with affected patience.

"It's about the massacre in the car park in the fifteenth arrondissement."

"The massacre?"

"Your car was parked in the car park of the shopping centre where two women were gunned down with a high-calibre gun . . ."

"I didn't do it!"

It's more than Vasiliev can take – he bursts out laughing.

"Yes, I assumed as much. That's not why I'm here. We've been talking to all the eyewitnesses."

"I didn't see anything."

"And I suppose you didn't hear anything?"

"Oh, I did, everyone did! I suppose you think because I'm old, I must be deaf!"

"Not at all, I'm just asking . . ."

"Give me the dog."

Vasiliev turns and picks up the puppy, surprised at how warm it is. He gives it to Mathilde, who places it on her lap, next to her ample belly.

"I heard blasts."

It's a touching scene. Vasiliev cannot help but wonder if he has slipped into a different world. He is in the process of investigating two crimes, probably committed by professional assassins, yet here he is, questioning a sixty-something woman – a mother according to official records – with a puppy on her lap who lives in the middle of nowhere and doesn't seem remotely fazed by his questions.

"They were gunshots," he says.

"What's the difference?"

"It doesn't matter. How many did you hear?"

"Three."

"Does the name Béatrice Lavergne ring a bell?"

"No, should it?"

"What about Maurice Quentin?"

"Nope."

"That's curious."

"What's curious?"

"You're the first person I've met who doesn't know that the industrialist Maurice Quentin was murdered in Paris last May – it was all over the news . . ."

"Oh, that Quentin? Yes, I've heard of him, of course, but that was ages ago. Why do you ask?"

"No reason."

"What do you mean, no reason? Why would you ask questions for no reason?"

"That's not what I meant."

"Well, what *do* you mean then?"

"Could you tell me what you saw in the car park, please."

"I wasn't in the car park, I was in a shop."

"And you heard the gunshots from there?"

"No, they came from the car park."

Vasiliev screws up his eyes, he's finding it difficult to understand.

"I'd just come out of a shop and was heading downstairs to my car when I heard the shots – but I didn't see anything, is that clear?"

"Just about."

"Good for you."

"Which level were you parked on?"

"Level two, maybe level three, I don't know, they all look alike, you never know where you are . . ."

Mathilde is not convinced that the inspector has understood anything at all.

"Have you just come back from a long trip?" he asks suddenly.

"No, why?"

"You were stretching when you got out of the car, as though you'd been on the road for a while . . ."

"A real Sherlock Holmes, aren't you? I also stretch when not coming back from a long drive. That's arthritis for you, you have to stretch if you've been in the same position for more than two minutes. You'll find out . . . Tall man like you, it's bound to happen sooner or later."

"I see . . ."

"Any more questions?"

"No . . . Well, I did wonder about your dog."

Mathilde nods at the puppy asleep in her lap.

"You want to know whether he was with me, whether he heard three gunshots?"

"No, I was just trying to work out why the head of your other dog, the Dalmatian, was separated from its body."

Mathilde glares at him.

"Your neighbour," he explains. "Well, he seemed to think the dog didn't have its head attached when you buried it."

If Mathilde were alone, she would get up, march into the kitchen, take the 9 mm Luger from the drawer, then go round and put three bullets in that bastard Lepoitevin's balls!

In fact, it's precisely what she will do as soon as this big lunk of an inspector has turned his back!

Unsettled by this unexpected hitch, she glowers, and Vasiliev can easily imagine the kind of grandmother she would have been, though from her records he has found no mention of grandchildren. Then, suddenly, her expression changes, she looks as though she is about to cry. Vasiliev feels ashamed of hurting this old woman.

"I found poor Ludo like that," she says, her voice barely audible. "Decapitated. Dreadful."

Mathilde looks as though she might break down, but pulls herself together.

"Do you also investigate dog murders?"

"No, not really, I was just wondering . . ."

"What were you wondering?"

"Where's the dog's body?"

Mathilde is still stroking the bundle of fur in her lap. Head bowed, she answers in a toneless voice bordering on a sob:

"I buried him, Commissaire. Dreadful, wasn't it?"

"No, no, you did the right thing."

"I meant, what happened to him is dreadful."

"It is . . . But when you buried him, you left his head in the garden?"

"I was in a terrible state, put yourself in my shoes . . . Such a beautiful dog . . ."

Vasiliev nods, yes, I'm sure he was, a big, heavy dog too, can't have been an easy task. "But . . . who would do such a thing?"

"These things happen out here in the country . . ."

"I live in Aubervilliers, we have lots of dogs, but I've never found one decapitated outside my building."

"In the countryside, I mean. You get these petty jealousies. I didn't want to bother the police about a dead dog."

"I understand."

He leaves a long silence and adds, as though to himself:

"I've heard of dogs or cats being poisoned, or even shot, but never beheaded."

"Neither had I. Until Ludo. But he'll pay for this, you mark my words . . ."

"Who?"

Mathilde nods towards the neighbour's house. She drops her voice to a whisper.

"I'm sure it was him. In fact, I'm going to press charges. Is that something I can do through you?"

"No, not through me . . . To press charges, you'd have to go to the commissariat."

"So, I'd have to go to that station, eh? But here I am blethering on and I haven't even offered you a drink."

Having said this, she doesn't move a muscle, as though there was no relationship between her words and her intentions. As indeed there isn't, since all she really wants, before she goes round to Monsieur Lepoitevin and settles his hash, is to get rid of this inspector who's boring her with his stories about dogs when he should be out catching thieves and murderers.

Vasiliev makes to stand up.

"Thank you, but I was just about to go."

"Is that the end of your investigation?"

"No, not really . . . In fact, while I'm here . . ."

Vasiliev stands, obstinately staring at the ground. Then, suddenly, he looks up.

"I wanted to ask you . . . On Wednesday the eleventh, the day of the shooting in the car park, what took you into the fifteenth arrondissement? It's not exactly close to home . . ."

"I was going to buy sandals. The straps on my old pair had snapped."

"And they don't sell them in Seine-et-Marne?"

"I wanted exactly the same brand."

She glances at Vasiliev's battered shoes.

"I don't know how much you know about buying shoes, but let me tell you, the only way to get the same pair is to go back to where you bought them in the first place."

Vasiliev nods.

"Did you keep the receipt?"

"Turns out they don't make that model anymore; I came home empty-handed."

Right. Vasiliev slaps his thigh, well, I won't take up any more of your time, then changes his mind.

"Where exactly did you bury the dog?"

Mathilde points vaguely: over there.

"Without the head . . ." says Vasiliev.

She gives an anguished nod.

"You're planning to bury it with the body, I assume . . . ?"

"I suppose so. Best to bury all the remains together, don't you think?"

"Yes, that makes sense. So, where is the head now?"

"Under the hedge, just to the right. Or at least I think so, because that's where the neighbour left poor Ludo's body."

Unaccountably, Vasiliev wants to see that damn dog's head.

He draws himself up to his full height and, without a word, walks towards the spot indicated.

She watches him go. The puppy in her lap whimpers; she had not realised she was squeezing him so hard.

Vasiliev can see the indentation of the dog's body in the long grass, but there is no sign of the head. He walks back to the terrace and stands by the bottom step. Mathilde has not moved; she is stroking the puppy.

"I couldn't see it."

"What the devil . . ."

Mathilde jumps to her feet, incensed.

She sets the puppy down on the chair and lumbers heavily down the four steps.

Vasiliev trails after her and the two of them begin to search the garden and the hedge, searching like an elderly couple who've lost a wristwatch on their way back from the beach. It quickly becomes apparent that the Dalmatian's head has disappeared.

As he comes to the corner of the house, the inspector spots a small mound of disturbed earth.

"Is this where you buried him?"

"Yes," says Mathilde, coming to join him.

They stand, rooted to the spot, studying the dog's grave without going any closer, like tourists surveying the results of an archaeological dig. The sun is still shining.

"Well, I'm going inside," said Mathilde. "I'm freezing out here."

Vasiliev lingers awhile, watching her trudge away, her ample buttocks swaying . . .

Then, suddenly, he sees the head. It is some two metres away, thrown up against the wall of the house, half buried in a bed of marigolds. He crouches down.

In his career, he has seen all manner of monstrosities, but what he sees here has a curious effect on him. Eccentric, he thinks, though he means truly bizarre . . . Ants have begun to devour it, worms have joined the banquet. He sees the remains of the pale, sunken eyes, the protruding vertebrae, the trachea, the matted blood, the swarm of flies. Still crouching, he turns and looks back at the grave, then reluctantly gets to his feet and ambles back to the house.

"The head is over there . . ."

Mathilde is no longer on the terrace, Vasiliev finds her in the kitchen, leaning against the countertop, her hands in the pocket of her pinafore clutching the 9 mm Luger she has just taken from the drawer.

"Just by the corner of the house," he adds.

Mathilde nods to indicate that she understands.

"Is that all?" she says.

"Yes. You'd be well advised to bury it or throw it away, it's pretty unsanitary, and it will bring all sorts of insects into the house."

"Thanks for the advice."

Vasiliev turns to leave.

"We'll still need you to come and make a statement," he says before he walks away. "Not about the dog, about the shooting in the car park. My colleagues at Melun police station will deal with it."

He takes the crumpled summons he fished out of the letterbox when he first arrived, clumsily smooths it flat against his leg, then hands it to Mathilde.

"Do you usually deliver a summons in person?"

"I thought, I'll just pop round, you know how it is . . ."

No, Mathilde does *not* know how it is. Vasiliev raises his hand in farewell.

"Goodbye," he says. "And thank you."

"You're welcome, Inspector . . . ?"

"Vasiliev, René Vasiliev."

"Vasifiev?"

"No, Vasiliev, with an 'l'."

He takes out a card and lays it on the formica tabletop, then gives a little wave, and pushes open the glass door to the terrace.

As he walks down the path towards the gate, the inspector turns and sees Mathilde Perrin, with both hands in the pocket of her pinafore, watching him walk away.

On the drive back, he tries to work out why he became so fixated on the dead dog's head, which is completely irrelevant to his investigation. Probably because there was very little to discover about the woman's presence in the car park.

Yes, that's probably it. Even so, the visit has left him depressed. These petty wars between neighbours can be vicious. Especially in the countryside, according to her, not that Vasiliev would know, he's always lived in the city.

For a long moment, Mathilde does not move. She stares pensively at the empty path.

Beside her, the puppy lets out high-pitched yelps. He's restless and anxious, perhaps he senses something electric in the air, a heaviness, an atmosphere.

Mathilde is not thinking about him, she is thinking about his predecessor and the head the idiot inspector went looking for in the hedge – she cannot understand why he was so concerned. It almost seemed as though the cast of the dead dog's head was more important than the murders in the car park murder.

She has planned to go and give Monsieur Lepoitevin a piece of her mind, sort things out in a neighbourly fashion (in her pinafore pocket, she strokes the Luger Parabellum she plans to use to settle the matter), but her intentions have been waylaid by the strange impression left by the policeman's visit.

Did he come all this way to talk about a dog's head – or did he come for *hers*?

The curious way he looked at her . . . And his constant harping on the same subject . . . She paces up and down the terrace as the puppy watches, bewildered – these constant comings and goings make him fretful. Mathilde tries to reconstruct the meeting.

The inspector has come because of her presence in the car park, but he starts out by stopping to talk to Monsieur Lepoitevin, and then, after that, all he can talk about is the missing head of poor Ludo, may he rest in peace.

They think I'm just a dozy, fat bitch . . .

Well, I'll show them what I'm made of! Starting with a little visit to Lepoitevin? No – the inspector is far more dangerous. Monsieur Lepoitevin isn't going anywhere, but the inspector . . .

Purposefully, she strides over to the telephone.

On the way, she encounters the puppy who has strayed from his basket and, with a furious kick, sends him crashing into the French windows. She snatches up the card left on the table.

Vasiliev, in Aubervilliers: he shouldn't be difficult to track down.

We'll see who cuts off whose head.

September 14

The commandant is never late. Except today. He pulls on his coat and dashes for his car. The reason for his tardiness is that, despite his best efforts to shrug it off, he is deeply distraught. Mathilde has become a loose cannon. He decided not to try and find out the story of "the Messin girl". Mathilde has gone rogue. She is a real and present danger. There is nothing to do except . . . By the time he gets to the booth, the phone is already ringing; he picks it up.

"I dealt with the matter today. This situation is in the process of being resolved."

He has only a few seconds remaining. The truth is nothing has been resolved yet; he is about to deal with it now.

It is not prudent to hang around an empty village square for too long. Even in the early hours. Villagers see without being seen. Along with television, curtain-twitching is the sole occupation of many villagers and one they find much more edifying. If a car pulls up, everyone knows. This is the last time he will use the phone box. He will go back to the one he used five or six years earlier; he randomly alternates.

Henri drives through the countryside. He has a car radio, but never thinks to turn it on. It stops him concentrating on his driving. Fragments of reality appear and disappear before his eyes, like visions from a dream. It's calming, almost hypnotic. He doesn't want to think about what he's doing.

He stops at the phone box, keys in a number from memory, leaves a brief message, steps out, walks a few steps, considers lighting a cigarette, but the phone begins to ring. A strong, clear voice. This is Monsieur Buisson. When Henri called on his services a year ago, his name was Monsieur Meyer. The conversation lasts four minutes.

The commandant climbs back into his car and drives some thirty kilometres to another phone box, one he has never used, set next to an old factory wall, no shopkeepers, only a few passers-by, an anonymous junction. He dials a number and requests a call-back.

For almost an hour, he waits, first in his car, then out on the pavement, he lights a cigarette, then another, as he paces up and down. The cold is beginning to bite when the phone finally rings. They speak in German. The conversation is longer and more difficult than the previous one as Henri explains the complications. In the end, he agrees to conditions that he would ordinarily reject outright, because time is running out.

"When can you be in Toulouse?"

His contact is called Dieter Frei. He is based in Freudenstadt. He can be in Toulouse in twenty-four hours.

The commandant hangs up. He has spent more money in the past two hours than he has in the past year; that is how these things go. And this time it is his own money.

It is not this that troubles him, but the sense that a section of his life has just ended.

He is overwhelmed by an immense wave of sadness.

Mathilde got up twice during the night to check on her new puppy, Cookie. There was no reason to worry, she simply wanted his warm presence. Eventually she took him up to her bedroom and let him sleep next to her. In the morning, when he whimpered, she just had time to grab him and run to the washbasin. That's it, baby – good thing Maman still has quick reflexes, because otherwise the duvet would be a shitshow.

She carried him down to the kitchen, gave him some kibble, then sat on the terrace in her rocking chair sipping her coffee and watching him explore the garden.

She thinks long and hard about Monsieur Lepoitevin. She'll deal with him later today. After what he did to Ludo, she's not about to let him go after Cookie. She'll sort him out. Actually – why wait until this afternoon, she could just as easily do it now, get it over with.

She gets up, puts her coffee bowl in the sink and stops in front of the saucer where Henri stubbed out his half-smoked cigarette. Such a waste! Obviously, it is not good that Henri smokes, but if he's determined to poison himself, he could at least finish his cigarettes . . . She empties it into the bin and washes the saucer.

She wishes he had stayed a while; they could have gone out for a meal. But she's happy that he came. She would rather he hadn't come all that way (from Toulouse!) just to criticise her work . . . But deep down, Mathilde is happy. He wanted an explanation; he got one. And he couldn't fault it. There are unforeseen circumstances in any mission. Henri knows this all too well. He simply needed something to tell Personnel in the event they hauled him over the coals, though that seems unlikely. When a contract has been carried out, you move on and that's that.

But as she is heading upstairs to wash and dress, Mathilde stops when she sees the notepad next to the phone. And the inspector's card. She'd forgotten that lumbering oaf. She picks up the card. Vasiliev. She jotted down the address she got from directory enquiries: 21, avenue Jean-Jaurès, Aubervilliers. Lepoitevin or Vasiliev? She has a lot on her plate today . . .

But, she thinks, as she goes up to her room, all things considered it would be best to deal with the cop first, she didn't like the cut of his jib, all those questions, and his dogged insistence made her distinctly uncomfortable. She can leave Lepoitevin until tonight or even tomorrow – the man practically lives in his garden, he won't be difficult to find.

The cop, now, he's a very different matter.

She knew it would be complicated. The cop knows her, he knows her car, and – just to complicate things – he takes the métro. You try shadowing someone under those circumstances! She watched him emerge from the offices of the Police Judiciaire, and his clumsy, gangling frame merely confirmed her earlier suspicions: she does not like this man. There is a single-minded stubbornness about him. She left him to shuffle away (If I were his boss, I'd give him a kick up the arse!) and headed to his address in Aubervilliers.

Once, for a contract in Geneva, she snuck into a target's home. It wasn't difficult, she had seen the guy leave a key on top of the door frame. That night, when he came home, she was sitting in an armchair, and as soon as he turned on the light, she plugged two bullets in his gut. In houses and apartments, a silencer is essential.

As she reaches the avenue Jean-Jaurès, she wonders whether she'll be lucky enough to get into the apartment and wait for him – but this, unsurprisingly, proves impossible. The building is all but impenetrable. The only access is through a large gateway whose heavy wooden door has long since gone. This leads into a long courtyard with the apartment buildings on one side and a row of garages on the other. The space is just about wide enough for a car to pass. She observed the other residents arriving. They are forced to drive very slowly, with their heads halfway out of their car windows so as not to scratch the bodywork. If the big lunk had a car, it would be perfect. Creep inside, hide behind the porch, then, when the guy is slowly inching into the courtyard, take advantage of the fact he's rolled down his window to put a bullet in his head and quietly slink out onto the avenue with no-one any the wiser. Almost a textbook case.

Problem is, the Russki travels by métro.

That said, the porch is still the best location so Mathilde adapts her tactics. Since cars leaving the complex have to drive across the pavement, a large mirror has been mounted outside so drivers can see any pedestrians. Making the most of the quiet afternoon, Mathilde slips into the courtyard. To the left, there is a small awning over an atelier where she sees two men with jewellers' loupes poring over clockwork mechanisms. At night, when the studio is closed, the area beneath the canopy is in darkness and the narrow concrete window ledge offers the perfect place to lie in wait. From here, she will be able to see passing pedestrians in the mirror, and so will see the lanky cop arriving. If she gets to her feet and takes two steps forward as he comes into the courtyard, he'll find himself face to face with her and won't have time to say "Jack Robinson". The only problem is that she doesn't know his routine or his habits. Does he usually come home on his own? She should have paid more attention. Was he wearing a wedding ring? Instinctively, she can't imagine him married with children. More like a forty-year-old virgin. Does he work late? Probably, given his job.

Try as she might to think of some other solution, Mathilde decides that this is the best and the safest. She has opted for a classic 7.65 mm Browning Short she found in a shoebox – she can't remember when she last used it, it must be a long time ago.

The watch repair studio closes at precisely 6 p.m. Shortly before eight o'clock, once night has fallen and the porch is in darkness, Mathilde gets out of her car. She's been watching the entrance and knows the cop has not come home yet.

She'll go and sit in the courtyard.

Be the welcoming committee.

Vasiliev went back to his office, wrote up his daily report and read through those of the officers who interviewed the other drivers who had been in the car park. Someone mentions that Commissaire Occhipinti is very nervous, and Vasiliev can well believe it. With the shootings now linked to the murder of Maurice Quentin, it is a terrible millstone around his neck.

The day before, Vasiliev did not go to Neuilly. After his last conversation with Tevy and the promise that he would get to see her somewhere other than Monsieur's house, going back so soon seemed in bad taste, as though he were desperate for the promise to be fulfilled.

This evening, when he arrives in Neuilly, he feels a vague confusion. He had naively assumed that Tevy's promise would be visible in her expression. But she has the same beaming smile as always and greets him with the same words, as though nothing has happened. He wonders whether they really understood each other.

Monsieur is more alert tonight than he has been in recent days.

"Good evening, René, it's a pleasure to see you," he says, though he seems uninterested.

He immediately goes up to his bedroom and starts to mumble.

"Don't upset yourself, Monsieur, I'm coming!"

Vasiliev hears Tevy settling Monsieur in his armchair in front of the television.

"He's having a bit of trouble putting tapes in the video recorder," she explains when she comes back to the living room. René listens carefully. He recognises the film soundtrack.

"That's *Army of Shadows*, isn't it?"

Tevy nods.

"Surely he's already seen it?"

"Four times this week. And every time is like the first."

Monsieur's bouts of amnesia are sporadic and unpredictable.

"He might lose his memory for an hour or two and then be completely lucid for the rest of the day."

"You knew this was happening long before you told me, didn't you?"

Tevy blushes.

"It's not a criticism," René says hastily.

Instinctively, he grasps her hand and is surprised to find himself holding it; a silence descends that neither knows how to break. They sit like this for a long moment. Then Tevy gets up and goes to Monsieur's room to see whether he needs anything.

"Could you help me put him to bed, René? He's fallen asleep in his chair . . ."

Once Monsieur is in bed and the lights are out, they go back to the living room.

"There's some soup and there's fruit," says Tevy.

It is curious that a woman as impulsive as Mathilde is capable of such patience. She truly was born for this job. She has been sitting on the concrete window ledge for over three hours and, apart from the pins and needles in her feet, she does not feel impatient, just a little cold. She pulls her coat tighter and reaches into her pocket to grip the Browning. Then she looks up and stares into the mirror that reflects the rare pedestrians on the avenue Jean-Jaurès.

There has been little coming and going in the courtyard. A few cars arrived, their owners raised the garage doors and closed them again. At about ten o'clock, the ritual of taking out the bins began at the far end of the yard. At dawn, someone will wheel them out onto the street before the binmen arrive.

No-one and nothing has disturbed her nocturnal vigil, except the biting cold that now means she has to take a few steps and shake her hands to keep them from going numb. She cannot stray far lest she lose sight of the mirror; if she moves too far, he is bound to show up – Sod's Law . . .

Here he comes!

No doubt about it, the tall, gangling figure. Mathilde draws her Browning automatic. Since she began her vigil, she has timed the interval between people appearing in the mirror and the moment they come through the gate; she needs to count to nine.

The inspector disappears from the mirror. Mathilde begins her count.

At six, she will take three steps forward.

At nine, the inspector will come through the gate.

At eleven, he will be right in front of her.

At twelve, he will be dead.

When she reaches five, she hears two voices somewhere to her left. Mathilde takes a step back but grips the gun.

"Shift your arse," says a voice.

Young. Three or four metres away. Automatically, Mathilde continues to count. She has reached eight when a flame suddenly flares in the gateway. A match. Two boys, about twelve or thirteen, are feverishly passing a cigarette and puffing on it.

"Look out!"

It is Vasiliev coming through the gateway.

It's not the first time he's surprised the two boys, and he always finds it amusing. He turns his head so as not to disturb them.

"C'mon, one last drag!" says one boy.

"Well, hurry up," says the other, "I gotta get back upstairs!"

The cigarette butt falls to the ground and is crushed by a foot.

The two boys run towards the door of the apartment building that Vasiliev has just entered.

Mathilde is livid.

If she doesn't find another opportunity to eliminate that big oaf soon, she's going to wish she'd wasted them all tonight, him and the kids.

September 15

At first light, François Buisson leaves the suburbs of Brussels behind the wheel of a L309D Mercedes van. He expects to reach Melun by 9 a.m. The hit is a last-minute job, and he is not in the habit of rushing things. His contact needed to persuade him, and in this business, money is the great persuader. The sum offered was worth it; he accepted the contract. The hitman is like the market trader: rush jobs are where he makes his money.

The van, which bears the logo of an imaginary cleaning company in Mons, is kept in a lock-up in the suburbs. Although he rarely uses it, he keeps it primed and ready: he has only to turn the key in the ignition and set off.

Buisson has never encountered any insurmountable difficulties, but when behind the wheel, he is always on the alert. Getting there is rarely a problem; getting home demands more care and attention.

Unlike the commandant – whom he has never met – Buisson loves his car radio. He always listens to it. He drives carefully, and is meticulous about traffic regulations. He is above suspicion.

Buisson is fifty-four. No need for nuance to describe him: he's a fat little man with receding hair, brown eyes, a low voice and stubby legs that can run very fast. To assume that this plump little man has a soft underbelly would be a big mistake. He weighs eighty-five kilos. He spent ten years working for the police. He was an outstanding officer. It was never his main job, but he regularly scored top marks at target practice and was considered a crack shot.

After his divorce, he sank into a deep depression. Booze didn't help matters. He had to leave the police before things got worse, he isolated himself from his friends, holed up in his house. He often considered suicide. It was the job that got him through the depression. He was assigned a contract, almost by chance, and it felt good to be working again. He carried out the hit with such care and efficiency that he was surprised he was not offered more contracts. Then, one day, he spotted someone tailing him. Personnel were considering recruiting him and wanted to know everything about him. He felt he had been reborn. He adopted a strict routine and set out to prove that he was a man who could be trusted.

Then, finally, he got another call. Simple missions at first, then gradually more complex hits. Until Buisson's final innovation, which was to offer both a sales and an after-sales service. This is what made his fortune. He no longer accepts more than three contracts a year, and he is happier to limit himself to two.

The job saved him from depression, and he is now a happy, well-balanced man.

No glasses, he has 20/20 vision. He wears a sober, boring uni-form that makes him look like an industrial cleaning operative. This is the occupation he lists on his papers and his tax returns.

He travels with a small bag for clothes and toiletries and an attaché case. If all goes well, a mission should not last more than a day. Two at most.

And Buisson is meticulous in his calculations; he is rarely wrong.

He sees the first sign for Brie-Comte-Robert, he turns off the radio, but rather than continuing towards Melun, he takes a right and drives for a long time along a dirt road spattered with chalky white. Those streaks of cement mean that he doesn't need to consult his map: he knows he's heading in the right direction.

And he is right. Eight kilometres further on, he pulls up outside the car park of a cement works in which there are some thirty vehicles belonging to labourers and foremen. He studies the iron gate, which is secured by a simple system of industrial padlocks that can easily be forced and neatly closed after use. He surveys the vast silos of concrete and tar. He will have to carry the body over his shoulder and toss it into one of the silos, but this does not worry Buisson; it will not be the first corpse he has carried. He inspects the security lights that sweep the area at night. He will have to cover two short distances in the light, but otherwise he should have no trouble, or at least nothing he cannot deal with.

Climbing back into his car, he heads for Melun.

From this point, he travels in silence, intent on the road ahead and on his mission.

There is nothing to be done, there is no alternative. The door into the apartment block is Mathilde's only chance to intercept the inspector. So, the following day, at 9 p.m., she parks nearby and waits for it to get dark before moving into position. Nervously, she toys with the Browning and, to pass the time, tries to remember the contract for which Supplies issued it to her. But in vain. It's like working for years in any profession, she thinks, everything gets muddled up. Just then, the inspector appears, walking along the pavement with his loping stride. So furious is she that he has come home early and spoiled her plans that she has to restrain herself from getting out and putting two bullets in his gut. She feels a wave of loathing. What is he doing coming home at such an hour like a civil servant? Another failed attempt. She pounds her fist on the steering wheel and takes a deep breath.

Perhaps he will go out again? You never can tell . . .

If he comes out and runs to the métro, she will have waited in vain, but that's the nature of this job. Like film actors, people in her profession spend a lot of time hanging around.

She decides to wait a little. She gives herself an hour, then she drives home. She puts Cookie out on the terrace, wrapped in blankets, because she doesn't want him to get into the habit of peeing on the kitchen floor. This thought evokes memories of Henri's visit. Did he really need to come all the way from Toulouse to check on something so trivial?

No, the real reason he came was to see her.

But strangely, they didn't discuss anything personal or intimate. They talked shop, and Henri left feeling reassured. Surely he could have taken an interest, asked what was going on in Mathilde's life, but no, he was straight in with his questions, his demands for explanations, it was tedious! She pictures him again, elegantly smoking his cigarette . . . She has such fond memories of him, so many beautiful images of the period when they would see each other almost every day. Of course, that was a long time ago, but it was the most glorious period of her life. Not only because she was young, but because she felt useful . . . And then there was Henri. Today, she blames herself for leading him on. Every time he tried to initiate a personal relationship, she rebuffed him, she was not about to throw herself at him . . . Did I let my one chance pass me by? And the day before yesterday . . . Why did she not take the opportunity to put her cards on the table?

To say, Henri, do you think we're too old to start something? Is there a woman in your life who is closer to you than I am? Would Henri have said yes, that there was a woman in his life? Mathilde smiled. No. Women can sense these things. Henri is a solitary man, he is lonely, desperately lonely; that was why he had come to see her, using work as an excuse. But, in the end, he hadn't dared. And nor had she. What if she had gone to visit him? She has visited him only twice in the space of thirty years, she can still picture the long, low, house, the English cottage garden – so typical of him. She is filled with an overwhelming urge to go there, to have it out once and for all . . .

There he is – the inspector! He has just stepped out of the gateway. He's wearing a suit. He looks like he's going to a funeral. Mathilde grips the steering wheel. Vasiliev is heading towards the métro, but before she has time to react, he hails a passing taxi, gets in. Mathilde turns the key in the ignition: there is still hope.

If he gives her an opportunity, however slim, she won't miss.

The Renault 25 follows the taxi.

Simply seeing the nape of his neck through the rear windscreen brings her black fury flooding back. She can almost hear his drawling voice: "Where exactly did you bury the dog?"

She feels something inside her flare up again, but it is simply the butt of the semi-automatic in her lap, under her raincoat.

Vasiliev has been dreading this evening.

Because he never knows what Monsieur will be like. And he is angry with himself for never letting Tevy know how much he appreciates her and all the trouble she goes to. Things must be very difficult at times. Oh, she keeps on smiling, but that's just the facade. He'll talk to her tonight. How hard can it be to say thank you? But he is also dreading this evening because he and Tevy have been in a state of suspense. They have made promises without really making them. They talked about meeting up one day, but when? I'm such a fool, he thinks, that's the problem . . . I need to go about things differently, I need to be more gallant. Gallant? Him? Good God.

For all this self-criticism, he behaves exactly as he usually does. I should have brought flowers, he thinks.

"Good evening, René, you're early this evening, aren't you?"

Always smiling . . . Vasiliev mumbles a few words but she is not listening as she leads him down the hall towards the living room. Monsieur's bedroom is in darkness.

"I'm letting him sleep a little, he seems very tired today."

She sits in a straight-back chair at the table. For the first time, he notices that Tevy never sits in an armchair as though this were her home. No, she is Monsieur's nurse.

Vasiliev sits opposite her. She looks at him calmly.

Has the time come to declare himself?

"So, how was your day?" he says.

Night has drawn in. Mathilde waits, hands clasped under her raincoat. The inspector has just gone into a building. Standing on the pavement, she scans the facade, checking the windows. Several are lit – how can she tell which is which? Mathilde wonders what would bring a blue-collar inspector to such a ritzy apartment building. A lover? She stifles a laugh at the thought of that lanky oaf with an aristocratic mistress. A fancy dinner party? It is at this point that another light comes on. A window.

Second floor, left. Obviously, it could just be coincidence, but then another window lights up on the same floor. She waits a few seconds more, but nothing else happens, the whole building is quiet. She closes the flaps of her raincoat, her right hand still gripping the revolver.

She goes inside. To the left, the lodge inhabited by the concierge, who has probably dozed off. She scans the plaque listing the occupants. Second floor, left: de la Hosseray. It sounds distinctly odd, and doesn't tally with that shyster inspector . . . She hesitates. Reads through the whole list. No particular name jumps out. There is nothing to do but trust her instincts. By the time the elevator reaches the second floor, the name "de la Hosseray" trips off her tongue. It has to be the right one. Slowly, she opens the elevator door, slips out, and wedges it open with her bag.

She steps forward, takes a deep breath. She is determined. In her mind, flickering images of Ludo's bloody head beneath the hedge and the head of the inspector. She is at the end of her rope.

No-one is going to fuck with her anymore! Gradually, her heartbeat returns to normal, her breathing slows. She takes both hands from under her raincoat, extends her right hand, the barrel of the gun pointing straight ahead, as, with her left hand, she rings the doorbell.

Twice.

Tevy tilts her head. Who could it be at this hour? A neighbour?

"I'll be right back," she says.

Before Vasiliev can move, she is on her feet and running down the hallway.

Tevy never looks through the peephole. If someone rings, you open the door, you don't play hide and seek with destiny.

She comes face to face with an elderly woman in a raincoat, well made-up, nice hair. She just has time to think that the woman obviously looks after herself, then, as she opens her mouth to ask what she wants, she sees the gun.

Mathilde raises her arm. She was not expecting a maid. And a Chink by the look of it. She shoots her between the eyes. The young woman crumples. Tevy will never know that her sacred tattoo is no protection against a 7.65 mm Parabellum.

Mathilde steps over her body and into the apartment.

Vasiliev can't believe his ears.

Was that a gunshot?

He jumps up and races out – why does he never carry his service revolver?

As he turns into the hall, he sees the woman he interviewed in her home standing less than two metres away. Why didn't I trust to my instincts?

Vasiliev has no time for further deliberation. The first bullet hits him in the chest, right next to his heart. Mathilde steps forward, puts a second bullet in his head, then turns on her heel.

She picks up her bag, gets into the lift, presses the button for the ground floor. She is calm because she feels relieved. Finally, people will stop fucking with her.

The whole building echoes to the sound of the gunshots. But it will be a while before anyone risks poking their nose out to see what's going on. Mathilde opens the front door of the building and walks across the deserted street to her car.

As she climbs behind the wheel, she takes a last look up at the second floor.

A frail old man in a dressing gown is standing at the window that was dark when she first arrived.

His face is lined and haggard, his eyes are wild. His lips look as though they are trembling but Mathilde is too far away to be sure.

He's obviously in a bad way. Should have put him out of his misery. But you can't be all things to all men, Mathilde thinks as she drives away.

Heading back to Melun.

I just hope Cookie doesn't catch a cold out there on the terrace.

I don't want to have to spend all day tomorrow at the vet's.

The gentleman who phoned had difficulty expressing himself, but he was clear enough for two uniformed officers to arrive at the apartment building just as the neighbours started screaming at the top of their lungs.

Dozens of them were milling about, it was impossible to move in the apartment.

Monsieur cannot bring himself to look at the bodies lying in the hallway, it is too painful. He sits in his armchair, which the forensic officers have placed in a corner of the living room since he was getting in their way. He does not weep, and it seems impossible that such devastating grief should have no outward sign. Someone whispers: "Do you think he really knows what's going on?" A rather pretty female officer says over and over: "Do you have any family? Anyone you'd like us to call?" He gestures vaguely towards the hallway: his whole family is out there, lying in a pool of blood.

The forensic team, the uniformed officers, the plainclothes detectives, the floodlights; it is all a little overwhelming.

Especially since the victim is a serving officer. Everyone at the Police Judiciaire is stupefied.

The murder of one of his own officers is bad news for Commissaire Occhipinti, especially since, although Vasiliev was a pain in the arse, he was also a first-rate detective.

When he arrives at the crime scene, he finds Vasiliev's body lying in a pool of blood and is struck that he looks even taller dead than he did alive. He feels sorry for the guy, he was so young. He stands, hands in his pockets, shaking his head, as forensic officers buzz around him – what a clusterfuck. He walks over to the body of the young woman and is surprised to discover that she is South-East Asian.

"She's the sister of the Tan brothers," an inspector tells him.

Occhipinti turns and takes the ID card that was found in her handbag. Every officer here knows the Tan brothers are vicious thugs who deal in street drugs and low-end prostitution.

"She was a carer. She was looking after . . ."

The inspector jerks a thumb over his shoulder towards the old man in the armchair with the dead look in his eyes. The commissaire's hunch is that the killer's target was the young Cambodian woman and Vasiliev was simply collateral damage. He is very proud of his instinct, which he calls "my nose" because he's a bit of a bloodhound. Obviously, they'll pursue both lines of investigation, but for the Tan brothers' name to crop up in a serious crime without them being directly involved would be a first.

According to what Occhipinti was told when he arrived, the haggard old man in the armchair is a former chief of police. A crestfallen Occhipinti gobbles a handful of peanuts as he stands in front of the former senior officer and attempts to question him. The old man does not seem to understand the questions.

Occhipinti turns to the female officer. Monsieur hears ". . . understand what I am saying? . . . you sure . . . ?" The commissaire turns back to Monsieur.

"So, you didn't witness anything, you just heard the shots, is that right?"

Monsieur stares impassively at the commissaire. He knows he should do something, that he should be tearful or enraged – anything but stare vacantly at the fat officer who smells of peanuts who keeps repeating his questions like a broken record. If Monsieur cannot put on a convincing performance, he will have social services knocking before long. So, he draws on his last reserves.

"Exactly. I heard shots, but I did not actually see anything."

His performance clearly passes muster, because the commissaire slaps his knees and gets to his feet.

This is partly because the examining magistrate has just arrived. He takes a long look at the crime scene as he listens to Occhipinti summarise the facts. The two men are in agreement. A warrant is immediately issued to bring the Tan brothers in for questioning. Meanwhile, some of the detectives will delve into Vasiliev's old cases, going back several years in search of any recently released cons who might have harboured a grudge against the man who put them behind bars. Occhipinti thinks this line of investigation is not very promising. Vasiliev chiefly dealt with rapes and serious sexual offences – not the kind of villains who exact revenge with a high-calibre revolver that could stop an elephant . . .

Then there's the Maurice Quentin case – the bane of his existence – not to mention the shooting of Béatrice Lavergne and the shop assistant in the car park. But it's difficult to imagine what

Vasiliev could have discovered that would lead to him being gunned down.

Right now, the Tan brothers are his strongest lead.

Occhipinti hopes he can solve this case quickly. He's already had enough grief over the Quentin and Lavergne cases; he doesn't want the unsolved murder of an officer from his department on his hands. That would be a very bad career move.

When the investigation magistrate has left, Occhipinti calls over the female officer and whispers to her, while staring at the man in the armchair. She seems to agree with the commissaire, who quickly follows the magistrate. Gradually, everyone drifts away, leaving only the pretty female officer and two of her colleagues. It is she who takes the initiative. She looks around the flat, asks where she might find a suitcase.

"You have no right to take me away," says Monsieur.

She finds a suitcase, but she is keenly aware of how much there is to do to gather up all the things necessary for a man of this age and in this condition . . . Better to leave it to social services.

"I demand to stay here. You have no right . . ." Monsieur insists.

The three officers have a whispered confab. They talk to the neighbours, who throw up their hands. If they had to deal with all the elderly people in Neuilly, it would never end.

Eventually, they give in. The young woman puts her card next to the phone, circling the phone number he should call if he has a problem.

After the police leave, a silence settles over the apartment. Monsieur looks at all the things that Tevy left behind, her knick-knacks, her dragons.

Her good luck charms.

September 16

The commandant always wakes at precisely the same time: 6.20
a.m. He assumes this is the time he was born. Tonight is a notable
exception. For the first time in ages – probably since the war – he
has barely slept at all. And what little sleep he's had has been
haunted by nightmares. His head feels heavy, his tongue pasty.
Henri rarely remembers his dreams. He likes to think that his
superego is bulletproof. But this is clearly not the case. During
the night, countless images he thought forgotten have resurfaced.
Mathilde is in all of them. The last image he remembers from
his nightmare was of Mathilde, smiling and radiant in a white
wedding dress as bloody as a butcher's apron.

At first light, Henri starts to tidy up. He takes out what he
calls his *antiquities*. He is shrewd and he is far-sighted; he doesn't
keep compromising documents. Thirty years ago, he developed a
tortuous labyrinth of trails and false trails, aliases, fake maildrops
real maildrops and false addresses that would make any attempt
to trace his movements long and chaotic, giving him more than
enough time to disappear. He has three numbered bank accounts,
and the few incriminating documents he has kept to give him
leverage in the event he ever has to negotiate with Personnel are
hidden in different locations to which only he has access.

This is the question that has haunted him all night.

Given that his life has hit serious turbulence since Mathilde
went rogue, should he implement plan B? Should he negotiate a

Peace of the Braves with Personnel? They allow him to leave in exchange for his silence.

He has come to the conclusion that it would be futile.

The whole reason he has spent decades devising a complex escape route is because he knows that Personnel will say they agree to his terms, and then let slip the dogs of war. It might take a few weeks, even a few months, but sooner or later a Buisson or a Dieter Frei will creep up behind him and settle the score. And his career.

At home, he keeps only official documents relating to his official life, and a collection of old clippings, letters, bills, letters and photographs that he would gladly burn, but feels he needs to provide set dressing for a single, isolated man of his age. Anyone breaking into his home – an unlikely eventuality before Mathilde's recent exploits turned his life upside down – would find evidence of an ordinary, boring man. In the year he first set up his complex security plan, Mathilde was not yet a colleague. But she appears in his personal archives as a former comrade in the Resistance, and as the widow of Dr Perrin. When Henri first brought her to Personnel, he considered getting rid of these reminders, but decided that their absence would look more suspicious than their presence, so he kept them.

It is 5 a.m.

Twenty-four hours since Buisson set off, so he should soon get to work, if he has not done so already. Not for the first time he wonders how things will play out. But the moment he tries to imagine what happens next, his mind balks – something inside him refuses to picture what will happen to Mathilde.

Coming back from the kitchen with a bowl of hot tea, Henri settles himself behind his rolltop desk, takes a cardboard box and removes everything that relates to Mathilde. There are some letters from the fifties and sixties; he recognises her neat, clear handwriting. Letters and postcards that invariably begin with "My dearest Henri". A postcard from Spain where she spent the summer with her husband ("Raymond loves the heat here, but I find it terribly oppressive"), a letter from New York on paper from the Roosevelt Hotel ("If it weren't for my husband's professional duties, I'd spend all my time wandering the streets"). She constantly complains about her husband, although the poor bastard seems to be doing the best he can. There are birthday cards. He didn't keep them all, but Mathilde never missed a year. When Henri realised this, he threw away most of them; the cards somehow sapped his morale. "Still as youthful as ever, I'm sure," she writes, though they haven't seen each other for years. Later: "You'll be the handsomest centenarian in the old people's home . . ." There is a letter from 1955 to which Henri has attached a black and white photograph with a paper clip. He and Mathilde standing side by side, ramrod straight. Mathilde's face is half hidden by the neck and the kepi of General Foucault, who is embracing her. Henri, intent and smiling, the Médaille de la Résistance he received a moment earlier pinned to his chest. Mathilde's letter came a few days after the ceremony. He attributed it to a bout of melancholy, she talks about old times with a slightly bitter nostalgia. "Just think about it, Henri, after all that's happened, we've finally won the recognition of the French people! I sometimes understand the soldiers who re-enlisted. I miss the war, of course, not just because we were young, but because we had something to do." She has underlined "something".

He finds a faded, misfiled photo of Mathilde in a print dress. He turns over the photograph: 1943. She is posing next to a military truck. He studies her intently and, more than ever, feels the powerful sexual allure of her beauty and the fascination she exudes by her cruelty. This is the paradoxical charm Mathilde has always wielded over him.

A death notice on a black-rimmed card. 1960. Memorial service for Raymond Perrin. "Thank you for coming, Henri, your presence (however brief) gave me great pleasure. When will you come back? Are you waiting for me to die?"

Henri checks that he has forgotten nothing. He tosses everything into the fireplace, sets it alight and sips his cold tea. He stares into the flames, somewhat hypnotised, then shrugs: staring into a fire is idiotic.

As a whole portion of his life disappears up the chimney, Henri thinks about himself.

He returns to a fact that has always seemed self-evident. All his life, he has had only one passion: to take action, to influence events. His success and his authority depend not on his leadership skills or his power, but on this secret obsession, the thrill he feels at being someone who makes history. A messenger of fate, if not fate itself. He thinks of all the lives that he has ended and those of the survivors, about whom he knows nothing, but whose lives he irrevocably changed. Suddenly, he imagines a vast family tree that maps out all the dead and all the living, and the unfathomable consequences of so many deaths, the marriages, second marriages, legacies, appointments, suicides, births, leavetakings, escapes, reunions ... A vast comédie humaine with Henri at its centre, since he is responsible for it all: not just the deaths, which would have occurred sooner or later anyway, but what lives – unexpected, sometimes unhoped-for – that those deaths made possible. He gets to his feet and wonders what he will do, now that it is his turn, now that his contract has been completed, now that Mathilde is no longer a presence.

Physically, Dieter Frei is the antithesis of Buisson. He is a tall, broad yet elegant man, with bristling hair and a flat stomach. It will take him just under an hour to get from Freudenstadt to Strasbourg. From here there is a direct flight to Toulouse, but Dieter Frei has a stopover to make in Paris. He is travelling under an assumed name.

In his brief layover in Paris, he collects an attaché case from a contact, pays him in cash and then boards the interminable train to Toulouse. The commandant warned him that he could not gauge the exact duration of the mission. One to four days. No more.

Dieter decided on three days and packed precisely enough clothes in his travel bag.

In Toulouse, he rented a car under his first alias. The whole journey took precisely twenty-two hours. He has two hours in which to get some rest. The attaché case contains a high-powered rifle with a scope. The only issue now is choosing an observation post.

Mathilde faffed around for a while, made herself some coffee. She feels grubby, there is a metallic taste in her mouth. She dismisses the thought of raiding the bathroom cabinet – when your husband is a doctor, you steer clear of drugs. She dozes over her coffee, feeling unaccountably fretful.

Outside, Cookie is waiting for his food. Mathilde gets up, opens the door for him, pours kibble into his bowl, then goes to

look at herself in the mirror. That face, good God! The haggard-
ness, the drooping eyelids. Truth be told, it's the same one she
sees every day, but Mathilde has reached the age when morning
has little to do with who you really are. It takes her longer and
longer to put her face on. She is working on this as it gets light.
It's half past seven. That's me, she thinks, staring at the mirror,
well, more or less, as much as possible. She pauses. She hears a
noise, a sharp scratch against the wall.

"Ludo!"

The dog doesn't come. Did she put him out in the garden? The
cocker spaniel tilts his head and looks at her, bemused.

"Shut up," she mutters, though the dog hasn't made a sound.

No, it's not the dog.

She goes over to the sink. Instinctively, she snatches up the
kitchen knife, peers out the window, sees nothing. The same
noise comes again. This time, there's no doubt that it's coming
from outside.

Cookie starts to whine. He can sense the mounting dread in
the room.

"Shut up!"

The dog sits, puts his front paws on Mathilde's legs. She bends
down, takes him in her arms and sets him on the countertop,
shut up, Ludo. The dog tries to lick her face while she strains to
listen for the noise – where is it coming from?

The dog insists, stop it, Ludo, she hugs him tightly, the dog
feels crushed and lets out a squeal, shut up, can't you see Maman
is listening?

The dog falls silent, though he is still afraid.

Setting him on the ground, Mathilde silently creeps over to
the grandfather clock, opens it carefully, never losing sight of

the garden door and the kitchen windows. She gropes blindly and pulls out an oily rag containing a Smith & Wesson that is locked and loaded. She takes a second magazine and slips it into her pocket and walks quickly to the door. She can hear her heart pounding. Flattening herself against the wall, she reaches for the doorknob and turns it slowly. Unlike the sense of detachment the commandant calls sang-froid, what Mathilde experiences is a dizzying lucidity. All-consuming moments when her every sense seems to converge on a seemingly insignificant detail. Her brain ceases to function, it is reduced to a keenly honed point fixed on a target whether real or imaginary she cannot tell.

Very slowly, Mathilde opens the door. As she steps out, she hears the noise again.

Looking up, she sees her bedroom shutter flapping.

In that same instant, perhaps because of the sudden relief brought by this realisation that the danger she feared does not exist, she has another funny turn, her legs feel like jelly, her hand falls to her side and she almost drops the gun. Slowly, she shuffles as far as the terrace chair and slumps into it. She tries to pull herself together. The puppy trots over. She picks him up, sets him on her lap and strokes him. They spend fifteen minutes like this.

What's the matter with me?

What am I so afraid of?

Get up, get moving, go shopping, make yourself useful. She goes to the grandfather clock, wraps the gun in the oily rag, then picks up her keys. The sense of dread has not dissipated, it is like a bitter taste in her mouth, or the fear of falling on a slippery pavement. A feeling that refuses to go away.

What should I do with Cookie? If I leave him outside, Lepoitevin might kill him – I know that bastard. Unless I go round now and sort him out once and for all. But she does not feel well enough to do that. Is she still overwhelmed? Her heart rate has not returned to normal; it is still beating erratically.

She puts the dog's basket and his blanket on the terrace, refills his water and food bowls, then walks unsteadily towards her car. If she should have a funny turn while she's driving . . .

Buisson accurately calculated the distance. He turns onto the narrow road leading to his target a few minutes before 9 a.m. The houses are set far apart and separated by perfectly manicured gardens. They all have preposterous names. He looks for La Coustelle, with its long gravel path and its wrought-iron gate. He is careful not to drive too fast. Turning a corner, he spots the house and its owner, because, as he drives past, her Renault 25 pulls out onto the road.

There can be no doubt: sixty years old, plump, too much makeup. He looks away and carries on driving, looks for a place where he can make a discreet U-turn, and finds one a hundred metres on. He heads back the way he came, slows as he comes to the house, checks the name on the gate, then speeds up. Plenty of time later to do a recce of the house, the garden, the neighbourhood. Right now, it's best not to hang around so as not to attract attention. Better to shadow the target. See how she behaves, how she walks, get a sense of her demeanour. And if he loses her, it doesn't matter: sooner or later, she'll come home and he'll be waiting.

Mathilde is feeling much better.

The moment she drove through the gate and turned onto the road to Melun, she felt rejuvenated. Her earlier unease has faded, her breathing has returned to normal. Phew. Like the flick of a windscreen wiper after a passing shower, the world is calm once more and her lust for life is renewed. She's made her decision: new shoes and a visit to a tea room. The high life.

There are four shops that Mathilde regularly visits. For some women, it's clothes shops, for others it's kitchen supplies, for Mathilde it's shoe shops – go figure! Mathilde laughs – oh, yes, she's bought countless pairs she's never worn, but so what? You only live once. She spends the morning in fittings, she buys two pairs, things are looking up. For lunch, she favours a tea room over a restaurant. She gorges herself on a huge Paris-Brest oozing praline-flavoured cream – I know it's bad for me, but I don't care!

And at about five o'clock she heads home.

Cookie has been as good as gold; he's overjoyed that she is back. My baby, she says, holding the puppy at arm's length. She uncorks a bottle of white wine, opens a packet of savoury crackers – too much salt is another thing that's bad for her . . .

She takes everything outside, determined to make the most of the terrace before the weather turns cold.

Sitting in her rocking chair, she stares at the hedge.

Going round to see Lepoitevin tonight is not feasible. Tomorrow, maybe. Or some other day, it's just a rain check, she can't let him get away with what he did to Ludo, she'll have to make that clear, but later, later . . . Right now, she thinks, just enjoy the balmy weather, Mathilde, cuddle your dog, drink your wine, stuff yourself with crackers, you deserve it!

Buisson did not spend long shadowing Mathilde. He quickly worked out the sort of woman he was dealing with. Shoe shopping, drooling over leather goods, visiting tea rooms – no need to labour the point. And he was glad he hadn't wasted any more time because finding an observation post in the dense woodland surrounding La Coustelle and the neighbouring houses proved more difficult than he anticipated. Having studied the ordnance survey map at length, he drove straight to the place he wanted, but as dusk began to fall, he thought he might have to climb a tree. Eventually he found the perfect place, a hunting lodge which clearly had not been used for some time. He broke two slats as he clambered inside, hugging the walls to avoid falling through the rotting floorboards. Even then, he was not out of the woods since he had to climb up onto the roof which looked as though it was on the point of collapse. But, in the end, he managed. From here, using his telescopic sight, he can see the target's house – only the southern elevation, admittedly, but that is by far the most interesting. At about nine o'clock, the terrace light went out. This was followed by an interminable ballet of lights being turned on and off upstairs and downstairs until only two first-floor windows still glowed – the bathroom and the bedroom, he assumed. Then, for a long time, only one. The bedroom. Buisson mentally drew a blueprint of the house; it did not seem to pose any problems.

At a quarter to ten, the last light flickers out. He waits for half an hour, then carefully climbs down, gets back into the van, drives off, stops at the village phone box to make a brief call, then comes back and parks in the woods.

He climbs into the back, crawls into a sleeping bag and falls asleep.

*   *   *

At about 2 a.m., Buisson, refreshed and ready for action, muffles the bell, lifts the garden gate so it doesn't squeak, walks across the lawn to avoid the crunch of gravel, then carefully circles the house. The kitchen door is a common model with a frosted glass pane and a standard-issue lock that he quickly picks. Once inside, he stands motionless for a long time until his eyes adjust to the darkness.

As he passes the puppy sleeping in the basket, he strokes it with one finger, kicks off his shoes and takes the Walther PPK fitted with a silencer from under his jacket.

He gingerly tests each tread on the stairs, and it takes him almost six minutes to get to the first floor.

Slowly and warily, he moves along the landing towards the bedroom.

The door is wide open: one less obstacle to overcome.

He sees the bloated figure of the target under the duvet. With infinite slowness, he steps forward. On the threshold, he feels a bump in the carpet. He realises that there is a blanket on the floor. With perfect focus, he brings his arm up horizontally and fires two bullets.

In fact, there are not two muffled gunshots, but four.

The first two from the Walther PPK fired into the bed.

The next two from the Browning semi-automatic, one in the back of Buisson's head, the other in the groin.

The explosions sound like the soft pop of champagne being carefully uncorked.

Mathilde turns on the light.

She is wearing a coat for fear she will catch a chill while waiting for this fuckwit.

Now that he's got what was coming to him, she can go and make a nice cup of coffee. What time is it? Three in the morning! Another night ruined.

September 17

Didn't I tell you, Henri? Your old friend Mathilde is still sharp as a tack, make no mistake!

She is standing in the kitchen, still wearing her coat, sipping a steaming bowl of coffee.

OK, Henri, I was a little lucky, I'll admit, but you remember what Napoleon said, don't you? "Never interrupt your enemy when he is making a mistake." Did she say that to Henri when he dropped by the other day or did she just imagine it? She can't remember.

Four in the morning. Things are looking up now, but it was a hell of a job! One that got off to a very bad start.

"Filthy pig!" she growls as she goes back up to the room.

The old rug and the blanket spread over the floor were intended to soak up the blood of the guy Henri sent to whack her. But the blood has seeped through to the carpet. And not just a little – it's completely soaked, there's a huge stain! Mathilde is apoplectic. You try cleaning that up! When it comes to stains, blood and ink are the worst.

Well, she thinks, what's done is done, no point complaining.

She'll do what she planned: roll the body up in the carpet and blanket, slide it down the stairs and just hope it doesn't get stuck halfway. Usually, with a neat package and no arms or feet sticking out, it's fine. But she has to move it quickly, before rigor mortis sets in, because after that she would have to wait, and

Mathilde is not the patient type. Besides, the bastard is bleeding like a stuck pig! I'm sure my new cleaning lady won't know how to get rid of the stain, the woman at the agency said she wasn't very experienced – come to think of it, I must have made a note of what day she's coming. Have to check.

She starts with a thorough search.

No ID, no papers on him. Normal.

Rubber-soled shoes and a Walther PPK – which she puts to one side, together with the keys to his van. Got to admit, Henri, you really know how to pick them. I don't mean myself – this guy was a pro. Actually, I'd have been annoyed if you'd sent an amateur, I'd have found it insulting.

Now I've got to track down his van, but first I need to get him bundled up. The things you make me do, Henri – honestly, I'm too old for this shit!

She remembered to get a roll of heavy-duty packing tape, but didn't reckon on the guy being this heavy, or falling diagonally across the blanket – which is why blood has seeped into the carpet.

For a second, she considers asking Monsieur Lepoitevin to help.

The thought of the neighbour brings back memories of Ludo. She makes a mental note to go and have it out with Lepoitevin, then gets back to work.

Mathilde kneels next to the corpse, panting for breath, then she gets to her feet, bends down and tries to lift the body onto the blanket, alternately gripping his shoulders, his jacket, his feet. It's a nightmare. It takes an age just to get the corpse into the right position. Then she rolls him up. This is not particularly difficult, but she's already exhausted. Now, to get him taped up.

She has to roll the body one way, tape one side, roll it the other way, tape the other side, then move a few centimetres and do it over and over again – no easy feat given that the bed is in the middle of the room – a logical place for a bed, but a pain in the arse when you're trying to roll a hitman into a rug.

She turns over her alarm clock on the bedside table. Good God, it's taken her nearly an hour to get him trussed.

Now, to push him down the stairs, and that's another Herculean task: getting him onto the landing, turning the body so it will slide straight down. This is the crucial moment, but Mathilde is exhausted. If the corpse should get stuck halfway down, it'll take brute force to shift and right now I'm shattered, Henri, I'm all in.

She props the body on the landing next to the top step.

She'll deal with it when she's got her strength back. She squeezes between the bundle and the banister, trudges down the stairs and sits in the kitchen. The puppy comes and rubs against her legs, she picks him up and puts him on her lap, she lays her head on her folded arms and falls asleep.

So, when the doorbell rings, it takes a moment for her to wake up, disoriented and numb, and work out where she is. The first thing she sees is that the puppy has peed on the floor, and that makes her angry . . .

"What have you done?"

She is furious. The puppy is cowering in a corner, she gets up and strides over, I'll show you, you little fucker, but the sound of the doorbell stops her in her tracks. She whips around and suddenly she is wide awake, because there are two men in suits standing at her gate. She can smell a plainclothes cop at forty paces. They can see her through the window that opens onto the terrace.

What are they doing here?

Up on the landing is the body of a hitman in a carpet ready to be rolled down the stairs . . .

In the bedroom there is a pool of blood that has soaked the carpet . . .

She runs her fingers through her hair, walks over and opens the door but does not step out onto the terrace.

"Come in, gentlemen, come in!"

She goes back into the kitchen, takes the Luger Parabellum from the drawer, quickly cocks it and carefully puts it back, leaving the drawer half open to save time.

Then she turns round and watches them walk up the gravel path.

The senior officer is on the right, he is shorter but he walks half a step ahead of a younger man. They're both as badly dressed as each other. The senior officer seems to be chewing something – gum?

Mathilde goes back to the counter and is wringing out a mop just as the two men step onto the terrace and stop next to the sliding door.

"Madame Perrin?" says the short-arse.

"That's me. Don't come in, the puppy's just had a little accident, you might slip. I'll be right there."

The two officers watch as this elderly woman with her haggard face bends down, sighs, and mops up the piss as she talks to the puppy.

"You have to learn, don't you, poppet? Maman can't be doing this every morning . . . You can come in, gentlemen, take a seat, I'll be right with you . . ."

The commissaire fumbles for his warrant card and is about

to introduce himself, but he doesn't have time. He shoots his deputy a puzzled look. This woman simply ushered them in and told them to sit down without asking who they are – it's strange and slightly unsettling.

Panting a little, Mathilde finishes mopping and comes to join them.

"Can I offer you some coffee?"

"I wouldn't say no . . ."

This is the young officer. He can't be more than twenty-five, and looks like he's fresh out of school.

"Madame," says the other, "we are . . ."

"Oh, I know who you are," Mathilde interrupts. "No offence, but police officers all look the same, don't they? So, coffee?"

The younger officer smirks, the commissaire, offended, takes a handful of something from his pocket.

"What's that?" says Mathilde. "What's that you're eating?"

"Cashew nuts."

"Well, you won't make old bones, let me tell you . . . Now, coffee . . ."

From the kitchen counter, where she is heaping coffee into the filter, she looks over her shoulder.

"Have you come about that incident in the car park?"

"Among other things . . ." says the commissaire.

Mathilde turns, beaming, as though this is splendid news.

"You mean there's something else?"

The overall impression is that she's a bored, elderly woman who's grateful to have visitors. Leave her to it and she'll spend the whole morning talking your ear off and when lunchtime comes, she'll set the table for three without even asking . . .

The coffee machine has started to hiccup, Mathilde comes over with cups, spoons, sugar.

"I thought I'd explained everything to your colleague – what's his name? Tall man with a Russian name . . . ?"

"Vasiliev?"

"That's right!"

She wanders off and comes back with the puppy snuggled in her arms, then slumps into the chair with a sigh.

"Do you want me to go through it all again? Well, the thing is, I went there to buy shoes, I know, I know, it sounds silly, but that's just how it is, you see I had this old pair—"

"That won't be necessary, madame," says the commissaire, "it's all in his report."

Mathilde makes a puzzled face, she doesn't understand why they are here.

"Our colleague died two nights ago, madame, so . . ."

"NO!"

The scream is genuine, Mathilde brings her fist up to her mouth.

"That tall young man who came to see me? He's dead?"

"Yes, madame, the day before yesterday."

"I thought he looked in fine fettle, I mean, his shoes were filthy, but I found him quite sympathetic, for a policeman . . . well, I mean . . . What did he die of?"

"He was murdered, madame . . . Maybe you heard it on the news . . ."

"Oh, I never watch the television, dear. I'm hopelessly behind the times. But who murdered him? And why?"

"Those are precisely the questions to which we are trying to find answers, madame."

Occhipinti is particularly pleased with this formulation, he gobbles another handful of cashews. He looks confident, but he feels a little at sea. The Tan brothers have been grilled for more than twenty-four hours with no result. He spent many long hours interrogating them himself before he was so exhausted that he let another team take over. He has spent so long switching between the Tan brothers theory and the Vasiliev theory that he doesn't know which way to turn. He feels as though he's missed something, as though everything is spinning, and he doesn't like it. When a team decided to re-interview the witnesses Vasiliev met while investigating the car park shootings, the commissaire offered to talk to the old woman in Melun. As soon as he got there and saw the old biddy, he kicked himself: has he really nothing better to do than interrogate a pensioner? It's a clear sign that things have gone wrong with the investigation. Starting with himself.

Mathilde turns to the younger man, who has barely said a word since they arrived.

"Would you mind fetching the coffee, dear, I'm afraid I can hardly walk this morning . . ."

The officer smiles, Mathilde reminds him of his grandmother, she's like that, she shoots from the hip.

"So, what can I do for you, Inspector?"

"Commissaire."

"If you say so."

To Mathilde, he seems a little prickly.

"I'd like to know whether anything – shall we say anything *significant* – happened while he was here. We're trying to get a sense of his comings and goings over the past few days."

Mathilde pulls a face: I don't understand.

"Well, we talked about that terrible thing in the car park, he didn't even have a coffee, he didn't stay long – no, honestly I can't think of anything."

The young officer comes back with the coffee pot.

"Is that a rug you have up there?"

"A rug?" the commissaire says. "What rug? Where?"

"At the top of the stairs," says the junior officer as he pours the coffee. "Rolled up on the landing . . ."

"It's for the local second-hand shop," Mathilde says. "The owner is coming to collect it this morning."

"Do you want me to bring it down for you?"

Such a thoughtful young man. But Mathilde is a little irritated.

"That's very kind, but you don't have to worry. The man from the shop will do it, that's his job, I've already rolled it up for him . . ."

As she says this, the commissaire wipes his hands on his jacket and takes out a crumpled piece of paper with spidery writing.

"This wasn't in Inspector Vasiliev's report, but it's from his notes . . . I can see he's written 'dog's head' – does that mean anything to you?"

In Mathilde's mind, two thoughts collide.

How can she play for time?

And how can she get up and go to the kitchen drawer without attracting attention? Because the black rage she felt for that fucking Russki cop has just come roaring back, and these two are going the same way.

"It was about him."

She nods to the spaniel puppy in her arms.

It's the first thing that popped into her head. It's like tossing a coin, it lands either heads or tails, and if this one lands the wrong way, it'll be too bad for them. They stare somewhat worriedly at the puppy.

"I think he had one like it as a boy . . ."

"But why dog's *head*?" says the commissaire. "I don't understand."

"He made this big thing about how his dog had exactly the same head. Personally, I think all cocker spaniels look the same, don't you? I don't mean to be rude, but I think maybe your colleague was a bit simple-minded."

The commissaire does not react.

The atmosphere in the room seems to be suddenly poisoned, something is bothering them, you can see it in their faces. The commissaire looks at the paper.

"There are a couple of other notes: 'neighbour' and later on 'hedge'."

"Means nothing to me . . ."

"But these are the notes he made just after his visit to you."

"Maybe so, but he could have been thinking about something else, I don't know . . ."

This does not seem to convince the officers who are silent and suspicious.

"Unless he went and had a word with my neighbour," she says. "But I don't see why he'd do that."

"That's possible," says the commissaire. "That's possible."

He stuffs the paper back in his pocket.

"Well then, we'll go and ask the neighbour."

There is trouble brewing. Mathilde is seriously pissed off. She looks from one to the other. She'll spare them a visit to Lepoitevin. She didn't go all the way to Aubervilliers and waste that long streak of piss only for these two idiots to show up on her doorstep.

She gets to her feet.

"I really need to take my tablets, otherwise . . ."

"I can get them if you like," says the young officer.

"No, no, you'll never find them."

As she goes back to the kitchen, Mathilde opens the sliding door since she will need room to aim. She's glad she remembered to cock the Luger, all she has to do is pick it up and turn . . . Mentally, she pictures the layout, the exact position of the older officer and the distance between him and his colleague. She'll shoot them in that order. She opens the drawer, lays a hand on the Luger.

Suddenly, the phone rings.

Mathilde stops dead. Who could that be?

Carefully she replaces the gun, closes the drawer, goes over to the phone and picks up the receiver. She turns to the commissaire.

"It's for you . . ."

He stands up.

"I gave them your number . . ."

"Make yourself at home," says Mathilde.

Occhipinti asked to be notified when the initial interrogation of the Tan brothers was over, and the Police Judiciaire have called with an update.

He steps forward, takes the receiver.

"So, what have we got?"

The commissaire is not one to mince words.

Mathilde goes back to the drawer. The hit is going to be much more difficult. The senior officer is now on her left – not her best side. His colleagues is four metres away, on her right. He is younger and probably faster, but the element of surprise should work in Mathilde's favour.

But before she can react, the configuration shifts.

The young inspector comes over to Mathilde and almost whispers in her ear.

"Why don't you let me bring that rug down for you?"

Without waiting for an answer, he heads for the stairs. Mathilde grabs the Luger. A second from now, she reckons, the commissaire and the inspector will be in the same line of fire, but only for an instant before the younger officer climbs the stairs. She has been stopped in her tracks.

"I'm afraid we have to leave, Madame Perrin," says the commissaire as he hangs up. "Duty calls."

Duty, in this case, refers to the examining magistrate. He wants to see him, to take stock. Occhipinti is going to get yelled at because nothing is happening. A junior officer has just told him that the Tan brothers are playing for time. They're saying nothing and running down the clock.

"For fuck's sake . . ." the commissaire mutters, scratching his head.

"Excuse me?" says Mathilde.

"I'm sorry . . ."

"I should think so too! I don't pay my taxes to have public servants swearing like navvies!"

On the second step, the young inspector stops and retraces his steps.

Mathilde glares from one to the other.

"What about the neighbour? I thought you wanted a word with my neighbour?"

"That will have to wait for another time, I think."

Before this has time to sink in, the commissaire says:

"Come on, lad, stop dawdling . . ."

"Thanks for the coffee," says the inspector, seeing the commissaire leave without a word.

"Yeah, yeah," Mathilde says between gritted teeth.

"All this kerfuffle and I'm no further on than I was before . . ."

Mathilde washes the coffee cups, feeds the puppy, then goes upstairs and realises that her plan to slide the corpse down the stairs won't work; she will have to change the angle . . . and drag it down.

As she eases the rolled-up rug centimetre by centimetre so as not to tire herself, Mathilde thinks about the impromptu visit of the two officers. Well, they had a narrow escape, didn't they, Henri, I bet you thought I was going to waste them . . . To tell you the truth, so did I!

What's bothering her now is that she's running late. It's already half past nine. If she hadn't fallen asleep, everything would have been done and dusted before they showed up . . .

After much heaving and hauling, the trussed-up corpse is finally downstairs, and Mathilde sets about rolling it out onto the terrace. Even through the thick rug she can feel that the corpse is as stiff as a board – good thing she acted quickly.

Once outside, Mathilde sits in her rocking chair to catch her breath.

The problem now is Lepoitevin. She needs to go and find the van the hitman must have parked nearby. With its Belgian number plate and the logo for a cleaning company, it's bound to attract Lepoitevin's attention, prompting a slew of questions and explanations, he'll be watching her every move, she'll never hear the end of it.

At the thought of Lepoitevin, Mathilde feels a wave of anger. When all's said and done, he's been the root of all her problems. including the little visit from Thomson and Thompson this morning! If he hadn't started blethering about the dog's head – where is the head, actually, she doesn't want Cookie finding it and poisoning himself. Must bury it, she thinks, only to forget a second later, because she is completely fixated on Lepoitevin. The only sensible thing is to deal with him right now. She will have to do it sooner or later, so why not just get it out of the way?

She opens the kitchen drawer, takes out the Luger, goes outside and walks towards the hedge. The idiot's probably hoeing or weeding or whatever, I just call him, he trots over all sweetness and light, I put a bullet between his eyes, job done.

"Monsieur Lepoitevin?"

Mathilde tries to part the branches, but the hedge is thick, so she needs to use both hands. She tucks the Luger into her belt.

"Monsieur Lepoitevin?"

She scratches her arms a little, but finally she manages to get far enough to see her neighbour's house. Parting the last branches with her left hand, she takes the Luger with her right.

"Monsieur Lepoitevin?"

Just then, she sees the garage door close and Lepoitevin's car drive off – he has a remote control that operates his gate. I should probably get one of them.

The tail lights disappear as he turns onto the road.

Oh well, another time.

She has just won a short reprieve (as has Lepoitevin). She will make the most of it to find the bloody van, and if her neighbour does come back in the meantime, she'll finish him off, double whammy, done and dusted.

As she gathers up the things she will need, Mathilde mutters to herself. Leave out food for Cookie, I'll leave you enough for three days, poppet, Maman will be back by then, don't you worry. A travel bag, a change of clothes, some toiletries, go up to the bedroom, come back down – at this rate, I'll have a stroke. Fetch the Smith & Wesson from the grandfather clock, the Luger, the Desert Eagle, and as much ammunition as she can carry.

When she has everything piled up on the terrace (shift yourself, Cookie, no, don't go licking that rug, you'll make yourself sick), she locks the puppy in the kitchen, Maman will open the door before she leaves, poppet. She changes her shoes. It's really cold. Let's go. She walks down the gravel path.

It feels strange to be taking this route on foot, because this is exactly where her car was two days earlier when she spotted the van driving slowly. At the time, Mathilde wasn't feeling very well. That banging shutter had given her such a fright that she was still tense and worried when the van drove past. She hadn't time to see the driver's face, but she saw the logo on the side for a Belgian cleaning company . . . A light went on in her head and instantly she felt much better. Because she knew, she was absolutely certain, that he had come for her. In a split second, she had worked out her plan. He would come during the night, there was no other option. She led him a merry dance, taking her time buying shoes, doing some window-shopping, and although she never spotted him, she could feel his presence. An experienced pro. He didn't put a foot wrong. Mathilde realised that she could not afford to make a single mistake. The whole thing went like clockwork. The problem with your boys, Henri, is they have a tendency to underestimate the target. A dumpy old woman, he probably thought he'd make short work of me. A classic mistake. You men have some strange ideas about women. Especially old women. Your boy won't get a chance to have a change of heart, Henri, but maybe you'll learn something from it.

As she broods about this, Mathilde scours the neighbourhood, where did that bonehead park his van? It can't be far, because he didn't have much time. And the further she walks, the angrier she gets.

Listen up, Henri, I'm going to tell you a few home truths: you like playing cowboys and Indians, but when it comes to efficiency, you're hopeless. I love you, Henri, you know that I love you, that I'd do anything for you. So why pull stupid stunts like sending a hitman after me when we could settle things between us, just you and me? Like we used to in the old days. I know you don't like to talk about the past, but we're not getting any younger, Henri, we're not getting any younger. You go first, Henri, you go first. All this fuss you've made over a gun. If I hadn't kept any of them, I'd be in a right pickle now! I'd be the one rolled up in a rug. And what about you, Henri? How would you feel knowing your dear old Mathilde is lying here, stiff as a board, huh? Did you even think about that? Oh, Henri, Henri, you never listen to me. You say to yourself: Mathilde is just a mad old biddy, she's a loose cannon, she does what she likes. So, you send a dumb goon who doesn't even know how to park his van properly.

Suddenly, there it is . . .

Parked in a side street where the only houses are still under construction. She opens the van. It is spotless. Have to hand it to you, Henri, your guy was well organised. He might have had antiquated views about women, but in terms of preparation and planning, he was a genius.

She makes the most of the quiet neighbourhood to explore the van. When she gets back home, she'll have no time to lose. And if Lepoitevin does show up, well, it won't be the end of the world (except for him), but she has so much to do already . . . !

In the back of the van, there is a full-width wooden cabinet fitted with drawers and pigeonholes containing everything you might need to do a clean job: ropes, tools, chemicals that are probably designed to burn away fingerprints or disfigure a body. It gives you a real buzz about the job, Henri, I swear, if I was twenty years younger, I'd sign up on the spot . . . The profession is really evolving and I'd love to get back in the game.

Ah – here is what she's looking for, the body bags. There must be a dozen. Either the guy worked overtime, or he was careful to the point of obsession.

Mathilde picks one up, but despite turning it over and over, she can't work out . . .

How the hell do you work these things, Henri?

Oh, here we go! My God, Henri, they're brilliant! Mathilde finds a nozzle into which she inserts something that looks like a bicycle pump, except that it sucks air out. It's genius. You slip the corpse into the bag, zip it up, it's airtight, then you pump all the air out. It might not create a perfect vacuum, but it will save precious time on the stages of decomposition. Chapeau, Henri, this guy of yours was a specialist, I love this thing, I can't wait to try it out.

As she pulls away, Mathilde is careful, since she is not accustomed to anything as big as the van. She carefully drives home, gets out to open her gate, gets in, pulls into her driveway, then gets out to close the gate again.

For whatever reason, she never got around to installing electric gates. But what used to be a pleasant ritual some years ago has now become an excruciating chore. She shakes her head. I keep saying I'm going to have electric gates installed, but I never do. She pulls up in front of the terrace. She is exhausted.

It's all very aggravating. You know that I don't need any aggravation, Henri, I've got a dicky heart, so why give me such a hard time? Haven't I always done what you asked? Well, I have my own way of going about things, and maybe it's not the same as yours, but surely what matters is the result, right? You've always been happy with the result, haven't you? And now you're hauling me over the coals about silly little details, honestly, Henri . . .

Thankfully, the van is equipped with an electric tailgate. It takes five minutes for Mathilde to find the button, but she does. All she has to do now is roll the corpse, get it up the ramp, haul it inside – Jesus fucking Christ, Henri, I can't do this! But the real danger would be to stop now. She draws on her last reserves of strength, and some fifteen minutes later, she has slid it into the body bag, attached the pump, and is sitting on a folding chair watching it shrink until it moulds itself to the package. Mathilde is thrilled by her new gadget.

She carries the pile of things from the kitchen to the van, she is worn-out, bathed in sweat, her knees and her arms are aching.

Not that I'm blaming you, Henri. All right, I flew off the handle, but that's just me, it never lasts. It's just that I got a bit of a scare when I saw that guy drive past in his death van . . . I know, it's all water under the bridge now, things will go back to how they were before, because deep down you love your old Mathilde – no, no, don't try to deny it, you adore your old Mathilde! Oh, things are different now, but there was a time when you would have done anything to take her in your arms, wouldn't you? Well, I can tell you now, Henri, I felt just the same. Silly, isn't it? Oh, I know, the circumstances were impossible, life was difficult, yada, yada, but it's silly . . .

She leaves the puppy on the terrace in his basket, locks up the house, leaves the sliding door ajar so that the puppy can run around the garden. Then she slowly drives down to the gate. Here we go again, get out, open the gate, back in, drive onto the road, get out, close the gate, such a bother, well, I've decided, first thing I do when I get back is have electric gates installed, I don't care how much they cost!

Mathilde shifts the seat forward, trying to find a comfortable driving position.

We were great friends, weren't we? And we pulled some brutal stunts, remember? Oh the things we did! Even back then, you were suspicious. Don't pretend you weren't! But I was just the same as I am now. It was all so long ago . . . Your little stunt this morning was just intended to scare me, I realise that, but it's not good enough, Henri, you don't do things like that to your friends.

"Well, well, so there you are!"

She has just passed Lepoitevin driving home.

"I'll see you later," she thinks.

It is 11 a.m. as she reaches the motorway. Right, let's see how fast this thing goes!

Because, the thing is, Henri, you and I need to have a little talk.

*　　*　　*

At noon, the commandant makes himself lunch as though this is just another ordinary day. Henri has been on his own since early childhood, so he has learned to do things for himself. And to think for himself.

He has been through his calculations and his theories countless times and is now certain that his plan has failed. Buisson's first call came at 12.34 p.m. the day before.

"Target located; everything is going according to plan."

"When do you plan to introduce yourself?"

"I'll confirm that later this evening, but I reckon it will be before tomorrow morning."

The second call came at precisely 10 p.m.

"Target has drawn the curtains, everything going to plan."

"And contact?" said Henri.

"I plan to make contact in three hours. Four at most."

And before Henri could pose the question:

"Will confirm contact first thing tomorrow morning at around 0600 hours, 0900 at the latest."

It is now half past twelve. Buisson will not call again.

So, Mathilde will be paying him a visit.

She won't take the plane.

She could be in Toulouse by tomorrow. It depends on how long she waits before making her decision.

Henri has dutifully done the washing up, drunk three cups of strong coffee and even treated himself to a cigar out in the garden – special events deserve special pleasures. He surveys the lush flowerbeds, the garage to the side, the barn he had restored some years ago. And as he studies his surroundings, he carries on thinking and considering the various possibilities.

What is going to happen is inevitable.

The fact that Buisson – who wasn't just some nobody – got caught off guard means that Henri has to take considerable precautions.

But he is not about to rush into anything. Life has taught him that things rarely turn out as you expect. To fully protect himself here, in this house, would be a difficult task. As he finishes his cigar, he shrugs philosophically: he'll have to trust to luck. Nevertheless, he goes into his garage and rummages on his workbench for the tools that he will need.

Occhipinti is deeply frustrated. He came back from the magistrate's chambers with pockets stuffed with bags of nuts, which he had to replenish two hours later. He is more nervous and more worried than ever. When he saw the investigating magistrate, he argued that Vasiliev was killed because of the nurse. He calls her the gook – to Occhipinti, Cambodians, Vietnamese, Laotians are all the same, they're gooks. The problem is that they're making no headway with the Tan brothers. The magistrate insisted they be released, unless he had hard evidence that they were involved in the Neuilly murders – evidence he doesn't have.

The Tan brothers are vicious, ruthless thugs, and the murder of their sister has sent them into a rage. Grief will come much later. They are not particularly intelligent. Their professional achievements have been very modest and owe more to their ruthlessness and lack of emotion than to strategy, because they have none. Occhipinti looks at them as they sit side by side. He is convinced the killer is to be found among the Tan brothers' enemies and rivals. The motive might be a turf war, a drug deal that went badly wrong. It has to be something pretty serious for their rivals to kill their sister; you don't send a warning like that without good reason. They've talked to informants, to the local cops, to the drug squad, but they've come up with nothing the Tan brothers could have done to trigger such a bloody retaliation.

"I'm telling you to release them," the magistrate told him.

Occhipinti will comply.

He feels awkward because releasing them from custody will have serious repercussions that are not lost on the magistrate. By insisting that this was the work of a rival gang, he has put the idea of revenge into the Tan brothers' minds. If they were not so stupid, he wouldn't worry, but their brains work in binary. He has opened Pandora's box and possibly triggered a gang war. Score-settling between criminals – particularly petty thugs – can easily turn into a bloodbath. Tit for tat attacks that go on for weeks; one murder leads to another and it's almost impossible to stop.

"Alright," says the commissaire, "let them go."

As they emerge from the offices of the Police Judiciaire, the Tan brothers look like two ferrets at the opening of hunting season.

The commissaire goes back to working on the Vasiliev theory, rereading the notes from the team who have been delving into the inspector's former cases. In reverse order, he sees all the grisly cases he palmed off on Vasiliev, the rapes and the sexual offences against women and children. He finally understands why he did it. Now that Vasiliev is dead, the commissaire naturally thinks of him as a decent guy and a first-rate officer, conveniently forgetting that he hated Vasiliev because he hates too many people, and considered it reasonable to delegate countless brutal and sometimes depraved sexual offences to a man who has never had a sexual urge. No-one has ever heard Vasiliev make the dirty jokes about women and gays that, since time immemorial, have been the stock in trade of locker rooms and police stations.

In hindsight, the commissaire cannot help but admire his former subordinate's mental health, because he finds such cases distressing, some prevent him from sleeping, he spends whole nights sitting up in bed next to his wife, gobbling handfuls of cashews.

The drive is long and tiring. The van may be state-of-the-art, but that makes it no less exhausting.

She could have taken a plane, but flying leaves a paper trail, you have to show your passport, go through security . . .

Mathilde has a fake passport.

That's something else to tell Henri. It was issued to her by Supplies four or five years ago for a mission in Malmö – a terrible mare's nest, so complicated that she really should have demanded a bonus (this is something else she should mention to Henri: her rates have not been increased for some time – not that she is in this for the money, but still). Needless to say, she was supposed to dispose of the passport as well as the gun, but she kept it. As a precaution. She has no idea whether she could leave the country under this identity, the passport may have been cancelled, although Mathilde suspects not, no-one will have bothered, it will have been forgotten. What was her alias for the Malmö hit? Oh yes! Jacqueline Forestier! She hates the name. Having to spend four days being Jacqueline was almost worse than the mission itself.

Long story short, Mathilde is going to Toulouse by road.

She has even decided to avoid the motorway lest she be spotted at a toll booth for some reason. The van is pretty conspicuous, someone might remember seeing it – but there are so many vans driving around with so many different logos you barely notice them. That said, the man Henri sent was a consummate professional. The kind who takes every precaution, so connecting the van to Mathilde Perrin will be difficult, perhaps impossible. Unless she screws up. Even then, she'll be able to wriggle her way out, because she's pretty much above suspicion, but she has to remain attentive and careful.

She finds the radio infuriating, there's never anything worth listening to, so she turned it off some time ago. Pick up a hitch-hiker? Too risky: you never know who you'll be landed with. Plus, she's not the ideal driver for this kind of van, so best to keep a low profile and show her face only when necessary.

So, she suffers in silence, she drives and drives and drives. And as the kilometres tick past, so do the memories. Perhaps because Henri is the focus of her concern at the moment, she finds herself thinking about her husband, Dr Perrin. Raymond. You always pretend you don't remember, Henri, but I'm sure you're lying. You remember how bitterly disappointing we found those first months after the war, a life that lacked the excitement and the intensity we'd grown to love. How, shorn of its context, the magnetic attraction that drew us together seemed like an anticlimax. But what was disappointing, what was anticlimactic, was a life that could not live up to our expectations. Goodbye to the tension and the tremors, to the feverishness and the fear, the glorious, incomparable, transcendent fear of dying. You were still a handsome man, Henri, but that was all you were. Everything was humdrum and ordinary. My father was a doctor and he wanted me to marry a doctor, my mother thought it would be wonderful if I followed in her footsteps, and I didn't oppose them because I no longer had a taste for anything in life. Oh, Henri, how I missed you. Not the Henri who came to visit bringing flowers and chocolates, no, the one from the Resistance, handsome Henri who made decisions, who gave orders, who was honourable and utterly imperturbable . . .

And so, Dr Perrin – what can I say? You know how hard I tried to be the wife that everyone expected. How tedious it was . . .

I only really understood why Raymond died on the day of his funeral. When I saw you among the mourners – you remember.

It's funny, when I think of that moment, I see us arm in arm, walking towards the church as though we were about to get married.

Mathilde is driving very slowly because tears are streaming down her face. She can hear bells. Are they a death knell tolling for the doctor, or joyous wedding bells? Actually, it is the sound of cars behind her honking their horns. She needs to stop. She pulls into a large car park that is deserted but for a few foreign eighteen-wheelers. She parks the van, she can't staunch the flood of tears. She blows her nose, tries to catch her breath. She is shattered. She doesn't know what time it is, where she is – nothing matters anymore. To avoid being seen, she attempts a painful feat of acrobatics and climbs into the back of the van. Eventually, she gets there, and lies down next to the vacuum-sealed corpse. In a corner is a neatly folded sleeping bag.

She crawls in, fully clothed. It doesn't smell of anything, certainly not the dead man, if it did, she wouldn't be able to sleep, but it doesn't.

By the time she closes her eyes, she has sunk into a dreamless sleep.

*　　*　　*

And at around 5 p.m. she sets off again.

It is curious, but after a while, Mathilde lowers her head close to the steering wheel as though she is riding a motorbike through a howling gale.

She misses Ludo. A dog is a wonderful companion, no question about it. It's hard not to want one, especially when you live alone in the country and have a garden. Dogs love gardens and her garden at La Coustelle is one of the most beautiful in the area. She thinks of the little spaniel and wonders if he will be smarter than Ludo. It wouldn't be hard. Ludo was sweet and affectionate, but he was never very bright, getting anything through his thick skull was hard . . . If Cookie doesn't turn out to be smarter, that'll be two no-hopers in quick succession.

When it comes to visiting her daughter, the dog has always been an issue. Her daughter doesn't like dogs, but then she doesn't like anything, and Mathilde doesn't much like her daughter, who has been a disappointment to her. Whenever she sees her, she is surprised to think that this child came out of her. She is a genetic mistake, or simply a mistake. Mathilde has never really liked children; she much prefers dogs. Even when she was young, she didn't like them much. Her husband criticised her for not wanting children, he claimed they are good for wives and make for happy marriages. Raymond was full of such ideas, inane bromides he parroted. The joys of motherhood were few and far between, Mathilde realises, thinking back. They were over by the time her daughter turned one. She did her duty. Mathilde likes to feel she is beyond reproach.

The dusk is slowly drawing in. Her midday nap seems long ago, and Mathilde tells herself there's no hurry, Henri doesn't know she's coming, he's not expecting her, so he has no reason to worry.

She's happy that she'll get to surprise him. But it won't be like your little visit, my old friend, a curt dressing-down before you turn and leave, oh no, my visit will be different, let me tell you, we'll have a full and frank conversation, you'll see, I've got a few surprises up my sleeve – no, don't ask, like I said, it's a surprise!

As she passes through a village, Mathilde slows when she sees a sign for an auberge. She finds the place a few kilometres on, in the middle of the countryside. It's nice, quiet, clean, exactly what she needs.

Since the only other guests are a sales rep and a retired couple, the owner is happy to come and chat with them after the dinner.

"So, you've come from Belgium?"

Mathilde frowns and then remembers – the van.

"Yes, I've been driving all day."

"I saw the logo – a cleaning company, right?"

"That's right," says Mathilde, "we're in the cleaning business."

Finding her uncommunicative, the owner goes to try his luck with the pensioners.

The bedroom is nice, the window overlooks the entrance, the gravelled car park. From here she can see the van. She needs to get petrol, she didn't check the fuel gauge, but it must be nearly empty. One last look at the van before she takes a well-earned rest.

And marshals her forces for Toulouse, which isn't going to be a piece of cake.

September 18

It is mid-morning before she notices the fuel gauge and realises that she will have to stop. She is worried that she didn't think to stop at a service station earlier ... She lifts her foot, grips the steering wheel – running out of petrol is the last thing she needs. She can't picture herself trudging down the road – what, five, maybe ten kilometres? She'd have to leave the van in open country, walk for miles, find a garage ... She has already got herself into a state when she comes to Peyrac, a tiny village, and, on the other side, a miracle, a petrol station! She could hug the attendant who had the bright idea of setting up shop here.

Mathilde pulls in, turns off the engine, takes off her shoes, wiggles her toes – bliss.

When she's dealt with this whole mess, she plans to focus on her own happiness. Forget her daughter and her fool of a son-in-law and find real happiness, by the sea, somewhere in the sun. Who knows, maybe Henri would be tempted to join her? They're too old to flirt and to fool around like they could have done once if they'd been less uptight, but Henri's getting old too, it's something they should have talked about long ago!

This is how she'll start the conversation.

While the attendant takes the keys and fills the tank, Mathilde puts on her shoes, gets out of the car and, as she strolls around, she allows herself be lulled by dreams of a little house with a fireplace for the winter – though the winters will be as mild as spring – dreams of a village with a fine restaurant where she'll go from time to time, a little break from routine. She and Henri will reminisce, but not too often. She'll tell him that, contrary to what he thought, she was never bored with Dr Perrin (this is what she called him, even when he was alive), she simply could do nothing with him, he was like a dead weight. And she'll finally be able to winkle out an answer to the question that has always been on the tip of her tongue: why did you never marry, Henri? With a little luck and a lot of honesty, he'll say it was because she was the only woman in his life. The days will drift past in a glorious tranquillity, afternoons spent reading on the veranda and stroking the dog, because they'll have a dog, and the occasional night out at the casino for a thrilling little flutter with all the money they amassed and didn't steal.

The pump attendant has just finished filling up and is working on the windscreen. Mathilde goes into the shop. She's a little hungry. Wandering between the shelves she picks up two packets of biscuits – so much for the diet! – and puts them back again. Better to be careful. Not that Henri is ever likely to be charmed by her sex appeal again, but he'll be more charmed by a Mathilde who's elegant and presentable than a dumpy old woman. Catching her reflection in the shop window, she arranges her hair falling in wisps over her forehead and she smiles at Henri. The cashier returns her smile. And not some foreign country, either! We didn't fight like hell during the war to end up in the Bahamas or in Sardinia, no sir! But then again, Mathilde crinkles her eyes, a little jaunt from time to time is good for avoiding a rut. A weekend in Florence or Vienna. Maybe a cruise. She's never been on a cruise. Henri will pooh-pooh the idea, but she'll persuade him, she always does. She knows how to handle him.

"A cruise up the Nile."

"Excuse me?"

Mathilde looks at the pump attendant.

"Nothing."

Mysterious Egypt? Is that a bit of a cliché? Yes and no.

When the attendant speaks again, it is Henri that Mathilde sees standing in front of her (such an elegant man, and never sick a day in his life, unlike her doctor husband, no, Henri is hale and hearty, which is for the best, she won't have to go through all that again, fetching the prescriptions, playing nursemaid, having dinner alone and spending her evenings listening to him pace up and down upstairs to ease the pain), yes, it is Henri that she sees, with the little cravat he wears tucked into his pristine shirt – that's another cliché too, Henri! The sea, the sunshine, the log fire, the pyramids, the dog and a little music, that's two hundred and thirty francs, madame.

Mathilde gets the money from her handbag, takes her change and leaves.

She could be in Toulouse by morning, but there's nothing to do there, better to get a little shut-eye along the way. Drive for a while then find a quiet place to take a nap. She'll have to be in top form tonight, so she can find the words to persuade Henri. She gets back into the van, hikes up her skirt so it doesn't crease, sets her bag on the passenger seat and pulls off.

And then she has a nagging doubt.

With her left hand on the steering wheel, she rummages through her bag, searching the inside pocket where she keeps her cash. She sets the bag back in her lap, and, with one eye on the road, she counts again. She is fifty francs short. There should be a fifty-franc note but it's not there. At any other time, Mathilde would have shrugged it off – money isn't everything – but she has her principles. And suddenly – whether it's the exhaustion or simply the time of day that has put her on edge – she is overcome by a wave of anger. She carries on driving, now obsessed by the idea that the petrol pump attendant accidentally short-changed her, or worse, ripped her off because he could see she was a little off colour.

Mathilde is looking for a place to do a U-turn, she's going to go back to the station and give the man a piece of her mind. And she hopes it won't be deserted, that there'll be customers so that everyone knows he's a thief, and she'll accept no excuses, she'll stay there until he gives her back her money, damn it.

But the road is flanked by fields and the verge is very narrow. She is getting further and further away, she can't afford to waste time with Henri waiting for her, eager to see her, never mind the fifty francs. Though she might stop by on her way back and tell him what's what. Taking advantage of an elderly woman is despicable!

Just then, she sees the dirt track through the fields. It is a sign. A handbrake turn and she goes back the way she came. Now that she's turned back, black rage roils inside her tired brain. Her face flushes red as she floors the accelerator. She slams on the brakes as she pulls into the station. There is no-one around. Pity, she can hardly make a scene if it's just the two of them. She stops in front of the shop, gets out of the car, and slams the door behind her.

There is no-one in the shop.

"Did you forget something, love?"

She sees him, over in the garage, lying on one of those things like a stretcher that mechanics use to slide under cars. He's just popped his out. He's a young man, she barely noticed him earlier.

One look at his face and you can tell he'd happily fleece an old woman for fifty francs. She strides over. He smiles, a little puzzled, happy to help. He grabs the bumper above his head, rolls the dolly out so that he can get to his feet. But he doesn't have time, he's still lying on his back trying to lever himself up when Mathilde grabs a tyre-iron from on top of an old oil can and swings it between his legs with all her strength. He lets out an agonised wail.

Mathilde swings the tyre iron again, brings it down on his head so hard that it lodges ten centimetres in his skull. Little bastard!

I think I've made my point, she thinks. She reaches into his pocket, pulls out a wad of notes, takes fifty francs and puts the rest back. Mathilde is nothing if not honest.

She heads back to the van, turns around, gobbets of brain are protruding through the skull, it's not a pretty sight. Luckily, none of it spattered on her – that would be all I need!

She climbs behind the wheel and reverses as best she can; she still hasn't got to grips with the size of the van. She opens the back doors, quietly lowers the tailgate, pulls the creeper from under the car and pushes it up the ramp. Looks like a stretcher, works like a stretcher, she thinks. She parks it next to the rolled-up rug. You two can keep each other company.

Then she gets out of the van. There's a pool of blood and brain in the middle of the forecourt, but fortunately there's also a can of sawdust nearby. That looks dangerous, someone could slip and hurt themselves, she thinks, as she covers it with a few handfuls of sawdust, then gets back behind the wheel and drives away.

Back on the road, she glances at her watch: what she really needs is a quiet spot so she can decant the pump attendant into a body bag.

Twenty minutes later, Mathilde pulls into a road on the edge of the forest. It takes less than half an hour for her to get the body into the bag and pump the air out.

She tosses the dolly into the bushes.

The two body bags sit on the floor side by side. This gadget is amazing, she thinks, I must tell Henri.

Just as Mathilde reaches Toulouse, it starts to bucket down. She'd been looking forward to doing some shopping, but there is no let-up, it's a real downpour. It's impossible to set foot outside without getting soaked.

She leaves the van in a car park in town, opts for the first decent hotel she saw on her way, and books herself in for two nights.

The weather makes it impossible for her to scope out the territory, and taking a taxi is out of the question, there's no surer way to leave a trail . . .

She changed her clothes (she didn't bring much with her; she won't be here long).

She spends the latter part of the afternoon driving around. At about six o'clock, she finds what she has been looking for: a quiet spot. She gives it some thought, decides she won't find anything better. Back at the hotel, she pores over the ordnance survey map she bought in a newsagent.

Henri's house is located outside a village, isolated – so like him. Our Henri doesn't mingle with the hoi polloi. She circles a few key places, checks her equipment – there is not a lot: a bag containing her tools, which is quite heavy; she smiles, she looks as though she's going to a small arms fair.

Unable to face going out again, she has dinner at the hotel restaurant, then goes back to her room, takes a shower, lays out her clothes and goes to bed.

Alarm set for midnight.

The ringing brings her out of a dense, dark dream, filled with dogs . . . Oh yes, Monsieur Lepoitevin . . . She keeps postponing their little talk; he doesn't know how lucky he is to have had a reprieve . . . She broods over what happened to Ludo, such a tragedy, and it would be so much easier for neighbours just to get along . . .

On the ground floor, in the hall, there are vending machines selling hot drinks and biscuits. She gets a coffee and some madeleines.

Beyond the hotel car park, it is pitch dark; a crescent moon radiates a milky light like the aurora borealis. She feels awake and alert; the moment has finally come to pay Henri a visit.

As planned, the commandant turned off all the lights at 9 p.m., except the one in the little corridor that runs from the living room to a bathroom. Behind this is a room that measures barely four metres square and a door, once boarded up, that he had reopened because he likes to walk in the garden after taking a shower. The hall light cast a faint glow over part of the living room. In the shadows, the commandant is sitting in an armchair, facing the door that opens onto the terrace, legs stretched out, hands on the armrests. He is listening to a silence filled with noises, a creak here, a rustle there. He carefully considers every sound, gauging its source, its origin. He has been doing this since nightfall, but he is no longer as young as he was when he spent nights standing guard, when his body was steeled to withstand fatigue. Gradually, his attention wanes and he is surprised by a sudden creak, an unexpected clattering, as though he dozed off and his subconscious has sounded the alert. The commandant is not asleep. He is just a little tired. Sitting in his armchair, staring at the door. Sitting here on a moonlit night, he can make out the trembling aspens, but since the crescent moon is on the far side of them from the window, they appear only as blurred, indistinct shapes. The commandant is in no hurry. He is merely waiting for a particular sound, the one that will tell him Mathilde has arrived. Assuming she gets this far. It's possible.

Unlikely, but you can never tell with her . . .

He waits calmly, from time to time he hopes she will come, he feels something almost like impatience.

The dashboard clock reads 1.15 a.m. as Mathilde drives past the tall wrought-iron gates protecting the grounds. On each side, a hundred-year-old drystone wall. For almost twenty years, Mathilde has had to listen to Henri tell her that it's crumbling in places and needs to be rebuilt. The way I see it, if the wall really was crumbling, dear old Henri would have done something long ago, he's not the kind of person to let things slide . . .

She pulls up two hundred metres further down the road.

She sits in the van, frantically thinking, but she finds it hard to choose. What should she take?

She settles on the Desert Eagle, because it holds the most ammunition. Experience has taught her that you rarely need much of anything. When you need a lot of ammunition, it's because things have gone pear-shaped, and she's too old, too overweight, too slow for something long-drawn-out. If she cannot resolve the matter quickly, her chances will be almost zero.

She gets out of the van, locks the doors and makes an unhurried survey of the property.

She was right, Henri has finally got round to tackling the problem: in several places, the drystone wall has been knocked down and replaced by a tall fence of strong wire mesh, not the kind you can manually bend. For almost an hour she feels her way around the perimeter wall. Though the sky is almost cloudless, she cannot see much. Finally, she finds an opening, just a small fissure that plunges into the brambles, only the topmost stones are missing. A boy could easily make the climb, but pudgy Mathilde is about as supple as a baobab tree: she doesn't stand a chance.

The most amazing thing about Mathilde is that she never doubts herself. Here she is, in the middle of the night, making a second tour of the property, creeping through the brambles, parting the branches with both hands, puffing like a whale, but moving ever forward, running her hand along the wall, testing the fence: the woman is a bulldozer. If she can't find a way in, she thinks, she'll have to adopt a new strategy, come back tomorrow, go about it differently.

And Mathilde amply demonstrates that pig-headedness sometimes pays off, because on her second tour (it is almost 2.30 a.m.), as she passes one of the new sections of fence, she notices that a fig tree has broken through a small section of wall. With both hands, she pushes one of the stones and it falls silently, cushioned by the long grass. It will be difficult to get through, she needs to looks for a stiff branch she can use to lever the stones into the grounds, she's panting for breath, that's all I need now, to drop dead of a heart attack just outside Henri's house, but this thought gives her renewed energy.

Within twenty minutes, Mathilde has made a hole just wide enough for her to try to squeeze through. It's a little high, she has to climb on a stone, then a second stone, and once in the breach, she has to sit down, let her fat legs hang, and – there's no alternative – she tosses her bag down and attempts to turn around, her fat arse hanging in the air as the toes of her shoes feel for the grass, the ground. In the end, she has no choice but to let go, she tumbles backwards, makes a loud noise, she has twisted her ankle, what a fuck-up, she's too old for this shit . . .

She gets to her feet, shrugs it off, this is the one advantage of having a fat arse, she thinks.

The hem of her dress is ripped, she's in a little pain and limping slightly, but there's nothing broken, nothing that can stop her from creeping through the grounds and visiting dear old Henri.

Sitting back in his armchair, the commandant mentally reviews every stage of the operation, oiling the door handle, stabilising the slightly loose concrete flagstone, sweeping the doorstep so no gravel comes in when it is opened . . . After that, it is a taut nylon wire just three millimetres off the ground. He can't see what could go wrong. Either she steps on the wire, or pulls it out, in which case he'll get the alert, or she unwittingly steps over it – but since there are six wires stretched around the terrace, she has almost no chance of not tipping one of them. It's possible, he thinks, but it's not likely. And if she does, he has a plan B. The commandant is not confident: in his business, confidence is a one-way ticket to the cemetery, but he is as confident as it's possible to be when you've tried to plan for every eventuality.

Henri is convinced that she will go around the house and enter through the back door. Unless something stops her first. This is what he fervently hopes: that she won't make it this far, that those taut nylon strings will never alert him to her arrival because something will stop her first.

This is exactly what Mathilde is thinking as she moves through the grounds very slowly, because she is tired, because she is limping slightly in her right leg and because it is so dark that she can't see her hand in front of her face. But none of this stops her from thinking, Mathilde says to herself, and she stops. She is thirty metres from the house. To her left, she can see the garage, to her right, the barn, and straight ahead – though it is barely visible – the French windows leading into the house, and behind them another door that leads from the kitchen into the vegetable garden, which is where she plans to enter.

If she makes it that far.

Because if this were me, she thinks, I wouldn't let a visitor get that far, I'd try to stop him first.

She brings a finger to her lips, let me think, let me think ... It's fun playing this little game with Henri, like chess players exchanging moves by post. The garage? The barn? Choosing is a risk, because she probably won't get a second chance. Let's go for the barn, thinks Mathilde, I can't hang around all night.

Slowly, she looks around. To get a feel for the place. She takes a few steps forward, but only for a few seconds, she does not like being in the open, so she studies the terrain, makes a mental note of the topography, then steps back. She has seen all that she wants to see.

For two or three seconds, Dieter had Mathilde in his sights, but she quickly disappeared. She is bound to reappear soon. From what he saw, she is a heavyset woman, no spring chicken, and she doesn't seem to suspect anything. She stepped forward without fear of being seen. Lying on the upper floor of the barn, the butt of his sniper rifle wedged into the crook of his arm, Dieter carefully scans the few metres the target has to cross to reach the house ... Just to be sure, he scans a wider area in case she takes a different route.

He does not wait for a few seconds, but for a minute, then two, then five, scanning the grounds over and over. Has she had second thoughts?

The moment she stepped back, Mathilde moved to her left, walking as quickly as she dared. Her bet is that if Henri has stationed a sniper on the upper floor of the barn (which is what she'd do in his shoes), he'll be expecting her to come down the centre path. When she doesn't, he'll get suspicious. If he doesn't see her advance, he'll assume she is making her way around, which is exactly what happens; when Dieter scans the area to the right of the barn, Mathilde has just passed. He missed her.

She's now standing in front of the heavy wooden door.

Two possibilities: either it creaks and groans and makes a racket, in which case there's no-one in there and I've screwed myself. Or it opens soundlessly, in which case someone has oiled the hinges and the head of Henri's welcoming committee is inside.

The door glides easily; barely a whisper. Mathilde slips inside, gently pushes it closed, takes out the Desert Eagle and stands, waiting for her eyes to adjust to the darkness. There is a tremulous silence. After a moment she can make out a jumble of old furniture and general clutter, but she focuses all her attention on the ceiling of wide wooden planks and the cracks that let in thin rays of moonlight dancing with specks of dust. Mathilde remains stock-still, her elbows pressed against her chest, gripping the gun with both hands, pointing the barrel upwards. This is one of her great skills: if she has time to settle herself, she can maintain a position for a very long time, much longer than the average person. A slow contest has begun between her and the person upstairs – if there is one – who will be lying on the floor with a rifle mounted on a tripod. Nothing happens. Nothing stirs. Mathilde mentally counts off the seconds (60, 61, 62 . . .). It is possible that she is mistaken, but there's nothing to do now but wait and see. She is firmly planted on her feet, her ankle no longer aches, her breathing is slow and steady, everything is fine. If nothing moves (103, 104), it means that the welcoming committee upstairs thinks she's in the barn, but since he cannot be sure, he too is forced to wait without moving a muscle (160, 161), to do precisely what she is doing. The first one to make a mistake loses. Or almost. Because in such situations, a lot of unexpected things could happen. Henri might show up, or someone else, Mathilde might get dizzy, the sniper upstairs might sneeze, anything could happen. The game is on. Mathilde smiles. Not a sound, bravo, but his presence has been betrayed by a little trail of dust falling through a crack that glitters as it passes through a ray of milky light. He's two metres away, to her right. Mathilde keeps a wary eye on the floor; now is not the time to trip and fall, she thinks. No obstacles in her path? Nothing?

Let's do this!

Mathilde takes two steps forward, raises her arms, points the gun at the ceiling and fires four times. The wood splinters, the worm-eaten planks crack and break, and Mathilde just has time to step aside before Dieter Frei falls through and lands like a heap of dirty laundry on the floor with a hole in his chest large enough for Mathilde to put both fists in. The rifle clatters after him. Sorted.

Mathilde approaches cautiously, the Desert Eagle still out-stretched. The man is obviously dead but she can't help herself, she puts one last bullet in his balls.

She frisks the body: nothing. No surprise there. She smiles. She is pleased that Henri has sufficient respect not to send a bunch of random losers to whack her.

She will probably need to spend some time with Henri, to talk things through, explain herself. By then, the guy will be as stiff as a board and impossible to handle if she leaves him spreadeagled like this. She tosses handfuls of straw over the pooling blood, then, with the tip of her shoe, she pushes his legs together, then the arms, so that at least he'll fit neatly into one of the body bags. This takes her another ten minutes or so.

Right: onward and upward!

She reloads the semi-automatic: she doesn't want to show up at Henri's empty-handed, it just isn't done.

Henri counted four bullets, and then, a little later, a fifth.

After an initial jolt of fear, he cannot help but be impressed.

Five bullets from what sounds like a semi-automatic: that wasn't the sniper he posted; it was Mathilde. What an extraordinary woman! And so like her to announce her presence in this manner.

In the end, perhaps it's for the best. The real beef is between the two of them. She will come through the back door and Henri, going out the front door, will catch her from behind.

He takes off his shoes, snatches the pistol from the floor – a Beretta (Henri is a traditionalist) – and tiptoes towards the door in the half-light. A moment later, he hears her walking on the terrace as stealthily as a Native American warrior. At her age . . . When Mathilde goes around the side of the house, he'll open the front door and follow her footsteps – but being behind her will give him a decisive advantage.

He knows he has to shoot without warning.

The second he sees her back, he needs to aim and empty his clip, leave nothing to chance. That, in this final moment, he will not be able to look at her is heart-breaking. Had circumstances been otherwise, he would have liked to talk to her, to explain, to apologise, but he is going to kill her because he has no alternative. He feels sure that, if they could talk, she would understand. But life is such that he'll have to shoot her in the back.

There's the signal, the little matchbox on the side table has quivered, Mathilde has reached the gable end of the house: it's time to go out. Henri gently opens the front door, the fresh night air brushes his face, he steps onto the terrace and instantly he feels the barrel of a gun against his temple.

"Good evening, Henri," says Mathilde, her voice soft and gentle.

Among his many other qualities, it must be said that the commandant has a keen sense of fair play, because he says simply:

"Good evening, Mathilde."

*   *   *

Henri is sitting in his armchair exactly as he was earlier that evening, except that this time the barrel of a .44 Magnum is pointed at his belly while Mathilde, pale and taut as a bow, sits facing him. They sit on either side of the unlit fireplace like two old friends chatting serenely and, as is often the case between old friends, innuendoes vibrate in the silent air. Mathilde, still wearing her raincoat, heaved a sigh of relief as she slumped into the armchair.

She did not ask Henri to turn on any other lights, and now that they have both adjusted to the darkness, neither wants to give it up. The atmosphere is propitious to conversation, to secrets and to death. Henri intuits more than sees her, backlit in the moonlight streaming through the window. Her hair has come undone and the wild tufts accentuate the age of the slightly disembodied silhouette before him.

She has not put down the gun, or shifted her aim, but otherwise she is as unaffected as always.

"The shit you've put me through, you old goat," she says. "Just look at this."

She nods to the torn hem of her dress, but Henri is too far away to see what she means.

"Not to mention my ankle . . . I'm sure it's swollen. I took a tumble. You've had your wall repaired, I see."

"I had sections of fence installed four years ago. I'm guessing that's where you got through."

"Yeah, I knocked down some loose stones, they'll need to be resealed. And that's where I fell flat on my face."

"I'm sorry, Mathilde."

"The ankle's swollen, isn't it?"

"Maybe a little, I can't really see from here."

They are both keenly aware of the price and weight of words in this moment. Henri has a vested interest in keeping Mathilde talking, in letting time tick by while he tries to think of a possible way out. Thankfully, it is Mathilde who breaks the ice, although the commandant doesn't like her strange tone of voice, tense and suppressed, the exaggerated way she enunciates, and the words she is saying, as though she were coming to her senses.

"Tell me something, Henri, do you really take me for a fool?"

Objectively, the conversation has got off to a bad start for Henri. So he sits back in his chair, folds his hands in his lap and tries to act as though his eyes are not riveted on the barrel of the .44 pointed at him.

"You do, Henri, you think I'm a fool . . ." Mathilde repeats as though talking to herself, as though the reproach is addressed as much to fate as to her old friend.

Now that the hardest part is over, now that she's safely reached Henri, Mathilde feels a kind of vertigo. Things, words and images are whirling in her head.

What she wants to say to Henri – dear Henri! – comes to her in snatches, but it's all a muddle, the accusations, the kind words, the confessions, the memories, the secrets. She cannot seem to get past this ill-chosen sentence, one she already regrets, blaming it on anger and irritation, on exhaustion:

"Honestly, that hitman in the barn was a dead loss, let me tell you!"

Henri shrugs.

"And nylon thread strung across the terrace? Really, Henri, you must think I'm a complete idiot!"

She finds Henri changed, different from their last meeting. I'm the one who's changed, she thinks, feeling a wave of tiredness sweep over her. She no longer wants anything, or rather she wants none of this to have happened, wants everything to go back to how it was before, long long before, back when she was just a little girl playing at boys' games.

Henri looks vaguely like her father, Dr Gachet. Past a certain age, all men of a particular class look more or less alike and Mathilde almost forgets the gun in her hand as she says "Henri", her heart pounding, her lips trembling.

"Of course not, Mathilde, I have enormous respect for you, you know that . . ."

His manner as he says it is calm but circumspect. It's important to keep her talking, but he can't afford to talk nonsense. He is unsure whether Mathilde has heard him. And he's right, because Mathilde is elsewhere, she is dreaming of the little piece of paradise where she and Henri would live. Henri doesn't move, doesn't say a word, he simply looks at her as at a little child from whom he expects excuses or explanations. The more she studies him, the more he looks like her father. Demanding and self-assured. Deep down, he has always been like that, overbearing, insufferable. Poor Henri. By association of ideas, an image of the petrol pump attendant flashes before her eyes. They are one and the same, they're interchangeable, they're both thieves. The man who is sitting stiffly in his Louis Philippe armchair is also a thief, he stole her life, and here she is, trying to defend herself in this absurd world, in the kingdom of the superannuated.

With calm impatience, Henri waits for Mathilde to say something else, something that will allow him into the conversation, something that will trigger a delirious torrent of words because that is what his life now depends on. But still Mathilde stares at him and says nothing. Although her face is in shadow, he knows that countless things are whirling through her mind. And he is right: images are flickering through the mind of this fat, fearsome woman. She is irresistibly reminded of the cliché that people drowning see their whole life flash before their eyes. Faced with the kaleidoscope of her life, she is out of her depth, and in that moment she is convinced that it is Henri who is going to kill her, that he will once again make her decisions for her.

For his part, Henri feels that the silence has gone on too long. For a while, silence was his ally, but if it allows Mathilde to drift away from the shores of reality, it will be counterproductive.

"Tell me something, Mathilde . . ."

She stares at him as at an abstract point.

"Tell me something . . ."

"What?"

"I've often wondered . . . Dr Perrin . . . how exactly did he die?"

To Mathilde, the question seems absurd.

"What difference does it make?"

"None at all . . . But I've often wondered . . . What was it that he had?"

"It was never really clear, Henri. You know that doctors make the worst patients."

"And the diagnosis?"

"All he ever said was 'the illness'. He didn't want to put himself through intrusive tests. He was resigned to it, poor Raymond. I did what I could. I made him soup, chamomile tea, eggnog, but it was useless. He didn't last long. A few short weeks and bang, Raymond was dead. Why are you asking me all this, anyway?"

"No reason. I just wondered . . . He was still quite young . . ."

"That means nothing, Henri. Your goon in the barn was – what, fifty? – and he's not around to argue."

"True, true."

Henri would like to carry on in this vein, but already Mathilde's eyes have glazed over. Their conversation has brought back memories of Dr Perrin. She respools the whole story. Her husband appears to her as he was when they first got engaged, then comes their house, their daughter, the war, Henri and her father, and, curiously, the day her mother slapped her for stealing money off the dresser, the munitions train in Limoges station exploding in a plume of red flames and black smoke, how ridiculous she felt the day she and Simon made love standing up in Attainville forest, and Ludo's decapitated body tumbling like a dead weight into his grave. Mathilde wiping her face on her blood-spattered forearm, and the German soldier, deathly pale, as his testicles join his five severed fingers in the bucket, while she feels perfectly calm and – what's the word? – fulfilled. It's strange to think of that now. Engrossed in her thoughts, she doesn't notice the gun in her hand weighs a tonne and is starting to droop, something that hasn't escaped the commandant's notice. Mathilde pulls herself together, but cannot shrug off the teeming images and vivid memories whirling in her mind . . . Henri still has not moved, and they could spend the whole night like this without saying a word. Now she is picturing Raymond's grave, remembering the aftershave of that brusque young sous-préfet who gave a long, rambling speech, and once again feels the surge of relief at the moment she shot him, her very first target, a man in an overcoat who looked like a provincial lawyer but was selling information to the Nazis, she remembers the day she went to Switzerland to open an account at the Centrale d'escompte de Genève (that's

Geneva!), the huge carpeted lobby of the bank, and, and still Henri says nothing. He is still waiting for her to say something, anything, as long as she starts talking. The silence is so oppressive and the images in Mathilde's cinema are spinning so fast: her parents' cat, a little tabby, fell into the well, and that's what's happening to her, she is falling down the well, she is falling and Henri is sitting there in front of her, Henri, the only person left who can do anything to save her, and she finds herself calling out to him, "Henri!", she needs his help so much she could almost cry, in a last, desperate gesture, she reaches out to him, but still he says nothing.

"Henri, how could you do this to me?"

The commandant feels a wave of relief: she has uttered the first sentence.

The second comes in the form of a .44 bullet that slams Henri against the back of his Louis Philippe armchair, leaving a hole in his chest as big as a lampshade.

The gunshot is so loud that Mathilde drops her weapon and claps her hands over her ears. The armchair has tipped backwards taking with it Henri, who looks like a bundle of rags. Hands still covering her ears, Mathilde opens her eyes again and looks at the bizarre scene: the feet of the armchair look like two pairs of eyes staring at her, the soles of Henri's shoes are bowed as though in prayer. Gripping the armrests, she hauls herself to her feet and takes two steps forward. She looks at Henri's chest, at the gaping wound gurgling with black blood. Henri's head is turned towards the wall.

Mathilde falls to her knees and starts to cry, foolishly cradling Henri's shoe in both hands. For a long time, she sobs as her head is filled with conflicting feelings and her nostrils with the acrid smell of poor, dear Henri's blood as it pools on the floor, and she decides that she will tell him about this little corner of paradise that would have offered the best solution for them both. She sobs, but she also smiles at the thought of all the peace and quiet that awaits them, all the pleasures of a time where nothing is at stake.

For a long time, she kneels there on the cold tiles. Then, at last, she stands up, she feels exhausted, such a tiring day, all that driving and her long conversation with Henri. They'll pick up where they left off tomorrow. She knows that she will be able to persuade him, but not tonight, tomorrow. Right now, she needs to sleep. She flicks a switch. The light in the living room is dazzling. She opens her eyes wide. Henri needs to sleep too, he needs his rest, otherwise tomorrow's conversation will be difficult. She goes back over to him, extricates his feet from the Louis Philippe armchair, puts his arms by his sides and his head straight so that he looks like a decent corpse. Tomorrow he can sleep in a body bag in the back of the van, he'll even have company if he feels like chatting. Then, despite the white spots dancing before her eyes, she manages to find her way to the guest bedroom. Henri always keeps it ready – I can't think who he does it for, I'm sure I'm the only one who ever visits. The minute she steps into the room, she slumps on the bed and falls asleep, without a single thought.

Occhipinti's fears were well founded. Vasiliev and the Tan sister have been dead for three days, and already three more people have been murdered.

Shortly after the Tan brothers were released, the body of a North African man, a lieutenant in the Moussaoui gang, was found in the Saint-Martin canal. The following day, the gang took their revenge, shooting two Cambodians in the head. The investigating magistrate has phoned several times, he wants this to stop and stop now.

His superior officers have taken over; things cannot carry on like this.

The only way to stop this bloodbath is to find the real culprit.

Occhipinti spent two hours racking his brain for a Talleyrand quote apposite to the situation, but drew a blank. Clearly, everything is fucked.

It is then that he comes up with an idea which he himself describes as genius. Since neither of their theories has borne fruit, might there not be a third possibility?

"Which is?" says the investigating magistrate.

Occhipinti puckers his lips.

"I don't know, it's just a thought . . ."

Back at the Police Judiciaire, he bawls out everyone, kicks up a stink. He finds it calming.

He goes back over the reports into Vasiliev's activities. Jesus H Christ, it has to be in here somewhere.

September 19

The whole house is cold, but especially the small guest bedroom in the northern wing. A shiver runs through Mathilde's whole body. She opens her eyes and it takes a moment for her to work out where she is. When she remembers, she stretches like a fat old cat, her fists clenched, her chest thrust out, her back arched, then falls back with her head on the pillow.

The bedcover is barely rumpled. Mathilde's mouth feels dry, she is in exactly the same position she was last night when she collapsed from exhaustion. The curtains were not closed, and through the window Mathilde can see the trees and a neatly symmetrical stretch of garden. She stretches again, then struggles to get up. Coffee, she needs coffee. She pulls off the bedspread and wraps it around her shoulders. She goes to the kitchen and hunts around for cups, coffee filters, toast, butter, jam. This is a bachelor pad, nothing is where you expect to find it. Arms folded, she leans against the kitchen counter while she waits for the coffee to be ready. Then she looks around for the tray but can't find it, so she has to make several trips.

The first thing that greets her in the living room is the upturned armchair and, behind it, the vague outline of the body. Despite the cold, Mathilde opens the French windows to let some air in. The place stinks! She makes two trips back to the kitchen, catches her foot in the bedspread and spills coffee on the floor before finally sitting down at the dining table opposite the empty hearth. She's starving. I hope there's hot water, because if there's one thing I hate it's a cold shower.

There is hot water.

The bathroom is a little spartan. Nothing essential is missing, but it is clear that, to Henri, a bathroom does not merit creature comforts. Spartan, that's what he was at heart. Not the kind of man to have affairs, nor even to strive for happiness. Mathilde is annoyed that she didn't bring all the things she needs, she doesn't even have her makeup bag. She manages to find a new toothbrush and a hairdryer. It's obvious that very few women have been in this house. Seeing her big breasts jiggle in the shower, she thinks about Henri's sex life. He wasn't a skirt-chaser and he certainly wasn't the kind of man who frequented brothels, always assuming such a thing exists in this freezing arse end of nowhere. That's another thing that was spartan about Henri – his sex life. The bare minimum. Probably Madame Palm and her five daughters. What a fool. Well, he won't miss sex wherever he is now. All the same, poor Henri. She dries herself and gets dressed. Before she leaves, she collects her .44 Magnum and she hovers for a moment, wondering whether she's forgotten anything. She looks down at Henri, dear Henri, but she is not one to be sentimental. It would be unworthy of us, Henri, wouldn't it?

She doesn't know whether Henri has a cleaner, a gardener, whether a neighbour will suddenly show up like that idiot Lepoitevin, and now that she's had a good night's sleep, the best thing is to get it over with and head home. She looks for the keys to the gate (Henri is a man of order and method, everything is neatly labelled next to the front door), walks through the grounds, fetches the van, which she parks outside the barn. She slides the sniper's body into a body bag and rolls it up the ramp.

Once he has joined the other two, she moves the van to the front of the house.

And performs the same operation on Henri.

Before long, Mathilde is aching. She didn't get much sleep last night, the bed was very uncomfortable. Honestly, Henri, you could have bought something decent. Not that I blame you. Single men never think about these things. But I have to say, I'm very disappointed. I felt sure that you'd like my idea of going away together, but you can't have everything.

She zips the bag over Henri's body, screws in the pump, then sucks out the air. You never think of anyone but yourself, Henri, you're a selfish old bastard. Well, you can drop dead, Henri, you can drop dead. I'm not about to make another proposal. It was a one-time offer. Take it or leave it. You left it – and that's your right – but that's not going to stop me telling you what I think: you're a rotten bastard, Henri, that's what you are! You've got everything you could want, you don't need to work anymore, but still you hang on to the past. Look at me, am I hanging on to the past? No! On the contrary, I'm hanging up my gun right now. Don't bother phoning me when you need help because we're done, do you hear me, we're done. I'm tired, you don't seem to realise. Right now, I'm heading home, I'm going to chuck out everything and then I'm going! Where? Don't ask me, I'll know when I get there!

After much pushing and pulling, she rolls the body bag up the tailgate. It's getting pretty crowded in the back of the van. And, she has to admit . . . it smells a little. Mathilde takes a deep breath, then steps into the van and sniffs. It's not very noticeable, but these body bags aren't as airtight as they claim.

It doesn't matter, she plans to dump it all, drive it into the river, the van and the cargo, and that will be the end of it. Though she'll have to do it pretty quickly before the stench gets any worse. In a few hours, she won't be able to drive it anymore.

She can't wait to catch a train back to Paris, back to civilisation. She won't be able to leave until tomorrow morning, but by tonight the worst should be over.

None of this has been easy. But getting to see Henri again, getting to talk to him, has cheered her up; she feels young and revitalised.

2633 HH 77.

A moment ago, Monsieur was certain of his facts, but now . . .

Everything in his head is so confused, he can never be sure whether what he is experiencing is real or a delusion, his mind does as it pleases, like a free electron, ideas and memories flash past, they scroll by, they telescope, they stop, everything freezes. He can spend hours like that: stunned, stupefied. He knows this because the other night when he was watching the news (or was it during the day?), his brain shut down and when it started up again, the credits were rolling. He has no idea what happened in between.

When he is reasonably certain he is conscious, he makes notes. But his hand shakes so badly he cannot always read what he has written and he has to throw it away.

That is how he feels about this number plate. He was certain. And the envelope with the number on it is right there in front of him, but now he can't think what it means, he has the impression that it was written by someone else, Tevy maybe, or René.

When he thinks about them, he starts to worry that before

long someone will come for him, that they'll send social services, cart him off, put him in an old people's home, but he doesn't care about that anymore. It doesn't bother him that they'll take him away – that's something he'll have to get used to – no, what bothers him is this number. It surfaced in his mind like an air bubble, he doesn't know where it came from, but maybe it's the right number. In a world where nothing works the way it should, even a stopped clock tells the right time twice a day.

So, this number plate.

He just needs to call the police and get them to check it out. If it's not a real vehicle registration number, they won't have wasted that much time, and they'll get over it.

It's a simple task, yet he can't bring himself to do it. It's almost a matter of etiquette. You check things out yourself, you call for help only if you need to. You don't pester the French administration for nothing.

The young female police officer called earlier. Monsieur assumes it was her, although he cannot be sure.

She just wanted to check on him, did he need anything, how was he coping . . .

Monsieur tried to answer and then, abruptly, he asked:

"Have you arrested the person who did this?"

The officer sounded embarrassed. You could tell that she wished she had something more reassuring than "we have officers looking into it", "we're following up a number of leads", in short, all the things you say when you're helpless, Monsieur used to be chief of police, he knows the score.

The real problem is that he never knows what will happen next.

A second from now, his brain may switch off, he'll have trouble remembering things, time will pass and he won't remember what he did, he might come to in the living room. Or out on the street. This is what the future holds in store for him.

Then he thinks of René and Tevy. They're dead. His grief is still immense, indescribable.

It's as though he longs to do something for them. Calling the police and asking them to run a vehicle check is probably the only thing he can do for them now that they're dead, it sounds ridiculous, but that's life, Monsieur has to make do with what he has. He puts on his glasses, checks the phone book for the number for the Indre-et-Loire police station, dials it and asks to speak to the chief of police.

"Can I ask the reason for your call?"

Standard, surly, police-issue tone.

"This is Monsieur de la Hosseray," he can hear the quaver in his voice, "I've had—"

"Monsieur de la Hosseray! I can't believe it! This is Janine Marival, you remember me . . ."

Monsieur does not remember her, but says:

"So lovely to hear your voice, how have you been?"

He lets the woman prattle on: she worked under him when he was préfet but now works the switchboard, she trades idle gossip about her superior officers, but the switchboard must be inundated with calls, he has to cut her short.

"So lovely to talk to you, now if you could . . ."

She puts him through to the préfet's direct line.

"Monsieur de la Hosseray, to what do I owe the pleasure?"

Once again, Monsieur has to fudge, to mumble meaningless platitudes, and it's tough because the préfet's name doesn't ring a bell.

"This is going to sound stupid, but what can you do? It's a petty matter involving car insurance."

In the space of two minutes, Monsieur manages to find an authoritative tone of voice, the right words, the appropriate phrases: someone has rear-ended his car, he got the number plate, but not the driver's name, so if the préfet would be so kind as to run a vehicle check . . .

When did he call?

Yesterday, the day before?

By now, Monsieur has forgotten.

Then the phone rings, it is someone from the police station "with the details you requested of the driver".

This sounds vaguely familiar.

"Do you have a pen and paper?"

"Just give me a minute."

The man turns everything upside down in search of a pencil and a scrap of paper.

"OK, I'm ready!"

His handwriting is barely legible, so he sits down at the kitchen table and copies it out in large letters:

Renault 25: registration 2633 HH 77.

Mathilde Perrin, 226, route de Melun, Trévières, Seine-et-Marne.

This is the woman who was here the other day.

This is the woman who murdered Tevy and René.

I need to phone the police to let them know.

Fifteen minutes later, Monsieur stumbles on the piece of paper again, but he no longer has any idea what it means. He tosses it into the wastebasket.

*   *   *

Because of the smell, Mathilde had to park the van out in the countryside. It was a long, exhausting day. Then she had to wait for nightfall, she couldn't do anything until then, but it was tedious. She made the rounds of the village cafés, sitting at a table for as long as possible, the afternoon stretching out like a rubber band.

Now, finally, here she is.

The best location is some twenty kilometres from here, near the river, just outside Chayssac, a middling-size town without an iota of charm or beauty, with a main street lined with white cement tracks. There are three building sites of differing sizes. The one that Mathilde is drawn to is the second, because it has everything she needs. It is a little after 8 p.m. when she pulls up in front of the iron gates and gets out. The German shepherd yowls and races towards her, lips curled, fangs bared, standing on his hind legs trying to bite her through the fence.

Mathilde walks up and smiles, which only serves to make the dog more furious, but this does not last long. Mathilde steps back, takes a ball of minced beef from the tin foil and tosses it over the railings.

This was something she worried about. Rat poison has a particular smell that dogs hate. Then it occurred to her to search her Belgian colleague's van. The guy was a real pro. In addition to the usual array of chloroform, emergency medications, bandages, painkillers, antibiotics, she found four capsules of strychnine and curare.

This site is not patrolled by a security company; it's simply not worth the cost. Nothing but the site owner's dog, who has been starved to make him more aggressive. He's a dumb mutt. He runs over to the meat, gobbles it down like a glutton, and savours it like a corpse as he is seized by a convulsion and falls dead, still slavering.

Mathilde has found a pair of bolt cutters in the van. The padlocked chain is quickly snapped, but, surprisingly, she finds that the gate is still locked. She has to go back, reverse the van, then floor the accelerator and ram open the gates in a shriek of metal, running over the dead dog in the process – nothing too taxing, she's back in business.

There are four site vehicles on the site, but Mathilde, who knows nothing about heavy machinery, cannot operate them. But there's also a dump truck. Which must work more or less like a car. She tries the door. It's locked. She goes to the site office, a little prefab with tiny windows. Mathilde steps back, gauges the angle of fire and puts a bullet through the lock. The door opens. She takes the time to survey the scene. Four desks, overflowing in-trays and – beneath tons of paperwork, invoices, oil-smeared delivery notes, junk mail and Pirelli calendars – two Bull computers and two state-of-the-art Olivetti typewriters. And on the wall is a corkboard with the keys of all the numbered vehicles. She glances through the window. The dump truck is number 16. She grabs the key and goes outside. The steering wheel is stiff: the guy who drives this piece of shit must be a beast, thinks Mathilde. She starts the engine and then quickly switches it off again. Everything is going to plan; she just has to keep moving. You never thought you'd see me drive a dump truck, did you, Henri? But you'll see, it won't be a problem!

She drives the van to the door of the site office, then takes the typewriters, the computers, the keyboards and the printers and unceremoniously tosses them into the back of the van. Yeah, sorry guys, I don't have time to tidy up, she says to the four body bags.

In the office, she also finds two small cashboxes, probably for petty cash and day to day expenses. She throws them into the van and slams the tailgate shut. She fetches her travel bag and sets it down by the door of the office.

It takes her two attempts to get the van onto the little jetty where flat-bottomed barges come to load and unload sand and cement. She is facing the river, which roils in the darkness. It's obviously been raining hard, since the Garonne looks set to burst its banks. She parks the van about fifteen metres from the end of the jetty, rolls down all the windows and releases the handbrake. She tosses a pebble into the water to try and gauge the depth, but it doesn't tell her anything.

It's a gamble; it's make or break.

Right now, I need your help, Henri, I need you to send positive thoughts, because if this doesn't work, I don't have a plan B.

She climbs behind the wheel of the dump truck, keys the ignition, drives it into the back of the van and starts to push. The engine whines. Her stomach churns as the two vehicles move off together. When the van reaches the end of the jetty, Mathilde floors the brake. Straight ahead, the van goes into a nosedive. And then comes to a juddering halt.

Panicked, Mathilde jumps down off the dumper truck and warily walks to the end of the jetty as though some wild beast might suddenly appear. The van is almost vertical, the front submerged in the river. It must have caught on a sandbank. This is the worst possible scenario. The rear of the van stands almost a metre and a half above the water. Mathilde looks around for something she could use to push, though she knows that, even if she could find something, she wouldn't have the strength to shift such a weight.

Looking at the van half sunk in the water makes her want to cry.

Nervously, she paces the jetty, glancing at her watch. She has very little time left, forty-five minutes. A gurgling sound comes from the van as water continues to pour into the cab. Suddenly, it lets out a long sigh, belches a huge air bubble and sinks below the water. Mathilde cannot believe her eyes. Then it stops for a few seconds. A few centimetres of bodywork are still visible above the surface. Go on, go on, Mathilde pleads, and the gods are clearly listening. As though it has received a sudden kick, the van sinks and disappears.

Oh, thank you, Henri! Thank you! We really make a good team! As soon as she has driven the dumper truck back and locked it, hung the keys on the corkboard and picked up her travel bag, she is walking through the gates, past the dead dog lying in a pool of blood. Hi Ludo! Have a nice nap!

It takes almost half an hour for her to make it to Chayssac, where the taxi she ordered is already waiting.

"So, where are you coming from at this hour, love?"

The driver is surprised to pick up a fare outside the town hall of the sleeping town.

Mathilde slumps onto the back seat, gives him the address of the hotel. Everything is set.

During the night or early tomorrow morning, someone will notice that the building site has been broken into, the dog has been killed and everything of value stolen; the local gendarmes will strut around, take statements and write up reports that will be filed away with the car thefts, the break-ins and the complaints from battered wives that generate nothing except statistics.

"I had to deal with the affairs of a friend who died recently. I did some clearing out, it was hard work, but now that it's done, I feel so relieved."

"Oh, I know exactly what you mean," says the driver as he pulls out. "After a hard day's work you get a good night's sleep."

"Tell me about it!"

September 20

I don't understand . . . Why is it taking so long for the bloody train to get to Paris?

This is what Mathilde wants to ask the ticket inspector, but she knows she has to keep a low profile, not draw attention to herself. Her conversation with the taxi driver last night must be the exception. She was careful to book the hotel room in the name of Jacqueline Forestier, but even so, no point tempting fate.

Jacqueline Forestier is the name on the fake passport that she kept, and she is drawn to it now. She rummages in her bag and finds it. The photo is old, but the passport is still valid. Has it been cancelled? If she were to use it, would she be stopped at immigration?

Up to now, Mathilde's luck has held, she doesn't see why things should change.

Because what she is thinking about now is leaving. Sadly, Henri didn't take the bait, but who knows, if she writes to him once she's found a place to live, perhaps he'll reconsider . . .

Mathilde allows herself to be comforted by this idea, which is new. She has no idea where she will go, but she's going to put La Coustelle up for sale, get the money from her Swiss bank account and – bam – the high life or more likely a quiet life, it's all the same.

She'll settle in a quiet little spot and look for a little house to buy. Les Marquises? Mathilde laughs, she doesn't even know where Les Marquises is. Italy? Spain?

Mathilde slaps the armrest: Portugal!

She went there once on a mission. The target stayed longer than expected, so Mathilde had to hang around in Lisbon, after which she trailed him to the Algarve and finally terminated him in some godforsaken village called Lagos or Lagoa – whatever it was called, she loved the place.

This is what she needs. She didn't fight like hell during this war and afterwards for nothing. She's entitled to a little sunshine, a little peace and quiet, damn it!

There, it's all decided, she'll close up La Coustelle, leave the keys with Lepoitevin, and contact an estate agent once she gets there.

And with all the cash she's put by, she can afford to buy a really nice place. She wonders whether maybe she might invite her fat lump of a daughter, she'll see. Suddenly, Mathilde is happy. She has a plan. She'll even get a dog.

Mathilde is so keyed up that her journey home becomes a dream.

She wants to move fast. Not that she has anything to fear, she's still above suspicion, but she wants to get it over and done with, to finally have some peace.

Mathilde falls asleep and snores peacefully.

Across the aisle, a clean-cut young woman smiles.

Mathilde looks just like her grandmother . . .

In the late afternoon, when the taxi drops Mathilde off outside her house, the excitement she felt on the journey home has not abated.

In fact, as she walks down the driveway to the terrace, she

feels a surge of joy at the thought of leaving this house. Which was never really hers.

"My, my, you've got so big!"

She picks up Cookie and hugs him.

"Well, poppet, the nasty neighbour didn't hurt you, did he?"

No: none of this has ever been hers, not this house, not this life. Not even her daughter. All she's ever had is her dogs. She'll be relieved to leave all this behind.

She sets the puppy down and stares at the hedge, in two minds about how to deal with Lepoitevin. She can't imagine leaving without having things out with him. Her sense of justice is affronted at the thought that someone who could do such a terrible thing to a poor defenceless dog like Ludo should go unpunished. At the same time, she has a vague memory that she shouldn't do it, but she can't quite remember why.

It'll come back to her tomorrow.

She puts down her bag, goes upstairs to take a shower, and sees the blackened bloodstain on the carpet in the doorway of her bedroom.

Oh, who cares, I'm selling the place, whoever buys it can deal with it.

They can do the clean-up.

September 21

Monsieur can't find that bloody piece of paper! He is sure he put it right here, on the dresser but it's not there now.

Without Tevy, life has become very difficult. It would be easier to give in, he thinks.

When he ran out of food, he went a whole day without eating before hunger set in. It was a curious feeling, needing to eat without wanting to. Maybe I want to die, thought Monsieur, but he knew he didn't. The following day the cleaner came. She was the one who offered to come twice a week rather than once. She's a rather elderly woman, kind and gentle, he doesn't know if she lives locally. When she tells him he really should move into a care home, he pretends he doesn't understand. But Monsieur was hungry, so he asked her to do some shopping. He gave her his debit card and the PIN that's written in large numbers on the fridge.

She came back with enough food to last him until her next visit. She handed him the receipt, put the debit card back in his wallet and went back to hoovering. She picked out simple food that requires no preparation, it's probably not very good for him, but she doesn't want him boiling water or even turning on the gas – with Monsieur the least little thing can be dangerous.

"You'd be better off in a home, Monsieur, honestly you would . . ."

He pretends he hasn't heard, but she's no fool.

Sometimes, Monsieur becomes aware that day has dawned or night has fallen and he has no idea what has happened in the intervening hours. The apartment changes, things are moved around, the cleaner whose name he can never remember makes no comment, she simply puts things back the way they were. She says something about René's funeral and Tevy's funeral. Monsieur cannot understand why there are two funerals: they died together; they should have been buried together. She told him the date they were being held, but no-one came to collect him, or maybe someone did come. If he'd been to the funerals, he'd remember, wouldn't he?

Soon, Monsieur will have to leave, to give up the apartment. He feels the net closing in, other people will make his decisions for him, it would be easier to make his peace with this fact, but Monsieur refuses. Sometimes he remembers why he is so resistant, but it is fleeting, the thought disappears as quickly as it came.

Just now, he can remember: he is not prepared to leave the apartment until he finds that scrap of paper. That's why he's still here. With that piece of paper, the police can track down the woman who murdered René and Tevy. He saw her through the window, he made a note of the number plate, he called the police station, they gave him her name, her address, but now he has lost it.

Her name and address.

He spent the whole afternoon looking for this paper. He asked the cleaner.

"You asked me twice already, Monsieur," she says. "I'm afraid I haven't seen it . . ."

So he resolves to call anyway.

But it is difficult. The young policewoman is not at her desk so his call is transferred to someone else.

"Monsieur de la Hosseray speaking. I'm calling about the Neuilly case."

"Is this about Inspector Vasiliev?"

On hearing the name, Monsieur starts to cry. Silently.

"Hello? Are you still there?"

"Y-yes . . ."

"Can I ask what it concerns?"

The woman sounds annoyed, impatient.

"I wanted to tell you that the woman who murdered them came here by car. I wrote it down on a piece of paper, but I've lost it."

There is a long silence.

"What's your phone number, Monsieur?"

He knows the number, but just now it escapes him.

"Just a minute, I'll get it . . ."

He sets down the receiver.

He thumbs through the directory, but cannot find his name under the letter H. Oh, there it is, on the front page.

"Hello?"

He can hear the female officer whispering to someone, she is talking about him . . .

"Yes, monsieur?"

"I have the number, my phone number, I can't find the woman's number. Her car number plate I mean, not her phone number."

He realises that it all sounds confusing, but it is the best that he can do.

"Look, monsieur, I'll ask my colleague to give you a call. Could you just confirm your name?"

Monsieur sits by the phone and starts his wait. He doesn't want to move from here. To risk missing the call. When he needs to go to the toilet, he drags the phone as far as he can and does his business quickly. From time to time, he picks up the receiver to check for a dial tone.

Then, finally, she calls. It is dark now.

"How are you doing?"

He should have taken the time to answer, to have a proper conversation, but all the time he was waiting he was rehearsing what he needs to say, so he opens the sluice gates and the words come pouring out.

"It's about the woman who came in the car and murdered them. I lost the piece of paper, but I saw her through the window, an elderly woman, rather fat, driving a light-coloured car, but the thing is I've lost the piece of paper, I've looked everywhere for it, I can't think where it's gone, I think it's the cleaning lady."

"The elderly woman?"

"Yes, I suppose she is old."

"And she came to your apartment . . ."

"She comes regularly, not every day, but regularly."

"And she's the one who killed Inspector Vasiliev?"

"No, no."

Monsieur is seized with a doubt.

"No, no, I don't think it was her, I'd have recognised her. The other one was fatter, I think . . ."

"I see. Tell me, is there someone there with you, Monsieur de la Hosseray?"

He is hanging on the end of the line, he wants to hang up, he knows he has failed, he can feel it, but if he hangs up now,

they'll come for him. They'll put him in a straitjacket, like they
do with lunatics.

"Yes . . ."

"Who is there with you, monsieur?"

"A cousin . . ."

"I see . . . Could I have a word with your cousin?"

"Um . . . He's just gone out to get some food, he'll be back in
a minute, I can ask him to call you . . ."

"Could you get him to call? Would that be possible?"

"Of course . . ."

Monsieur is devastated by his failure. He knows exactly what
he needs to say, but the words don't come out in the right order,
ideas flutter all over the place. What a fiasco.

With great difficulty, he gets to his feet. Sitting on this stiff-
backed chair has left him in agony.

Slumping into an armchair, he spots the crumpled piece of
paper in the wastepaper basket. He picks it up and reads:

Renault 25: 2633 HH 77.

*Mathilde Perrin, 226, route de Melun, Trévières, Seine-et-
Marne.*

He must call the policewoman back . . . But he doesn't move.

They won't believe him; they think he's insane. By tomorrow
morning, social services will be coming for him.

Calling the police will do no good: no-one understands him,
no-one believes him.

He screws up the piece of paper and wipes away the fat, silent
tears streaming down his face.

Never has he been as inconsolable as he is in this moment.

*　　*　　*

The following day, Mathilde is up with the lark taking coffee on the terrace. She was woken by a sudden thought: the perfect idea would be to leave . . . today.

The plan is crazy enough to make her delirious. She giggles to herself. She grabs a paper and pen and writes down everything she needs to do to leave Melun before nightfall, and none of it seems insurmountable. She goes upstairs to shower, takes the Luger, her passport and some cash, and when the travel agency opens, Mathilde is the first through the door.

The woman behind the counter vaguely reminds her of Madame Philippon from the temp agency who promised to send someone to clean her house but never did. Because of this resemblance, she is instantly suspicious of this woman, who beams at her and says:

"Portugal! But what a good idea!"

"Why?"

"Excuse me?"

"You said it's a good idea, how is it any better than going to Geneva, Milan or Vladivostok?"

The agent is a little confused, but she is an old hand, she has her fair share of moody clients, she is not about to let herself be riled.

"So," she says, spreading out some catalogues, "let me see . . . Portugal . . . Which part of the country were you thinking?"

"South," says Mathilde, who can't remember the name of the region. "Right down at the bottom."

And this momentary lapse upsets her, she feels that the agent's smile is condescending, it's intensely aggravating. She slips a hand into her bag.

"The Algarve?"

She has just clasped the Luger when the name comes back to her.

"That's it! And I'd like to leave today."

"Today, really?"

"Is that a problem?"

"Well, let's just say it's a little last minute."

"What's the problem?"

"Availability, madame. Finding a flight . . . I'm guessing you'll also need a hotel?"

"You guessed correctly."

This client with her brusque replies and her hand buried in her bag as if she's about to take out a tear gas canister is making the agent distinctly uncomfortable. She leafs through the catalogue.

"I think I've got good news for you, madame . . ."

"That would make a nice change."

"Just a moment."

She picks up the phone, calls a colleague, and while going through the necessary information, she keeps a wary eye on her client, especially on the hand that remains invisible.

But the miracle comes to pass. There is a flight from Orly Airport tonight at nine o'clock, a car to meet her at the airport and:

"Just take a look at this," she says, showing Mathilde photographs of the luxury hotel, with its swimming pools, orange groves and terraces. All at an off-season price.

Mathilde takes out her passport.

"I'll be travelling with my dog. And I'll be paying in cash."

"Well, the thing is . . . it all adds up."

"Don't worry, I've got enough," Mathilde says, rummaging in her bag and bringing out a wad of large notes.

The agent feels a wave of relief: that's why she kept her hand in the bag! She is once more warm and winning.

"And I'd like to rent a car," Mathilde says.

"You're pushing the boat out!"

Mathilde spends the rest of the morning shopping: a travel basket for Cookie, sunglasses, summer shoes, a hat, because she remembers that, even at this time of year, the Algarve will be quite hot.

She has paid for a two-week stay. She'll spend that time looking around for a house to rent or buy, and once that's done, she'll send Henri some photos, if he only comes for a few days, she'll persuade him to stay a little longer, and one thing will lead to another . . .

Back at home, she gathers up clothes and packs a large suitcase, together with the paperwork she needs to transfer money from her account in Geneva or Lausanne or wherever. She arranges a taxi for seven o'clock so as to get to Orly by eight; the flight is at 9 p.m., so it should be perfect.

Mathilde laughs. She thinks about the four bodies in the van at the bottom of the Garonne. Four bodies? Who were they again? The goon Henri sent after her – no! – the *two* goons Henri sent. Then there's Henri himself, but she can't remember the fourth, never mind, it'll come back to her.

But the police are not going to trace them to her, not for a long time; if they ever do, she'll be sitting on the hotel terrace wiggling her toes, perhaps even in her own home, if she finds a house she likes.

Mathilde has been weaving between the raindrops for more than thirty years, so it seems only logical that in her well-earned retirement, she'll slip beneath the radar as she has always done before.

* * *

"Still nothing?" says Occhipinti.

They are waiting for the magistrate to issue a warrant.

The young woman shakes her head. Another man would pound his fist on the desk, Occhipinti merely gobbles a fistful of pistachios.

On his desk are the details of Mathilde Perrin, a sixty-three-year-old widow and mother, and decorated hero of the Resistance ... Not at all the profile he was expecting, but it's all he has!

The call from the old man, the former préfet, was both strange and unexpected.

"Disjointed?" said Occhipinti, somewhat surprised.

Very disjointed, to say the least. It was difficult to tell who he was talking about. He seemed to be confusing his cleaner with the woman he thought he saw.

"Some fat old biddy came and murdered Inspector Vasiliev? Do you think maybe the old man is a bit senile?"

The female officer found this remark disrespectful, though the commissaire has a point. But they have no leads to go on, they have officers raking over all of Vasiliev's old cases and meanwhile the Tan brothers and Moussaoui's gang are killing each other.

The young female officer personally visited Monsieur de la Hosseray, but the old man wasn't himself. He didn't remember calling the police, even the name René Vasiliev didn't seem to ring a bell, he pretended that he remembered but it was clear to her that he didn't.

This time, the policewoman did not ask what he wanted. The moment she left the apartment, she called social services. They will come and fetch him this evening. Or tomorrow morning at the latest.

What really upset her was that when Monsieur made the call, he seemed lucid. More or less. He sounded sure of his facts.

"That's typical of senile dementia," said the commissaire. "They are completely convinced of what they're saying, that's the reason we should be wary. I should know, my mother-in-law had dementia. Every night she thought she saw her sister who'd been dead thirty years, and she mistook me for the pharmacist she'd been cheating on her husband with for twenty years."

The thorny fact remained that Monsieur's description broadly matched that of the woman the commissaire had gone to question near Melun.

"There are thousands of overweight elderly women," the policewoman objected.

"Hang on, hang on . . ."

There has only ever been one fat elderly woman with a light-coloured car in this investigation. Admittedly, she doesn't have the profile of a killer, but, even so, it's disturbing.

"My mother-in-law could sometimes be completely lucid, but because she talked rubbish most of the time, we never believed her."

So, the commissaire called the investigating magistrate to request an arrest warrant.

"If you could issue a search warrant too, that would be very helpful," he said.

If he has to go all the way to Melun, he may as well go prepared.

The magistrate could not be reached, so he left a message.

Eventually, shortly before 6.30 p.m., the magistrate phoned back and agreed to issue the warrant.

It is now 6.45 p.m., a courier has just arrived with the document. They are about to head for Melun. Occhipinti takes two officers.

"Perfect, we should be there by eight o'clock."

Just before they leave, the young policewoman calls Monsieur de la Hosseray, in the hope that his memory will have returned, that he will be able to give them more details of the strange visit of the "old woman", but no-one answers.

She calls social services.

"We picked him up earlier," she is told.

The commissaire will never have the pleasure of arresting Mathilde Perrin.

It's already too late.

By the time he executes the search warrant and discovers the huge cache of weapons, he will have missed his chance . . .

Because just as the commissaire's team is leaving the Police Judiciaire, a taxi pulls up outside La Coustelle. The driver calls through the gate.

"Is this the right address for a Madame Perrin?"

Mathilde is sitting on the terrace, wearing a coat, next to her is a large suitcase and the travel basket in which the puppy whined at first but then stopped. She stares at the taxi driver, who is flailing as though communicating in semaphore.

Arsehole – here I am with a suitcase the size of a wardrobe and you're asking if it's the right address . . . She leans over the basket. Ah, Cookie, I'm think we've landed the dumbest taxi driver in all of Melun . . . She stands up and gives a tired wave, come on in, you bloody idiot . . .

The driver beams, he opens the gate, gets in the car and drives slowly up to the terrace, turns the car, then gets out.

"I was wondering whether I'd got the right house!"

He is a cheery chappy.

"And did you come to a conclusion?"

He looks at the woman with the suitcase and the dog basket next to her.

"Haha! Yeah, yeah, I think this is the place! Haha!"

He walks to the foot of the steps.

"I'm fifteen minutes early!"

This is clearly a source of great pride. He goes up, takes the suitcase and carries it back towards the car.

"What time's your flight?"

"Nine o'clock."

"Oh, you'll be there in plenty of time! At this time of night, it's an easy run to Orly!"

At this, Mathilde makes up her mind. All day, she has been upset at the thought that she did not have things out with Lepoitevin. Every time she thought about going round, there was something she needed to do. Then she forgot about it. But since they're running fifteen minutes early, she can go and sort it out now.

"Just give me a minute," she says as the driver picks up the dog basket and sets it on the back seat.

"What kind of dog is it?"

"A Dalmatian!" she calls from the kitchen as she gets out her Smith & Wesson.

The driver leans in and looks at Cookie through the little grille.

"I didn't know they looked like that . . ."

He closes the back door of the car as Mathilde appears, a bag slung over her shoulder, locks the sliding doors and comes down the steps.

"I'm just going to drop the keys round to my neighbour, I'll be right back."

"Do you want me to drive round?"

"No, there's no need."

Mathilde is suddenly furious. For a long time now, she has had it up to the back teeth with Lepoitevin, she's happy to give him a little send-off. She'll say, "This is for Ludo, remember him?" and put a bullet between his eyes. She's fitted the gun with a silencer, the driver won't hear a thing. She'll throw the gun into the hedge. Not that it matters. She'll be long gone.

By the time they start looking for Mathilde Perrin, they'll need a miracle to find Jacqueline Forestier.

By then, I'll have had time to die ten times over, she thinks as she walks briskly towards the gate.

The driver calls after her.

"Don't take too long, will you?"

She is halfway down the drive when the beat-up Ami 6 suddenly appears.

The engine shrieks, the car is in second gear, the rear wing hits the railings, the car swerves, corrects its course and accelerates. Shifts into third gear.

It has taken Monsieur almost two hours to get here. He couldn't seem to work the gears, especially fourth. He lost the right front wing leaving Paris when he swerved to avoid an oncoming car. He was determined to drive here, he said it over and over, I need to drive there. To see for myself. Since the police don't believe me.

Finding Trévières was no mean feat. He didn't want to ask for directions. In fact, he was so convinced that someone would stop him that he didn't stop. Even for red lights. Or stop signs. He heard the honking horns and the insults. Gripping the steering wheel, his face forty centimetres from the windscreen, Monsieur had only one thought: to get to Melun.

When he saw number 226, he turned sharply, now here he is on the gravel driveway.

And standing right in front of him, this woman petrified by the appearance of the shrieking car.

He recognises her. This was the woman he saw getting into the car, the woman who came and murdered René and Tevy.

Mathilde could take three steps and avoid the Ami 6 barrelling towards her, especially since the driver does not have the reflexes to steer towards her.

It is Monsieur's face that stops her.

She instantly recognises the wild-eyed, haggard old man she saw through the second-floor window. Her fleeting amazement is fatal.

The Ami 6 is doing fifty when it hits her head on.

Rather than being knocked aside, Mathilde falls forward onto the bonnet and is swept forward by the car as it brutally crashes into the terrace.

Mathilde is thrown against the sliding door, which surprisingly remains intact. Both her legs are already broken and her chest has caved in when her skull hits the glass with shocking force and her body crumples onto the tiles.

When he sees Monsieur open the car door, slowly climb out and stagger back down the driveway, his face streaming blood, the stunned taxi driver tries to say something but doesn't know what to do: help his fare, who is lying bleeding next to the sliding door, try to stop the tall, emaciated old man who looks as though he might trip at any moment, or call the police. In the end, he does none of these things. Stunned by the unexpected violence of what he has just witnessed, he climbs into his car, takes his head in his hands and, curiously, he starts to cry.

Social services had indeed sent a team to fetch Monsieur but they didn't find him: he had already left, in a screech of burning rubber, to meet his fate.

He was later found bleeding, his face bruised and swollen, wandering the streets of Trévières.

The subsequent investigation took some considerable time, it was more than three months before a permanent place was found for him.

He now lives in a nursing home near Chantilly.

Pass by at any time, except at night, and you'll see him standing at the window of his room. He spends his days staring at the trees in the grounds.

The little smile on his untroubled face lends him the gentle and serene air of a man who is not afraid of death.

Acknowledgements

My thanks to François Daoust, whose help was invaluable.